Julia Roberts was born in Nottingham and was inspired to write her first play at the age of ten after winning second prize in a writing competition with a short story called 'The Foundling'.

Throughout her forty-two year career in the entertainment industry, initially as a dancer before becoming a TV presenter twenty-five years ago, she has written articles for magazines and newspapers and for the past five years a weekly blog on qvcuk.com where she has worked for twenty-one years.

Although she had always wanted to write a book Julia was a busy working mum so it wasn't until her two children left home that she finally fulfilled her dream and finished her first book, a memoir entitled 'One Hundred Lengths of the Pool'. Two weeks after it was published by Preface Publishing, Julia went on holiday to Mauritius and was instantly inspired to write a novel, Life's a Beach and Then... the first book in the Liberty Sands trilogy.

She now lives in Ascot with her 'other half' of thirty-seven years and occasionally one or other of her children and their respective cats.

Life's a Beach

and Then...

Julia Roberts

A ripped Book

ISBN 978 0 9932522 0 4

Copy edited by Justine Taylor
Book cover illustration Angela Oltmann

Published by ripped

life's a bitch and then you die

Julia Roberts

x

CHAPTER 1

Holly sank back into the comfortable leather seat of the air-conditioned, chauffeur driven car that the Plantation House hotel had sent to meet her at Sir Seewoosagur Ramgoolam International Airport. She was grateful to escape the vicious heat of the early afternoon Mauritian sun, which had caused a trickle of perspiration to run down her spine in the short walk from the terminal building. It was a complete contrast to the freezing temperatures she had left behind in London twelve hours previously.

The flight from Gatwick had been delayed by three hours, initially to wait for some passengers arriving on a connecting flight from snowbound Paris, and then for the de-icing procedure which had kept them sitting on the tarmac for over an hour, unsure whether or not they would be leaving for their exotic destination.

Holly didn't mind too much, after all it wasn't her hard-earned cash paying for the trip to Mauritius and besides it gave her the opportunity to do a bit of people-watching, a pastime she indulged in a lot these days. The only thing that had made her slightly nervous was the engineer repeatedly making his way from the flight deck to the economy-class section, torch in hand, to peer through the porthole windows checking the condition of the flaps during the de-icing procedure. Holly had comforted herself with the thought that the pilot would not risk his own neck, or that of his crew, just to appease a bunch of holidaymakers.

By the time the flight eventually took off Holly's eyelids were feeling heavy and she was asleep before dinner was served. Since she was a small child mechanical motion had a sleep-inducing effect on her, as her father had discovered when she was a teething baby. He would bundle her into her car seat and drive around their council estate in a suburb of Nottingham until she was lulled to sleep.

Holly bit her lip to stop it trembling as she thought of her father and wondered what he would have made of her travelling to a five-star resort on an island paradise in the back of a limousine. He would probably have been quite sad that I am on my own, she concluded.

She turned her head to look out of the window at the passing countryside but also to avoid making eye contact with the driver through his rear-view mirror, particularly as her eyes were filling with tears. She reached into her handbag for a tissue. At this sign of movement the driver, who had introduced himself as Sachin when he had held the car door open for her at the airport, tried to strike up a conversation.

'Is this your first time in Mauritius?' he asked.

It was a standard opening gambit and Holly was very tempted to say 'No', which would probably have saved her from further conversation, but it actually was her first time and she knew from past experience that the information her driver/guide would impart could be very useful.

'Yes it is,' she replied and settled back to soak up all the local information, occasionally interrupting his flow with a question of her own.

At least it made the journey pass quickly and in no time at all they were making a right turn onto a road signposted to Flic en Flac and she saw the small town at the bottom of the hill, with the beach and ocean beyond. Sachin drove through the town, still indicating points of interest, until they reached a T-junction with only a stretch of grass, scattered with tall trees, between them and the beach.

'Are they pine trees?' Holly asked, as Sachin turned the car to the left.

'They are filaos trees,' he replied. 'They help to prevent sand erosion.'

Less than a mile later the car turned into a sweeping driveway at the end of which stood the Plantation House hotel, a striking colonial-style building, which was to be Holly's home for the next seven days.

'Pretty impressive,' said Holly almost to herself as the car door was opened for her by one of the uniformed reception staff. She noticed the slight nod of the head, the smile and the look of pride in the man's eyes. Obviously he is happy in his work, Holly thought, as she thanked Sachin, handing him a 200-rupee tip, and climbed the half dozen steps to the front entrance.

This time she kept her thoughts to herself as she found herself in a double-height reception area with a vaulted ceiling and a view straight through to the beautifully manicured gardens, against a backdrop of the deep blue ocean.

'Welcome to the Plantation House, Ms Wilson,' said a tall slim man in a light-coloured linen suit. 'My name is Vikram. Please follow me and we can get you checked in as quickly as possible. I trust you had a pleasant journey?'

'Yes thank you,' said Holly, as she followed Vikram through to a comfortable seating area which, although not air conditioned, had a pleasant breeze blowing through the glass-less windows and overhead ceiling fans to assist the flow of air.

'Please take a seat,' he said, indicating a low rattan sofa, 'and I will have my colleague attend to you.'

Moments later a waiter appeared carrying a tray, on which there were three glasses containing a peach-coloured liquid, complete with a bendy straw and a cocktail stick piercing a piece of fresh pineapple and mango.

Holly took one glass and allowed her eyes to follow the waiter as he delivered the two remaining drinks. She instantly recognised the distinctive middle-aged couple who had been sat several rows in front of her on the plane, in the business-class section. The man had been very attentive towards his travel companion making sure she was comfortable throughout the long journey. Holly had thought at the time that it was good to see that chivalry hadn't completely died out and it had made her wish that she had someone other than her darling son Harry to care for her. As the man took his drink he noticed Holly and raised his glass in acknowledgement.

Oops – caught, she thought, raising her glass in his direction and feeling the warmth in her cheeks as she flushed slightly. I must be tired. I don't normally get caught people-watching.

'Ms Wilson,' said Vikram, clearing his throat slightly to gain her attention, 'there is a short registration form to fill out and then we will transport you to your room.'

Five minutes later Holly had completed the form, making sure she had ticked the box for premium Internet access so that she could work in her room and not just the public areas. She finished her drink and was escorted back to the front of the hotel, smiling at the couple from the plane as she passed.

A golf buggy, already loaded with her silver Antler suitcase, a purchase she had made eight months previously with the first paycheque from her new job, was waiting to take her to her room. The buggy carried her through the colourful gardens, past the tennis courts which unsurprisingly were unoccupied in the heat of the afternoon, and the children's play garden, again completely deserted, despite being located under the shade of giant trees with huge waxy leaves, eventually coming to a halt outside a two-storey building housing a dozen rooms.

After Deven, the porter, had finished his explanation of how everything in her room worked she pressed a 100-rupee note into his hand. It always helped to have a good relationship with the hotel staff.

Holly sat on the edge of the bed taking in her surroundings. The decor was in neutral shades of ivory and taupe with dark wood furniture. There was a flat-screen television, which Deven had explained showed not only the local channels but also DVDs of recent movies played out from the hotel reception. The en-suite bathroom had a bath and a shower and was separated from the bedroom by a glass-less window that had a Venetian blind for privacy, a necessity as her room was on the ground floor. This meant there was a terrace rather than a balcony, complete with a small table and chairs, and two sun loungers, and her room was less than twenty metres from the adults only pool.

This is perfect, she thought, reaching for the telephone receiver and dialling 0 to speak to reception. It was answered on the second ring.

'How can I help you, Ms Wilson?' asked the receptionist.

'Oh, hello, I'm sorry to trouble you but my room doesn't have a sea view,' Holly said.

'I see. Did you request one when you made your reservation?'

'Yes I did,' replied Holly, mentally crossing her fingers.

There was a tiny pause before the receptionist said, 'I must apologise for our mistake. Please give me five minutes and I will see what I can do.'

CHAPTER 2

Robert closed the door to the terrace as quietly as possible. He didn't want to disturb his sleeping wife. The flight had taken its toll, particularly with the three-hour delay in London, and Robert was beginning to wish they hadn't agreed to meet Philippe for dinner that evening, but it had been difficult to turn down the invitation after their friend had driven across the island to meet them at the airport. Robert had said it would be just as easy to take the transport laid on by the hotel but Philippe had been insistent.

'You are my friends,' he had said, 'and friends help each other.'

Besides, Rosemary really enjoyed his company and had spent the journey catching up on all his news and laughing at some of the scrapes he had got himself into. It was almost like she was flirting with him at times, especially when she referred to him as her 'toy boy', but Robert knew that deep down she viewed him as the son they had never had.

Robert cradled his wine glass in his hand and swirled the red liquid around gently to warm it. He smiled as he thought about the unnecessary action, after all the early evening temperature was still in the late twenties and would warm his Chateau Neuf du Pape without any intervention from him. A shiver trembled through his body as he looked at the deep red of the wine. It reminded him of blood and there had been so much blood over the last two years. He shook his head to try and clear morbid thoughts, then lifted his gaze to admire the beautiful sunset. It was one of his and his wife Rosemary's favourite things to do. He thought briefly about waking her but decided instead to deal with her annoyance at missing nature's awesome display later. He breathed in the warm air scented with frangipani. The decision to come to Mauritius had been the right one, even though it was against the advice of the doctors. The break would do them both good in preparation for the tough road that lay ahead.

The orange globe of the sun was now halfway over the horizon and almost as if she knew what she was missing Rosemary opened her eyes and focused first on her beloved husband and then the glorious scene beyond. She swung her long legs effortlessly to the floor, slipped her feet into her favourite flip-flops and went out onto the terrace.

'I didn't want to wake you,' Robert said. 'You looked so peaceful.'

She looked into his chocolate brown eyes reproachfully and planted a gentle kiss on his still firm lips.

'We've already missed too many sunsets,' she murmured softly as she arranged her shoulders under his waiting arm and rested her head against his chest.

CHAPTER 3

After dropping off his friends at the Plantation House hotel, Philippe had spent longer in the shower than usual in the hope that the sharp driving needles of water would refresh his mind as well as his body. Unfortunately they hadn't. He stared at the computer screen, which he had been in front of for more than an hour, and re-read the two paragraphs he had written.

'*Merde*,' he cursed under his breath and then started to laugh.

In his head he had dramatically ripped a piece of paper out of a typewriter, screwed it into a ball and thrown it across the room into an already overflowing wastepaper basket. He hit the delete button which was not so theatrical but it had the same effect of condemning the nonsense he had written to the 'trash'.

'Why do I always swear in French?' he asked himself.

Philippe had not lived in France since his

English father had left his French mother when he was thirteen years old. There had been no fight for custody, his mother, Veronique, had decided she couldn't cope with bringing up a teenage boy on her own and had agreed to Philippe returning to England with his father. She had open access to visit them in Kent whenever she chose but sadly she didn't choose to visit very often. He believed that his mother loved him in her own way, and he loved her unconditionally, of course he did, she was his mother, but theirs was not the close relationship he witnessed between some of his school friends and their mums.

It had been hard for Philippe at the time, having only a masculine influence for most of his teenage years, however it had provided the basis for his widely acclaimed first novel, *Maman*. How easily the words had flowed. He rested his head in his hands for a moment and then lifted his gaze to admire the view that was supposed to be the inspiration for his second book.

Jo, his editor at Ripped publishing, was so certain that *Maman* would be a success, she had managed to secure him a three-book deal with a healthy advance. The advance had enabled him to leave his job as a journalist for a tabloid newspaper to concentrate on his new career. The idea for the second novel had come very easily, but when he had submitted the first fifty pages Jo had said the characters lacked warmth and believability.

'It's like reading a travel guide about Mauritius,' she had criticised, 'with a bit of romance thrown in, but no real story.'

The words had stung at the time but Philippe knew she was right. He had taken all the background information from the Internet and glossy travel brochures. He had never set foot on the island of Mauritius and it showed. The success of his first book was because he knew the subject matter intimately. He needed to experience Mauritius first hand so he had booked a two-week holiday staying at the Plantation House hotel. That was where he had first met Robert and Rosemary.

They had come to the hotel for dinner in Waves restaurant one evening and because it was so busy had asked to share his table in the bar afterwards to watch the local cabaret show. He had sworn Rosemary to secrecy before revealing he was the author of *Maman*, a book she had wept buckets over. He had explained that he had come to Mauritius to research and gain inspiration for his second novel and that was when Rosemary had come up with the idea of renting the house they were staying in at Tamarina Bay and staying in Mauritus to write it.

Philippe was unsure.

'But what if you want to come back on holiday and I'm still here writing?' he had asked.

'No problem,' she had assured him. 'We usually stay here at the Plantation House but we're thinking of buying the house at Tamarina Bay for our retirement and we wanted to try before we buy to see if we like it. In a way you would be doing us a favour. If you are renting it on a long-term lease it might put off other prospective purchasers.'

'And do you like it?' Philippe had asked.

'No,' Rosemary had answered, with a twinkle in her eye. 'We absolutely LOVE it.'

'So you will buy it?' asked Philippe.

She had looked at her husband and squeezed his hand. 'I think so, we just have to sort out a few things in the UK first.'

Less than a week later Philippe had signed a six-month rental agreement on the house at Tamarina Bay, with an option for a further six months. He had used part of his book advance money to pay the rent up front. He hadn't even needed to fly home to sort out his flat in Pimlico. His friend Jason, a former colleague on the newspaper, had been sleeping on his couch for several weeks since splitting up with his girlfriend, and he was happy to cover the rent in return for sleeping in a decent bed. It had fallen into place like clockwork. There was just one problem: no matter how hard he tried, Philippe had an almighty case of writer's block.

The tinkling sound of a piano being played brought Philippe back to the moment. It was his computer going into sleep mode which it did if there had been a lack of activity for ten minutes. He now knew the tune by heart as he had heard it so often over the last nine months.

He swiped the touch pad to stop the music. The twelve-month deadline to deliver the finished manuscript of his book, so that the editing could begin, was getting perilously close. He searched the horizon, now bathed in the pink and orange of a glorious sunset, desperate for inspiration.

CHAPTER 4

Holly ran a hairbrush through her freshly washed hair knowing that it should really have been a comb. She had spotted one or two grey hairs in her dark mane lately but nothing that a pair of tweezers couldn't deal with. That was something else she knew she shouldn't be doing, tweezing out grey hairs. She furrowed her brow trying to remember who had told her the old wives' tale about each grey hair you plucked out being replaced by two? It certainly wasn't her mum. For a brief moment she wondered what her mum looked like now.

The last time Holly had seen her was at the funeral eighteen years ago and, even taking the circumstances into consideration, she had looked considerably older than her thirty-eight years. Looking at her own reflection it was hard to believe that she was now the same age as her mum had been then. Holly was fortunate that she had inherited her dad's dark hair and olive skin tone, which was on the oily side, so she had almost no sign of any ageing lines, even though she spent quite a lot of her time nowadays in sunspots around the world.

She leant closer into the mirror to inspect her 'elevenses', the two lines between her eyebrows. They had always been quite pronounced, even as a teenager, when her skin, that she was now so thankful for, was spotty and the bane of her life. No wonder she hadn't had a boyfriend throughout the entirety of her secondary school education. No one wanted to get up close and personal with the 'pimply princess' as her school mates had so unkindly nicknamed her.

She deftly twisted her damp hair into a scrunchie while she applied her eyeliner, mascara, lip gloss and a touch of blusher, and then released it again to dry naturally in the warm evening air. She opened the Venetian blind in her bathroom, which she had closed to protect her modesty while she was showering, although she doubted that anyone could see in now that she was occupying a first floor room.

The reception staff had been very helpful in assisting her move to a sea view room, even though she hadn't requested one when she had made her reservation. It had allowed her to sit on the balcony watching the sun disappear into the ocean before getting ready to go to dinner.

Holly looked across at her suitcase and decided she would unpack that in the morning, she had everything she needed for tonight in her hand luggage. She always carried all her skin-care and make-up, a day outfit and an evening outfit, a change of underwear and a bikini in her hand luggage after the incident in the Bahamas when her luggage had gone missing for twenty-four hours.

Holly didn't usually make the same mistake twice.

The main restaurant at the Plantation House hotel had double-height vaulted ceilings with ceiling fans and was open to the terrace that bordered the freeform swimming pool. Dining was either under the stars or in the slightly cooler interior. There were two other choices of restaurant, Waves, which as the name suggested was on the beach, or the Italian restaurant, Roberto's.

Holly had chosen the main restaurant as it was buffet-style so there would be no waiting around to give her order and then more waiting for her food to be prepared and served. She was suddenly ravenously hungry which was not surprising really as she hadn't eaten since lunchtime the previous day, apart from fruit salad for breakfast on the plane.

She could only have been standing at the entrance for ten seconds before a waiter appeared and asked her whether she would like to sit inside or out.

'I think I'll stay inside tonight please,' she replied, acutely aware of the beads of perspiration that had formed on her nose and upper lip in the short walk from her room to the restaurant.

'Certainly madam, please come this way.'

Holly was shown to a table for two near an open double door at the back of the restaurant, directly under a ceiling fan. Obviously the waiter has noticed how warm I am, Holly thought, flushing with embarrassment, as she sat on the chair he had pulled out for her, and allowed him to place a crisp white napkin across her lap.

'What would you like to drink, madam?'

Holly thought for a moment. She normally stuck to soft drinks, usually water, but she could murder a crisp white wine.

'I'll have a glass of the house white please and a bottle of still water.'

As soon as the waiter had left to get her drinks she headed for the buffet, but instead of picking up a plate and piling it high with food she approached a member of staff in a smart cream linen suit who she presumed must be the restaurant manager.

'I'm sorry to be a nuisance,' she said, smiling up at the man whose name badge identified him as Rajesh. 'I was just wondering if there is a special area of the buffet to cater for vegetarians?'

Without a heartbeat of hesitation Rajesh accompanied her to the islands where all the pre-prepared salads were and pointed out the green labels signifying that the food was suitable for vegetarians. He then introduced her to the head chef, Soobis, who assured Holly that there would always be plenty of vegetarian options.

'And if you ever want us to prepare something especially for you please let us know by 2 p.m. and we will make sure it is ready for you, madam.'

Holly was impressed. She hadn't told the hotel she was a vegetarian when she had booked and yet seemingly it was not a problem.

She then helped herself to a selection of the salads, cut herself a slice of crusty bread and made her way back to her table where, in her absence, the waiting staff had discreetly removed the second place setting. Her bottle of water was already in an ice bucket at the side of her table and as she sat down the waiter reappeared with a bottle of white wine.

'Would madam care to taste it?' he asked.

'No,' replied Holly, 'I'm sure it will be fine.'

The waiter poured her a generous glass and left the remainder of the bottle in the ice bucket alongside the water. She took a sip of the wine, allowing the sharp fruitiness to burst on her tongue before swallowing and taking another sip. This was definitely the right decision, she thought, twisting the bottle round in the ice bucket so that she could read the label. She was not surprised to learn it was French, after all Mauritius had been a French colony until the British took over in 1810, and French was still widely spoken, albeit a creole version of the language.

Being positioned towards the rear of the restaurant was perfect for Holly to indulge in a bit of people-watching while she tucked into her starter. There were plenty of people to watch but it was a large restaurant so it didn't feel crowded.

The table closest to hers was occupied by three generations of a Chinese family. The elderly parents were very traditional in manner and dress, but the couple who looked to be in their early thirties, and their two young children, a girl of around five and a very young baby, were much more modern in style. Holly wasn't sure if the baby, who was dressed in a Burberry romper suit, was a boy or girl but there was a certain irony about it wearing the very British brand

Burberry which had probably been made in China.

She cast her gaze further afield to several tables whose occupants she guessed to be British. It was the clothes that were the giveaway, with the men flagrantly breaking the 'no shorts to dinner' rule and the women wearing just a little too much make-up and slightly too few clothes.

Holly herself was wearing a simple coral-coloured shift dress, not too short and not too low-cut, showing off her curvy body to perfection without being too obvious. People often thought she was Italian with her dark looks and stylish clothes, mostly acquired from charity shops. That assumption occasionally came in handy when she wanted to pretend she didn't understand English so that she could eavesdrop on conversations.

Dragging her eyes away from the sparkly, six-inch stiletto-heel sandals one of the women was wearing, Holly noticed that the couple she had checked in with earlier were just arriving at the restaurant.

A different kind of British, Holly thought, as she lowered her eyes back to her salad to avoid being caught out people-watching for the second time that day. The woman was blonde, but not in a brassy way, very slender and tall, almost as tall as her husband even though she was wearing flat shoes. The man had the look of an ageing rock star or trendy photographer from the 1960s. His grey hair was tied back into a small ponytail at the nape of his neck, something Holly normally hated but somehow it seemed right on this man, and although he was tall his shoulders were slightly rounded and he had a bit of a middle-aged paunch. Even so, he was a handsome man and they made a very attractive couple.

At that moment the waiter, whose name she had noticed was Antish, arrived to refill her wine glass and remove her starter plate. Holly was shocked that she had finished her wine so quickly, it was most unlike her. I'd better go and select a main course to soak that up, she thought.

As she made her way across the dining hall again, she saw the British couple were deep in conversation with another man in a cream linen suit. That's a bit of overkill, she thought, two restaurant managers on duty on the same evening.

CHAPTER 5

Philippe would have liked to make eye contact with the stunning woman in the coral dress but he had his back half turned to her and she had only glanced in his direction for a moment before returning to her table. He wondered who she was dining with. How annoying that his view of the back of the restaurant, where she had been heading, was obscured. Maybe he would leave by the rear doors of the restaurant later in the hope that she would still be there. He dragged his attention back to his friends.

Robert must have made some kind of joke or amusing comment because Rosemary was laughing.

'The suit, Philippe,' repeated Robert. 'Had you forgotten that cream linen is what the restaurant managers here wear?'

'Actually I had,' replied Philippe, joining in the laughter. 'But I have no choice, I only have one suit and I like to make an effort to dress well when I am dining with you two. I haven't been here since your last visit, this place isn't the same when I don't have you for company.'

Rosemary shot a warning look at Robert as he opened his mouth to speak, and quickly jumped in with, 'It's nice to be missed. Let's eat outside on the terrace tonight and enjoy the warm air.'

'Wherever you like, my beautiful English rose,' he said, linking his arm through hers and guiding her towards a waiter so they could be seated.

Robert followed, delighted to see his wife happy and smiling.

CHAPTER 6

Holly gazed up at the night sky, full of bright twinkling stars, and tried to spot the constellations. She could see the plough and Orion's belt but she was struggling to find Venus. Her dad always said that when Venus was bright he knew she was happy.

Am I happy? she wondered. Well, I'm not unhappy so I guess my glass is half full at the moment which is how my wine glass has been all evening, she thought.

Holly didn't usually drink alone. She had seen the devastating effect that taking a step onto that particular slippery slope could have. She shuddered and decided there would be no more solo drinking on this trip, which meant she wouldn't be tasting the colourful cocktails currently being delivered by waiters to others who had come to sit by the moonlit beach, until she began to socialise.

She looked around at the couples and groups of friends. Holly was the only person on her own. She decided to head back to her room before anyone took pity on her and invited her to join them. Normally that was exactly what she wanted, but not tonight, the drink had made her slightly lightheaded and it wouldn't do to be caught off guard and say something that would blow her cover.

Holly had fully intended to do some work but as she put her key in the lock tiredness engulfed her and a mere five minutes later she was fast asleep.

The hum of the air-conditioning unit, churning out freezing cold air, woke Holly. She shivered and pulled the blanket over her shoulders. She was used to sleeping in air-conditioned hotel rooms however, when she went to bed in her slightly inebriated state the previous evening she had forgotten to adjust the dial and had thrown her blanket to the foot of the bed, sleeping with only the sheet for cover. No wonder the slight noise of the air-con had disturbed her. She was too cold so deep sleep had evaded her. She glanced at the luminous hands of her travel clock. It was only ten past six, which meant it was just past two in the morning back home. It was a good job she had such a long sleep on the plane otherwise she wouldn't be able to think straight today and she needed her wits about her.

As a thoroughly honest person, Holly struggled with the little white lies that were a necessary part of her job, but at least she would probably make a better poker player now than she had at university. She had never played the game before she met her then boyfriend Gareth, but he and his rugby-playing mates used to play late into the evening after their Saturday matches and if she wanted to spend time with him she had to join in. Although they were all downing pints of beer like it was lemonade, and she was actually drinking lemonade, they were still able to read her like a book when she was bluffing.

'It's like taking candy from a baby,' they would joke, as she watched the pittance she had earned from working long hours behind the student's union bar dwindle to nothing. Gareth would always sub her, even though she would protest that she wouldn't be able to pay it back.

'You'll pay it back in kind,' he would tease, not unkindly, winking at his mates.

Holly wasn't so fond of this side of Gareth, showing off in front of his friends, but whenever she confronted him about it he would say, 'It wouldn't do for them to see my softer side. I'm the captain of the rugby team. They need to believe I'm hard and ruthless, so that they will trust me on the field.'

Lying in his arms Holly would always accept this explanation because she trusted him completely. It didn't matter what other people thought, she knew the real Gareth, at least she had thought she had.

Holly shivered again, unsure whether it was the overactive air-conditioning unit or the memory of her first true love that caused this involuntary action.

First true love, she thought, only true love would be more accurate. She felt the familiar weight in the middle of her chest and swallowed hard, blinking her eyes to stop herself from crying. It amazed her that even after all these years merely thinking about

Gareth could provoke such a strong reaction.

Suddenly she kicked off the bed covers, slipped on her robe, crossed to the French doors and flung open the curtains. She unlocked the door and stepped outside breathing in huge gulps of warm damp air to calm herself.

Why can't I accept that he left me because he didn't love me as much as I loved him? she thought. Why can't I just let it go?

It was barely light outside, but there was already some activity in the hotel gardens. The ground staff were raking the sandy paths and collecting fallen coconuts. The Italian restaurant to her right didn't serve breakfast so the shutters were firmly closed, but she could hear the sounds of cutlery being laid on the tables of the main restaurant, even though the breakfast service didn't start for almost an hour.

An hour, thought Holly, wondering how best to fill the time. Shall I work or walk?

Moments later the decision was made. She threw on a pair of frayed denim shorts over a bikini, twisted her unruly dark curls under her red Yankees baseball cap, slipped her feet into her Havaianas and headed for the beach.

It was deserted. No one had yet appeared to reserve their sunbeds with brightly coloured beach towels and it was a bit too early for most people to take a pre-breakfast stroll.

Flip-flops in hand she stood at the water's edge, with the shallow rippling waves caressing her toes and looked out to the reef. The sound of the waves crashing against it created a constant background roar which was comforting and very different from the rumble of traffic she was used to at home. She began to walk in the direction of Flic en Flac, carefully avoiding the pieces of coral that had been carried in by the tide.

Holly had always loved the feel of sand beneath her feet and the smell of the ocean, which was quite odd as she had grown up in Clifton, a suburb of Nottingham, one of the most inland cities in England. There hadn't been any exotic holidays throughout her childhood, not even a package holiday to the Spanish costas, but she could still recall the thrill of racing her dad down the long expanse of beach at Skegness into the chilly waters of the North Sea. They weren't joking on the sign that welcomed you to the little seaside town that announced, 'Skegness Is So Bracing'!

That was one word for it, Holly thought, but at least she had been able to enjoy a week's holiday away from home each year at the caravan park in Ingoldmells, something she hadn't been able to provide for her own son, Harry. He had made do with pitching a tent in their pocket handkerchief-sized garden when the weather allowed.

A different sound cut through the background rumble of the waves on the reef. Holly couldn't place it at first but it seemed to be getting louder. She raised her chin to look up from under the peak of her baseball cap but couldn't see anything, other than the groundsmen from the various hotels that fringed the beach raking up the needles that had fallen from the filaos trees and burying them into the holes that they had dug.

The sound, she now realised, was coming from behind her and it was horse's hooves approaching at a gallop. She turned to see a blond man, stripped to the waist, astride a big black horse less than a hundred yards away. He galloped past, and a vision of Brad Pitt in the movie *Troy* flashed into her mind. The expression on the man's face was totally focused, almost trance-like, and she doubted that he had even noticed her as he passed by, but she had certainly noticed him, tanned and handsome in a rugged way, and not dissimilar to Gareth. She felt flustered as she stood watching the horse and rider retreating into the distance, realising that she had almost called out 'Gareth', had the sound not been strangled in her throat.

Moments later horse and rider had rounded the headland and if it wasn't for the hoof marks carved into the sand Holly might have believed him to be a mirage or a product of her imagination, the result of too much alcohol and not enough sleep.

It couldn't be him, could it? she wondered, a tiny glimmer of hope rising in her as it had done hundreds of times over the years, only to be quashed by her sensible side. Don't be ridiculous, it said, Gareth's gone.

Her heart was thumping in her chest as she turned and strode purposefully back towards the hotel. The sun was already starting to heat up and she hadn't applied her sun protection yet. It wouldn't do to get sun burnt on her first day.

CHAPTER 7

Rosemary watched Robert cross the small expanse of grass to place their towels on the sun loungers closest to their room. She loved to sit on the beach and gaze out to sea or read a book but these days she did it from the shade of a beach umbrella. Gone were the days when she would lie out in the sun from ten in the morning until the sunset with no SPF to protect her skin and a liberal application of coconut oil to help her 'fry'. Thank goodness her mother had instilled in her the need to use good quality skin care products from a very early age which had minimised the damage caused by the sun. One of the reasons that she loved coming to the Plantation House hotel was the range of beauty products that the hotel spa carried. She really enjoyed the decadent treat of facials and full body massages.

This was her favoured end of the hotel complex away from the swimming pools surrounded by families and the 'body beautiful' types. She had nothing against either group but she had nothing in common with them either. In the not-so-distant past women would envy and men would admire her slender body, with her long lean legs, rounded bottom, flat stomach and small pert breasts. She still felt confident of her appearance in cleverly designed clothes but there was no hiding in swimwear.

Robert, or Bobby as she called him, was making his way back towards her, having reserved their place on the beach for when they had finished breakfast. She had long since stopped nagging him about his posture. His rounded shoulders and rounded belly were a consequence of the many hours he spent at his drawing desk or more often these days at his computer. Just like all other areas of modern life computers played an increasing role in the work of an architect. They were a wonderful technical aid for producing the stunningly quirky buildings he had been working on recently in Dubai but they couldn't give the human touch to turn a structure into a place where people felt comfortable spending their time.

'I don't suppose you'd care to join me for breakfast would you?' he quipped, extending his arm for her to link hers through.

'Why I don't mind if I do,' she replied in a southern American drawl, mimicking the accent of her favourite movie character, Scarlett O'Hara.

CHAPTER 8

Holly was anxious to get back to her room to start on the work she should have done the previous evening. Fleur, the travel company representative, was already ten minutes late, which was not creating a very good impression on Holly or the other guests who were waiting to see her. They were all gathered in the lounge area where Holly had checked in the previous day, but noticeable by their absence were the British couple that had arrived at the same time as Holly. She hadn't seen them at breakfast either, but then she had gone quite early.

Breakfast had been a delicious combination of fresh fruit, followed by griddled tomatoes and a poached egg on toast. Holly's request for HP sauce had been met swiftly and her coffee cup refilled several times without her having to ask. The only cause of disappointment was the fruit juice which was reconstituted rather than fresh – a big black mark in Holly's opinion.

Holly glanced at her watch. The rep was now fifteen

minutes late. Holly stood to leave just as a short dark-haired woman, clutching a clipboard, rushed into the lounge.

'I'm so sorry,' apologised Fleur. 'The traffic was terrible this morning.'

'Really?' said Holly, genuine surprise in her voice, after all this was Mauritius not the Marylebone Road.

'Yes,' said Fleur, oblivious to the sceptical looks all around her. 'A bus had broken down on the hill out of Flic en Flac and the police were directing the traffic, but they were only allowing a few cars from each direction at a time. Anyway I'm here now, and I'll try and make-up for my lateness by speeding through the boring bits.'

There were a few mumbles and grumbles but Holly liked this woman's sincerity so she sat back down to listen to the 'Welcome Speech'. True to her word, Fleur had finished all the basics in less than twenty minutes.

Most of the other people stood up to leave, but Holly remained seated.

'Is there something else I can help you with?' Fleur asked.

'Actually there is,' said Holly. 'I'd like to have a look around the island. Would you recommend that I hire a car and make my own way or would it be better to organise a car with a driver for the day?'

'I would strongly recommend that you book a day with one of our driver/guides. They know all the best places to visit and they will be able to get you discount on some of the entrance fees. Was there anywhere in particular you wanted to go?'

'I liked the sound of the coloured earth that you spoke about,' said Holly, 'and the dormant volcano, but I'd also like to visit the north of the island to see what the coast is like up there.'

'The tours are normally either in the south, where the coloured earth of Chamarel and the Trou aux Cerfs crater are, or the north where you can visit the botanical gardens to see the giant water lilies and then go to the beach for lunch, but I can ask if any of our drivers would do it.'

'Perhaps you could ask the driver who brought me from the airport,' said Holly, hoping that the 200 rupees she had tipped him would be enough to persuade him, particularly if he thought there might be another tip.

'Do you remember his name?' asked Fleur

' I believe it was Sachin,' Holly answered.

Ten minutes later, after a phone call to Sachin and paying the fee on her credit card, the trip was arranged for Friday, giving her three days to sit around the pool and beach and mingle with the other hotel guests.

Right, thought Holly, now I really must get on with some work.

Holly patiently typed in the premium access code for the Internet for a second time and pressed 'enter' again. Perhaps she had hit a wrong key. The same message flashed up on her computer screen:

Access currently unavailable.

She reached for the phone and dialled 0.

'Hello Miss Wilson,' said the receptionist,

answering her call on the first ring. 'How can I help you?'

'I'm having a bit of trouble getting on to the Internet using the premium code you gave me. I keep getting a message saying "access denied"', Holly explained. 'Am I doing something wrong?'

'I am very sorry, Miss Wilson, but the Internet access for the whole resort is currently down. Is there anything else I can help you with?'

'Do you know when you are likely to have it up and running? I have an email I need to send quite urgently.'

'We should have it back by tomorrow morning at the latest,' replied the receptionist. 'It's rarely off for more than twenty-four hours and it only went off this morning.'

'Okay, thanks,' said Holly replacing the receiver. There was no point getting cross with the receptionist as it was beyond her control. The only person Holly was angry with was herself.

It's my own fault, I should have done this last night, she admitted. Well there's no point crying over spilt milk, she thought, it will just be late.

She pressed 'save as', typed in 'First Impressions' and then turned her notebook off. She locked it, her passport, her purse and her jewellery in the room safe, picked up her beach bag, already packed with a book to read, a notepad and pen, her camera, towel and battered straw hat, popped her sunglasses on her nose and headed for the beach.

It was just after midday, so Holly needed the shade of a beach umbrella. There were plenty to choose from on this stretch of the beach. Although the resort had seemed quite busy, judging by the number of people in the restaurant at breakfast, they were obviously nowhere near capacity and anyway this was the quieter end of the resort away from the two swimming pools.

She hadn't even finished reading a paragraph of her book when the first beach seller approached her.

'You like to buy sarong,' he questioned, holding up a brightly coloured piece of fabric printed with hibiscus flowers. 'Only 600 rupees.'

Holly smiled, shook her head and went back to the pages of her book. She had deliberately left her purse in the safe in her room so that she wouldn't be tempted to buy. She didn't need anymore colourful beach sarongs, she had a dozen or more back in the UK plus the four she had brought with her on this trip. Even so she knew she would have bought something if she had any money on her. That was the beauty of All-Inclusive, you didn't need to carry money with you for anything.

The beach seller hung around for a few seconds to see if she would change her mind and then moved along to the next occupied sun loungers. Holly watched as a young woman with short dark hair fingered the fabric and then said something which she couldn't quite hear as they were too far away, but it must have been a question regarding other colours or designs as the beach seller dropped his sports bag to the sand and started pulling out other options. The woman was engrossed in her selection and the man with her was on his mobile phone so neither of them noticed their toddler wandering towards the sea a few yards away. Holly sprang to her feet and called out to attract their attention. Within moments the woman had scooped her daughter up into her arms and carried her, wriggling like crazy, across the sand and sat her down on the sunbed. She hadn't shouted or smacked the child, as some mothers might have, she simply handed her a piece of coral to play with while she completed the sarong purchase. The man had continued his phone conversation throughout the episode.

The little girl was very cute with dark curly hair.

It's funny, thought Holly, that's exactly how I had imagined my baby would look, but Harry was blond and blue-eyed, like his father. She only realised she was staring when the baby's mother waved and called out,

'*Grazie!*'

'*Prego,*' responded Holly, making use of the tiny Italian vocabulary that she knew.

Several other beach sellers approached Holly over the next hour or so, offering necklaces made of beads or pearls, T-shirts and little carvings of dodos, the national emblem of Mauritius. She refused them all with a smile. She knew she would succumb eventually, after all they were only trying to earn a living, but she really must get through her first morning without making a purchase otherwise they would pester her for the rest of her stay knowing she was a soft touch.

She closed her eyes behind her sunglasses and must have dozed off briefly because the next time she looked across towards the Italian family they had gone, although their towels were still there so they were obviously planning on coming back.

They've probably gone for lunch, thought Holly, what a good idea.

The condensation formed on the cooled beer glasses as soon as they came into contact with heat of the Mauritian early afternoon. Holly had been tempted to order a beer to have with her lunch but had decided to stick to sparkling water, just as refreshing, no calories and no more drinking alone.

She had chosen a table at the back of Waves restaurant so that she could see everything that was going on around her while pretending to look out at the view. She waited for her lunch, a simple Greek salad, and observed the efficient service of the waiters and waitresses. No one waited for more than a minute before being shown to an available table, and the drinks order was usually taken immediately. There was the right mix of friendliness and respect for the paying guests, with particular warmth and attention directed towards the children, not that there were many children of school age. Early March was term time in the UK and probably most other countries around the world, Holly thought.

She scanned the restaurant for the Italian family but could not see them. She did however notice the British couple who she had missed seeing at breakfast. They were talking to another man in a linen suit and as he turned she realised she recognised him. His face had smiled out from the cover of the resort magazine that had been pushed under her door at some point that morning. He was the resort manager. He might have been doing his job, mingling randomly with the hotel guests, but Holly sensed a degree of familiarity.

I need to strike up a conversation with those two, she thought, they could be very useful.

At that moment Holly's lunch arrived and she was about to protest that she had been given the wrong order when the waitress, Ornelia, smiled and said, 'Enjoy your Greek salad.'

It was like no Greek salad Holly had seen before. It was stacked, having come out of a mould, with a layer of cucumber at the bottom, followed by a layer of fresh chopped tomatoes, topped with cubes of feta cheese and sprinkled conservatively with black olives. It looked amazing and tasted even better.

She was so engrossed in her lunch, trying to eat from around the edges towards the middle without it toppling over, that she didn't see the British couple leave.

CHAPTER 9

'If she's still on her own tonight we should ask her to join us,' Rosemary said to her husband as they strolled through the gardens hand in hand. 'I thought that maybe she was meeting someone here but every time we've seen her she has been on her own.'

'Well, no harm in asking,' Robert said, 'she can always say no.'

'I'm sure she won't be able to resist your charm,' Rosemary teased. 'I know I never could.'

Changing the subject to avoid further teasing Robert said, 'The old girl's still looking pretty good.'

'Robert,' exclaimed Rosemary, a look of mock horror on her face, 'that is no way to talk about your wife!'

'You know full well I didn't mean you,' he said smiling indulgently and gazing up at the hotel building. 'I think they've only painted her twice since the renovation works were finished and that must be sixteen years ago.'

'At least,' agreed Rosemary. 'We celebrated our first

wedding anniversary here the week she opened and it's our eighteenth in November, assuming we make it,' she added.

'Don't talk like that, Rosie,' he said, 'of course we'll make it.'

'I don't know what you were meaning,' she quipped, 'I was meaning if I can put up with you for that long!'

She let go of his hand and ran down the sandy path towards their room with Robert in pursuit. To onlookers they may have looked like a couple of young newly-weds except that when they reached their terrace a couple of minutes later they were both terribly out of breath. He swung her round to face him and kissed her full on the mouth.

'Why do you persist in joking about it?' he asked, as he unlocked the door to their room. 'It's really not funny.'

'You know I'm only teasing, Bobby,' she said, sitting on the edge of the bed and kicking her sandals off, 'and you used to like me teasing you.'

He pushed her gently back onto the pillows and kissed her again, allowing his tongue to push between her slightly open lips. He felt the familiar arousal. He still fancied his wife like mad. The back of his hand stroked her cheek and then travelled down her neck to rest on the top of her breast.

'I'm sorry, Rosie,' he said breathing heavily, 'do you want me to stop?'

She pulled the top of her swimming costume down to reveal her still firm breasts and moved his hand to caress them.

'I'm dying, Bobby,' she said, looking deep into his eyes. 'I'm not dead yet.'

CHAPTER 10

The bubbles were beginning to dissipate and the temperature of the water was decidedly on the cool side which was not surprising as Holly had been relaxing in the bath for half an hour or more, reflecting on an interesting afternoon chatting to a group of young people whose mobile phone company was rewarding their high achievements with a five-day stay in Mauritius. It wasn't quite the holiday they had been expecting as each morning they had lectures or team-building activities, but at least the afternoons were their own before they had to meet up for dinner.

They were mostly a good ten years younger than Holly but she was used to being around younger people and was delighted when they had asked her to join in a game of beach volleyball. It had been fun at the time but she was already starting to feel her muscles tightening up despite the soak in the bath.

I might have to book my complimentary massage at the health spa for tomorrow, she thought, as she pulled the plug out and allowed the water to drain away, while climbing out of the bath and wrapping a generous but not overly soft towel around herself. She had hoped for an invitation to have dinner with the group but apparently that was not allowed by the corporate organisers, although cocktails by the beach post dinner were mentioned if she was 'up for it'.

To add to her disappointment the group were taking over the whole of Roberto's, the Italian restaurant, where she had been intending to dine that evening. She sat on the bed, wrapped in her towel and read through the resort newsletter to find out what theme the cuisine would be in the main restaurant that evening. A smile crept across her face as she discovered it was Italian anyway so she could indulge in the pasta she was craving.

Half an hour later Holly stood at the entrance to the main restaurant waiting to be seated. It was busier than the previous evening, probably due to Roberto's hosting the private event, and most of the tables inside seemed to be occupied. She looked out to the terrace and noticed the British couple just being seated near the edge of the pool. The man raised his hand and waved to her just as a waiter came up to show her to a table.

'You know Mr Robert?' he asked.

Holly looked at him questioningly.

'Mr Robert,' he said, indicating the man who still had his arm mid-air in a wave. 'You know him?'

'No,' replied Holly smiling and waving back to 'Mr Robert'. 'We travelled here on the same flight yesterday and our paths seem to have crossed a few times.'

'I think he wants you to join them,' said the waiter.

Sure enough the man was gesturing for Holly to go across to their table.

What a stroke of luck, thought Holly, it saves me having to make the first move.

'Well that would be lovely,' said Holly, following the waiter as he moved between the tables in their direction.

As she approached, the man she now knew to be Mr Robert said, 'It's a bit busy in here tonight so Rosie and I wondered if you would like to join us,' and then hastily added, 'unless of course you are meeting someone?'

'No, I'm not meeting anyone,' said Holly, 'and it's very kind of you to offer. My name's Holly,' she added, holding her hand out to shake his and then repeating the process with his wife.

'I'm Robert,' he said, 'and this is Rosemary.'

While they had been making their introductions the waiter had brought an extra chair for Holly, and a second waiter had laid a place for her.

'The waiter called you Mr Robert,' said Holly, 'I thought that was your surname.'

'They've always called me that. I think Mr Forrester sounds too formal and Robert is too familiar, so we settled on Mr Robert,' he explained.

'It sounds like you come here a lot,' Holly observed, wondering what this man did for a living to enable him to afford frequent trips to a five-star resort in Mauritius. Maybe he really was a retired rock star, although he didn't look familiar.

'Robert's an architect,' said his wife. Holly was surprised. Had Rosemary read her mind about his occupation? 'He designed and built this hotel and the owners were so pleased with the result we are allowed to come and stay whenever we want, provided they are not too busy. They even named the Italian restaurant after him,' Rosemary explained, positively glowing with pride.

'What an amazing coincidence,' said Holly. 'My—' she stopped herself just in time and recovered. 'My goodness, what a lovely building.'

Robert and Rosemary were both looking at her expectantly, waiting for her to explain the coincidence but she knew better than to deviate too far from her cover story and create too many lies as at some point she might forget a lie she had told. Instead of referring back to her slip she pushed her chair back and said, 'Shall we get some food? I'm really hungry after a rather energetic game of beach volley ball I played earlier.'

When they sat back down at the table, their plates filled with delicious-looking antipasti, the waiter, Siraj, approached with a bottle of red wine.

'Do you like red?' Rosemary asked. 'The waiters know it is our preferred tipple so they don't bother to take our order any more.'

'I think I will stick to water this evening,' said Holly. 'I enjoyed rather too much of a bottle of white last night, I'm afraid.'

'Are you sure, because we can easily ask for a glass of white if you would prefer that to the red. After all, you are on holiday,' Rosemary said.

Holly thought she noticed just the tiniest hint of a question at the end of Rosemary's statement but she ignored it and answered, 'No thanks, I'll just stick with water although I may go crazy and have sparkling if that's okay?' she said to Siraj.

'No problem, madam,' responded Siraj, leaving the bottle of red wine on the table for Robert and Rosemary to help themselves.

'So do you often holiday on your own?' persisted Rosemary.

There was no escaping the direct question but Holly had been expecting it so she was well-rehearsed with her answer.

'No, I used to holiday with my husband,' she said in a slightly faltering voice, fingering the gold band on her left ring finger. Funny how the little token of affection that Gareth had given her all those years ago helped to validate her cover story. Holly was pretty sure it wasn't real gold so it was just as well she didn't have to wear it all the time or she may have ended up with green-fingers and not of the gardening variety.

There was an awkward pause during which they all concentrated on eating the food on their plates before Rosemary ventured, 'Are you not together any more?'

'He's dead,' Holly said quietly, a single tear rolling down her cheek. It was a reaction this lie always produced because if it had been the truth she would have cried, and Gareth had been dead to her from the moment she had lost contact with him when he went to America.

The older woman reached across and placed her hand on Holly's arm.

'I am so sorry,' she said with genuine remorse in her voice. 'I didn't mean to pry.'

Holly looked into Rosemary's eyes and immediately wished she hadn't. They were full of compassion and concern. It was the look she had hoped for from her mother when she had told her about the baby but instead she had been met with a look of revulsion and disgust.

Holly shook her head to clear the image of her mother from her mind, wiped the tear away and said, 'It's okay, I'm getting used to being on my own,' which was the first truthful thing she had said in several minutes. 'We came to Mauritius on our honeymoon and I felt a need to come back, a kind of closure I suppose.'

Rosemary nodded her understanding and Robert remained silent with his head down, seemingly concentrating on his food.

Holly was glad that the lie had the desired effect of closing the conversation about her private life, just as it always did, but she was feeling terribly guilty about Rosemary's reaction to it.

CHAPTER 11

After Holly said goodnight to Robert and Rosemary, she didn't feel like going for cocktails on the beach with the youngsters from the mobile phone company, choosing instead to return to her room and check if the Internet was back on. She was relieved to find that it was for two reasons. She would be able to send the work she had done that morning and, more importantly, she suddenly felt the need to chat to Harry.

She was still feeling upset about lying to Robert and Rosemary, which was strange considering she had told the lie about her dead husband dozens of times to scores of people over the last eight months since she had started this job. It was Rosemary's reaction that had unsettled her, looking into her eyes with such love for a person she barely knew, and she could have sworn she had seen a tear fall from the end of Robert's nose onto his fried whitebait.

They really were a lovely couple, Holly thought, and obviously still very much in love. They hadn't mentioned how long they had been married, probably not wanting to rub salt into Holly's wound, but they had both looked sad when she asked if they had any children and Rosemary replied that they hadn't been blessed with that gift.

Perhaps that's why I'm feeling so wretched, thought Holly. I fell pregnant a few months into a relationship with a man who obviously didn't love me as much as I loved him, and they are happily married and would have been able to offer a child so much. It just didn't seem fair.

Even though she had been frightened and alone, after her mother had refused to speak to her and warned her dad that he mustn't either, Holly had never once contemplated having an abortion. She had no idea how she was going to manage financially but she had loved her baby from the moment she had felt the first tiny fluttering in her swelling belly.

She hated denying Harry's existence to her new friends but the less anyone knew about her real life the better and besides it had only been a part untruth when Rosemary had asked whether Holly and her husband had ever had any children.

Holly had never been married so technically she had no children with a husband, but it had still felt wrong not to tell them about Harry, although she had almost let it slip when Rosemary had revealed Robert's occupation.

She reached for her iPad and pressed the Facetime button and then selected Harry's number.

Moments later her son's smiling face popped up on the screen.

'Only a day late, Mum,' Harry said in his good-natured manner. 'I noticed your blog wasn't up so I wondered if you had been snowbound at Gatwick?'

'Hi Harry, sorry but the Internet was down and I haven't got 3G on this thing. It was pretty bad at Gatwick as it happens, we were probably the last flight out. What's it like in Bath?'

'Two feet of snow,' he enthused. 'It's been brilliant. We just got back from a snowball fight and we've been racing down the hills on campus on trays from the canteen. Look.' He stood up and moved his iPad behind his back to show his mum a big wet patch on his bottom.

'Harry, you're such a child,' she teased. 'Have you been sitting on your sofa in your soaking wet jeans?'

'Oops,' he said. 'Not to worry it will have dried out by the time I get home from work always assuming there are any buses running. I'm not risking Toby on those roads.' Toby was their nickname for the ancient green Vauxhall Corsa he had inherited when his mum had bought a newer car with her extra earnings. The number plate started with T and ended OBY so the pet name had been obvious. 'You okay?'

'All the better for seeing you,' she said in a jokey manner, but meaning every word. 'I had dinner tonight with a couple who were on the same flight as me yesterday. They seem really nice so I hated having to lie to them. You'll never guess what the man does for a living?'

'Brain surgeon, astronaut, prime minister ... am I close?'

Holly laughed indulgently. 'He's an architect, he

designed and built this hotel. How weird is that?'

'Shame you can't tell him about me, he might have been useful when I've finished my degree. Contacts and all that. Gotta go, Mum, I've got a bit of coursework to finish before my shift at the pub. Love you.'

Holly just had time to say 'love you too' before Harry hung up at the other end.

She marvelled at the young man her son had turned into, and so handsome too. She hoped he wouldn't break some young girl's heart like his dad had.

She turned her iPad off and picked up her laptop, as she preferred writing with a proper keyboard. Reading through her work from that morning, she made one minor adjustment and then pressed send. Her shoulders were starting to ache from the beach volleyball as she settled back onto her pillows to make a start on Day Two.

CHAPTER 12

Life's a Beach ... in Mauritius

Even after a twelve hour flight from the UK, which had been delayed three hours due to snow, I wasn't too tired to appreciate the look of the Plantation House resort, designed by British architect Robert Forrester, as we approached. As the name suggests it is built in the style of the colonial sugar plantations, but on a grander scale and with some clever modern features.

The entrance is at the top of half a dozen steps but this wouldn't be a problem for you if you are in a wheelchair as there are ramps either side.

The reception area was a pleasant cool relief from the heat of the early afternoon sun with ceiling fans and a breeze from the glassless windows. The view is fabulous as the hotel gardens meet the beach. I felt like kicking my shoes off and making a run for the sea. You know me, I love the feel of the sand between my toes.

Check-in was very civilised, seated in a lounge

sipping a cocktail, and loads of staff on hand. It beats queuing up at a desk for the next available receptionist. It only took about fifteen minutes and then I was taken to my room on the back of a golf buggy. I should imagine if you are in the main building you might be expected to walk to your room with a porter taking care of your bags.

The staff seem very attentive and eager to please without being intrusive, and they all have their names on little metal name badges to give a personal touch. I deliberately requested a room change, even though there was nothing wrong with the one I was in, and my request was met with no suggestion that I had put them to any trouble.

My room is a deluxe double with a sea view so I can sit on my balcony and enjoy the sunset, which last night was spectacular. The balcony is a decent size with a lounger and a table and chairs, but the terraces on the ground floor are bigger so you could request that if you need more space.

The room itself is easily big enough for either two double beds or a king size and there are two comfy chairs and a table as well as a writing desk... handy for me! The furniture is generally a bit dark and old-fashioned, but the decor is neutral and there is a flat screen TV. The deluxe rooms have a bath and a separate shower, and the loo is in its own little room. My favourite thing in the room is the venetian blind at the glass-less window that separates the bathroom from the bedroom – a little bit of privacy if you close it but quite sexy for newlyweds when left open and I would definitely recommend this hotel as a romantic honeymoon destination or even the perfect location for a beach wedding.

I had dinner in the main restaurant tonight which is buffet style and seems to cater for most dietary needs. There is a different theme each evening with tonight's being Asian cuisine. I opted for the Thai green curry and I can highly recommend it.

There are two other restaurants on the complex which I shall try out during my stay, purely research of course, so I'll let you know how much of the menu is available to you if you are travelling 'All Inclusive' like me.

Time to try out the comfort level of my bed and pillows... I'll let you know tomorrow.

Liberty Sands xx

Rosemary nestled into her husband's shoulder as he stroked her hair. She had always found his touch calming and soothing which was just what she needed after hearing Holly's tragic story. Rosemary had sensed a sadness in the younger woman the moment she had noticed her sitting on her own in the departure lounge at Gatwick airport. She hadn't looked like someone going on holiday, nor had she the look of anticipation of meeting up with friends or her partner in Mauritius.

'What a terrible shock it must have been for her,' Rosemary said, voicing her thoughts, 'to lose someone you love so much. At least we will have time to say our goodbyes.'

Robert continued stroking her hair, not trusting himself to speak. It had taken him years to find the person he wanted to devote himself to for the rest of his life and he still found it difficult to believe he was going to lose her.

The diagnosis had come out of the blue, after

a routine health check, but the experts believed they had caught the chronic myeloid leukaemia in time, particularly as the early results with the oral chemotherapy drugs had been so encouraging.

No one could have predicted that Rosemary would develop the rare mutation known as T3151 that stopped the medication from working. Her body thought it was being clever by finding a way around the block the drugs provided but the reverse was true.

They had been told by the doctors that there was still hope that newer, experimental drugs might work even though they had worse side-effects, and she was put on the register for a suitable donor for a stem cell transplant, providing the leukaemia could be brought sufficiently under control.

After three months on the drug most likely to work, during which time Rosemary had experienced hypertension, severe headaches, nosebleeds and a skin rash, a bcr/abl blood test revealed the condition was not improving.

She was given another drug that had made her so sick that she couldn't keep any food down. After a month of being violently sick after each dose of medication, even though there was nothing but bile in her stomach, she had lost two stone in weight, and there was still no improvement in the leukaemia. That was when she had told Robert that she was going to come off the medication. He remembered her words with absolute clarity. *'I'm sorry Bobby, I'm just too much of a coward to carry on,'* she had said, which was not true as she didn't have a cowardly bone in her body.

She had cried then for the first time since the diagnosis eighteen months earlier and he had cried with her.

Rosemary broke into his thoughts.

'You're very quiet,' she said. 'What are you thinking?'

'I was just thinking how much I love you,' he replied, hoping she wouldn't notice the wobble in his voice. 'And what a kind person you are to care so much about Holly when we've only just met her and you have your own troubles to deal with.'

'You know me, Bobby. I'm a sucker for a sob story, and besides I get the feeling that there is much more heartbreak in Holly's life that she has kept bottled up inside,' she said, arching her neck so she could look up at him with her cornflower blue eyes. 'I want to help her.'

'Well let's start by asking her to dinner with us again tomorrow,' he said. 'Maybe she will open up a bit more when she knows us better.'

Her husband had clearly forgotten they were dining with Philippe the following evening but Rosemary hadn't.

'That's an excellent idea,' she said, a smile touching her lips.

CHAPTER 14

The smooth even strokes running up and down her back, and the heady aroma of frangipani in the body oil were working their magic on Holly. Good decision to book the spa treatment for this morning, she thought, particularly as it had rained overnight and was still looking grey and threatening. Not only that but every muscle Holly had used during the beach volleyball game was now hurting, even her fingers.

Maybe her aching muscles were the reason she hadn't slept particularly well again. It wasn't the air conditioning this time. Perhaps the heavy rain beating down on the corrugated iron roof had disturbed her, or possibly the mattress was a little too firm for her liking.

Most likely it was the guilt she was still feeling at lying to Rosemary and Robert. That feeling hadn't lessened at all when she had bumped into them as she was leaving the restaurant after breakfast and they had invited her to dinner that night. She had been about to say no and fabricate some excuse, after all she was working and her best blogs were when she mixed with as many diverse groups of people as possible, but there was something about the woman's expression that meant that before she knew it she agreed to meet them for dinner in Waves restaurant at eight o'clock.

I will still be working, Holly reasoned, as I'll be finding out what's on the menu if you're all inclusive and a vegetarian.

Holly was regretting her decision to claim to be vegetarian on this trip, wishing she had gone for gluten-free instead so that at least she could have sampled some of the delicious-looking seafood. I'll have to go to dinner away from the resort one night, she thought, as it would be such a shame not to try at least one of the local fish recipes.

Without warning the masseuse started kneading very firmly into her shoulders and she had to bite her lip to stop her crying out in pain.

'Madam is very tight,' he said, which made Holly giggle into the massage bed, despite the discomfort.

The word tight could mean so many different things in different situations. He could mean she was tight with money, which in Holly's case was usually true as she didn't have a lot of cash to splash around. He could have been alluding to the growing closeness between Holly and her new friends. He could even be suggesting, in urban speak, that he thought Holly was stylish and cool. That was the one that made Holly giggle as nothing was further from the truth. She made as much of an effort with her appearance as was possible on a limited budget, but she would never describe herself as stylish. Maybe she was just a little bit cool, at least that was what Harry's school friends had thought.

She was quite different from the other mothers at his school. She was younger than the majority, she dressed in jeans and T shirts most of the time, she worked in publishing and she allowed Harry to drink beer and wine at home.

Nothing cool about that, she thought. Holly knew he would have experimented with alcohol anyway so at least by allowing him to drink at home she could keep an eye on him and not make it seem so special and grown-up.

Holly's plan had worked. After the initial interest, when he was about fourteen, Harry could take or leave alcohol.

He's probably the most sober second-year university student in the UK, Holly thought proudly, and yet, judging by their Facetime call the previous evening, he still managed to have a good time. At least he can remember the fun he's had, she thought.

The masseuse was now rotating Holly's left arm and digging his fingers into her shoulder blade. This was more like a form of torture than the gentle massage she had been expecting. He moved around the table and repeated the process on her right arm and then pulled both arms behind her forcing her shoulders up from the table.

At that moment the rain started again, rattling on the corrugated iron roof, and Holly realised what was missing from this treatment room. There was no soothing, relaxing background music and the lighting could have been a bit softer too. It was more like the rugby club physio room, where she had occasionally been allowed to spend time with Gareth after a particularly physical match, than a luxury hotel spa. It was a shame really as the entrance was beautiful walking through the Japanese style water garden to the treatment rooms. It was just the rooms themselves that spoilt the overall experience.

The massage had moved down to her legs now and the gentle pressure of thumbs against her sore calves felt good.

Ten minutes later her time was up and she was led back to the reception area to sign for her complimentary treatment.

'Do you sell nail varnish remover?' Holly asked. The polish had chipped off one of her nails and Holly hated the unkempt appearance it gave.

'I'm afraid we don't,' said Diana, the girl behind the reception desk, 'but you should be able to get some in the hotel shop, or if you fancy a walk into Flic en Flac it would be cheaper in the chemist's.'

'Thanks for the tip,' said Holly smiling. 'How long would it take me to walk into the town?'

'About twenty minutes along the road, or thirty minutes along the beach,' she replied. 'Or you could take the bus. It stops right outside the hotel and it's only a few rupees.'

Very honest and helpful, thought Holly as she flip-flopped her way towards the hotel shop, splashing the back of her legs with water that had yet to dry up from the recent rain shower.

The grey clouds had cleared away by the middle of the afternoon, leaving behind a few of the white, fluffy variety in an otherwise clear blue sky. Holly decided to walk along the beach in the opposite direction to Flic en Flac to check out what some of the other hotels had to offer in terms of location and style.

In the near distance she could see a small cluster of houses which she surmised must have incredible views of the entire beach. Beyond them were the mountains of the south of the island with dark grey rain clouds shrouding them like old men's beards.

It was very warm so Holly was wearing factor 50, her baseball cap and a loose cotton kaftan to protect her shoulders. As she walked she couldn't help but notice how sunburned some of the people were who had arrived with her two days previously. Holly couldn't understand the logic. What was the point of sitting in the sun and turning red? It was one of the topics of the welcome speech that Fleur had most definitely not skipped or even hurried through.

It annoyed Holly to see that some people had ignored her sound advice for themselves, but she found it upsetting to see children with red shoulders and faces still playing in the full glare of the sun.

She had noticed how particular the Italian couple had been with their little girl the day before, just as she had been with Harry when he was a baby, even though they rarely ventured beyond their back garden where it wasn't exactly tropical. The baby had let her mum put the thick white lotion onto her arms and legs and tummy and then she had 'helped' her mum to rub it in. Her mum had carefully smoothed it over the little girl's face so that it didn't go in her eyes and had put a sunhat with a big brim on her daughter for extra protection.

They had come onto the beach near her again today, just as she was about to set off on her walk, and had volunteered to watch her stuff, which Holly had happily agreed to, not that there was anything worth taking. She was carrying her camera with her to take some pictures for her next blog and everything else of value was locked away in the safe in her room. It was nice of them to offer though and it would give her the opportunity to talk to them about the facilities for families with young children if they were still there when she got back from her walk.

Holly had passed several hotels fronting onto the beach, all quite different from the Plantation House. Most of them were set back from the beach a little so that you had the hotel gardens and swimming pools to relax and enjoy the view but a couple fronted directly onto the beach and in these places the beach appeared more crowded. There was quite a variety in style too from the ultra modern, boxy Mar et Ciel built almost entirely of glass, to the more traditional grass-roofed huts of La Badamier, named after a local tree whose big waxy leaves offered shade from the heat of the day.

Eventually the beach gave way to vegetation and Holly decided to turn back rather than tackling the damp earth and giant tree roots in her bare feet. It was a shame as the pretty houses of Tamarina Bay were almost in touching distance now.

Maybe another day, she thought as she carefully

picked her way across a mound of coral washed up by the tide. She pulled out her camera to take a photograph of the thousands of weirdly shaped pieces. She zoomed in to get a close-up but with a shudder realised that it looked like a desecrated graveyard with the bones of corpses piled high. She trained her camera lens on the houses at Tamarina instead, wondering idly who might live there.

CHAPTER 15

At two minutes to eight Holly stood at the entrance to Waves restaurant waiting to be shown to her table. She was a couple of minutes early, one of the habits she had formed when picking Harry up from school. She couldn't bear the thought of him standing alone and frightened at the school gate as she herself had on so many occasions as a child.

The waitress, Ornelia, who had served her lunch the previous day approached. 'Table for one madam?' she enquired.

'No,' replied Holly, 'I'm dining with the Forresters this evening.'

'Oh yes,' Ornelia said, 'they mentioned they were dining with friends tonight. Please follow me.'

Had Holly misheard? Had the waitress just said friends, plural?

Holly could see Robert and Rosemary now, standing next to a table right at the front of the restaurant, chatting to the same manager in his cream linen suit that she had seen them with on her first evening. Friends in high places, thought Holly, as she made her way across the restaurant. Very useful for getting the best table in the place.

At that moment Rosemary saw her, said something to the two men and they turned and watched as she walked the final few steps towards them.

'Holly you look beautiful,' Rosemary said as she pulled her into a warm embrace. 'There are so few people who can wear yellow, but it really suits you.'

Holly had dressed for the occasion in her favourite shift dress and twisted her dark curls into the bejewelled Butler & Wilson hair clip that Harry had bought her for Christmas. It was the name which had attracted him to it, a little private joke for the two of them to share, but Holly had fallen in love with the clip the moment she opened the shocking pink box and wore it whenever she needed an extra boost of confidence. A light application of make-up completed her look.

'Thank you,' she said, blushing slightly. 'So do you.'

Rosemary wore a full-length floral dress in pink, which fell away from her body beneath the bust disguising her thinness. Her golden wavy hair gathered softly on her shoulders and her smile lit up her startlingly blue eyes.

'This is Philippe,' said Rosemary, gesturing to the man in the linen suit.

Philippe took Holly's hand and raised it briefly to his lips. '*Enchanté*,' he murmured.

Holly hardly noticed what he said. This was the horseman from the beach the previous morning, the one who had reminded her of Brad Pitt and

Gareth. On closer examination he wasn't that much like Gareth at all apart from his colouring and his physique. His facial features were sharper, particularly the thin, slightly hooked Gallic nose and his piercing green eyes which were looking directly into her own olive ones.

She blushed again, aware that she hadn't said anything.

'Nice to meet you,' she stammered.

Philippe released her hand, and moved behind her to pull the chair out for her sit down. Robert had done the same for his wife before taking his seat opposite her. Regaining her composure, Holly sat and then was a little surprised when Philippe took the fourth chair at the table. Dining with the paying guests was not completely unheard of but it was quite unusual and she wondered if the hotel group was aware that their managers fraternised in this way when clearly on duty.

At that moment another restaurant manager, who Holly hadn't seen before, approached their table with the menus and asked what they would like to drink.

'We'll start with a bottle each of the house red and white,' said Robert. 'If that's all right with everyone?' he added.

'Fine with me,' confirmed Philippe.

'May I also have a bottle of sparkling water please?' Holly asked.

'Certainly madam,' said the manager, whose little metal badge gave his name as Vij. 'I will come back and take your order presently.'

'Are you not drinking again this evening?'

questioned Rosemary. 'The house wine here really is very good.'

'I know,' smiled Holly. 'If you remember I sampled rather too much of it on my first evening,' she admitted, regretting her confession immediately. She didn't want to sound like a lush but she didn't want to appear anti-social either, so she continued, 'I'm sure one glass won't do any harm but I do enjoy the refreshment of sparkling water when I'm in hot countries.'

'I agree,' Rosemary said. 'Nothing is quite like water for quenching a thirst.'

Holly smiled appreciatively at Rosemary, grateful for her help in getting out of the hole she had just dug for herself. She opened the menu, which thankfully was big enough for her to hide behind, so that she didn't need to speak for a few moments. She hadn't expected another person to be joining them for dinner and it had caught her off guard especially as this Frenchman was so good looking. She risked a glance over the top of her menu to find that Philippe was looking straight at her.

'Were you wearing a coral dress on your first evening here?' he asked. Rosemary and Robert both turned to look at him. 'And your hair was loose, yes?'

Holly nodded.

'I remember seeing you in the restaurant and wondering who the lucky person was that you were dining with, and now it's me.'

There was an awkward pause before Robert joked, 'I think we could safely call that the direct approach.'

'I'm sorry if I have embarrassed you, Holly? It's

just that I couldn't help but notice such a beautiful woman.'

Holly smiled. 'I'm flattered rather than embarrassed,' she said, lowering her eyes back to the menu.

Vij returned and placed a basket of various breads on the table, before pouring the wine and taking their food order. The other three had all ordered fish for their main course and once again Holly regretted her decision to claim to be a vegetarian.

'So how long have you worked at the hotel, Philippe?' she asked, savouring the fruity crispness of another good quality French wine.

Philippe looked puzzled, but Robert immediately understood the confusion.

'It's the suit, Philippe,' he laughed. 'I told you that you looked like one of the restaurant managers in it.'

Holly could feel she was blushing again. That would explain why he wasn't wearing a little metal name badge. Why hadn't she just asked him what he did for a living rather than assuming he worked at the hotel just because he was wearing a cream linen suit. Never assume anything, she mentally admonished herself, it makes an ass out of u and me!

Thankfully Philippe had now joined in the laughter with Robert and Rosemary.

'Let me rephrase that,' Holly said. 'What do you do for a living?'

Before Philippe could speak Rosemary said proudly, 'He's a writer.'

Philippe quickly interrupted, placing his hand on Rosemary's arm to remind her of her promise. 'I used to be a journalist, but now I'm trying to write a book.'

'Really? What is your book about?' she asked.

Philippe had a mischievous look on his face as he answered, 'It's a travel guide about Mauritius. I've been living here for the past nine months to really get a feel for the place.'

How weird that this man should be a travel writer too, thought Holly, albeit he was writing a book and she wrote blogs.

'Really? Well I'm going on a sightseeing trip of the island on Friday. Perhaps you would like to come too and do some more research?' she teased, assuming that he had already traversed the island several times before embarking on his travel guide.

'I would like that very much,' replied Philippe. 'What time shall we meet?'

Holly had inadvertently backed herself into a corner. As it didn't look as though Rosemary was going to come to her rescue this time she simply said, 'I'm being picked up at nine thirty from the hotel reception.'

'Well, that's a date then.'

Was it a date? thought Holly. What on earth am I doing? I'm supposed to be working.

'It'll be good company for you, Holly,' Rosemary chipped in. 'Much better than going on your own.'

Holly knew she couldn't really retract her offer and anyway she might be able to pick up some useful information from the handsome Frenchman. Besides, she quite liked the idea of spending a day in his company.

CHAPTER 16

It had been a thoroughly enjoyable evening, Holly thought, as she unlocked the door to her room having said goodbye to her dinner companions. The food had been delicious and then the four of them had moved through to the bar area to watch local dancers in colourful costumes performing their national dances, accompanied by musicians beating out the rhythm on a ravanne, a tambor-style drum.

When the show finished they went to sit on the comfy sofas next to the beach, in close proximity to the bonfire that was lit every night at dusk. Holly had seen them building the fires in a pyramid shape in specially dug out pits each afternoon but this was the first opportunity she had to enjoy one, and how nice to be sharing it with friends.

Friends, she mused. I've only known Robert and Rosemary for two days and yet I feel like I've known them a lifetime.

And now she had met Philippe. Holly was no fool, she realised that she had been set up. The invitation to dinner was deliberate so that they could be introduced to each other but she didn't care. He was handsome and funny and she was flattered by the attention he paid her and his obvious attraction towards her.

Philippe didn't seem to want the evening to end and had persuaded the others to join him for a nightcap by the beach. Robert and Rosemary had sat on one sofa and she had sat next to Philippe on the other. By this time he had removed his linen jacket and rolled his shirt sleeves up as the night air was so warm. At one point they had both reached for their drinks at the same time and their arms had touched, skin against skin. It was like an electric shock running through her body as she had quickly withdrawn her arm but not before realising that the attraction he felt for her was not one-sided. She had coloured up again and she felt breathless and light-headed but not as a result of alcohol. She had kept to her promise of just one glass of wine, and her nightcap was fruit juice.

It had been a long time since Holly had allowed herself to be attracted to a man, not that there had been much opportunity until she had started her job writing secret travel blogs for the Soleil Hotel Group. Prior to that she had worked mostly from home, apart from the two mornings a week that she volunteered at the local charity shop while Harry was at school.

There hadn't been much chance of meeting Mr Right there, she thought wryly.

All the other volunteers had been at least twice her age and predominantly female, apart from Bert, whose surname was ironically 'Wright', but who was definitely not her type!

Do I have a type, she pondered?

There had only ever been Gareth. He was the only man she had ever truly loved. Maybe that was all the attraction to Philippe was? A passing similarity to the love of her life.

No, she thought, it's more than that. There was definitely chemistry. She had felt comfortable in his company, chatting about his writing and his time in Mauritius. What a shame I'm only here for a week, she thought, he is someone I would like to spend time with and get to know better.

She smiled at the pleasurable thought of having a whole day with him on Friday on the sightseeing trip.

Holly had been expecting Philippe to ask what she was doing in Mauritius on her own but he didn't, so she presumed Robert and Rosemary had filled him in on her tragic cover story, however he had asked whether she worked. She had been expecting that question too so the lie came easily. She didn't mention her freelance copy-editing job, nor her incognito travel blogging. Instead she said she worked for a charity, which was only a little white lie.

Holly turned on her computer and logged into Wordpress. She was relieved she had written her blog about the day prior to going for dinner. Her head was full of thoughts about Philippe and she doubted she would have been able to create the standard of work her readers were used to and that she demanded of herself. She went on to her dashboard and clicked the publish button.

CHAPTER 17

The silvery moon was casting a broad sparkling path onto the dark ocean. Philippe wondered why the path always seemed to lead to the person looking at it. There was probably a very simple explanation but he didn't have a scientific brain. He was a wordsmith, although that was debatable at the moment.

He loved the view from this window both day and night. It was no wonder that his friends wanted to buy this house. He had been surprised to learn, when they had dined together on Monday night, that they still hadn't reached a decision about buying it. At his question they had exchanged glances and made the same vague excuse about things to sort out at home before quickly changing the subject. He didn't think they had money worries and he couldn't imagine what else might be holding them back from buying the home of their dreams.

The lights of torches twinkling in the shallow waters near the shore caught his attention. When he had first come to stay at the house he had thought that maybe it was some kind of smuggling operation, letting his writer's imagination run riot. When he mentioned his suspicions to Delphine, the woman who came to clean for him once a week, she had started to laugh.

'No no, Mr Philippe,' she had said. 'It is the local fishermen looking for prawns.'

The next time she arrived to clean she brought him a child's plastic beach bucket filled to overflowing with prawn and other local delicacies. Philippe was not a great cook, despite his French heritage, another failure on the part of his mother, but he had made a very passable bouillabaisse from a recipe he had found on the Internet.

This was the first of many deliveries of fresh fish and although Delphine insisted she didn't want any payment, Philippe always added a few hundred rupees to her cleaning money envelope. She never made reference to it and the additional rupees were worth their weight in gold for the local information he was able to glean from Delphine. The best restaurants and bars for a bit of local colour, help in buying his battered old car and even, on occasion, a bit of adult company. Philippe didn't like the idea of paying for sex but he certainly didn't want the complication of an affair, or worse still falling in love, while he was trying to work on his book.

And now I fear it has happened, he thought, as he remembered the electricity that had shot through him like a lightening bolt when he had accidentally touched arms with Holly earlier that evening.

He had initially been annoyed with Rosemary for inviting someone else to join them for dinner, but when he had turned and seen the vision in yellow walking across the restaurant towards them he couldn't believe his luck. His heart had skipped a beat as she had held her hand out to shake his and he instead had brushed the back of it with his lips. How he had wished he was kissing her full pink lips instead but he was hopeful that would come. He knew he had been very forward inviting himself on her sightseeing trip but he hadn't been able to stop himself. And she didn't say no, he thought triumphantly.

When he had arrived at the restaurant, ten minutes after the designated time of 7.45 p.m., Rosemary had quickly filled him in on Holly's tragic recent history.

'I want to make her happy again,' Rosemary had said. 'I want to see her smile reach her beautiful eyes.'

Philippe pictured those dark olive eyes and he knew exactly what Rosemary meant. There was an underlying sadness buried very deep and he was determined to release her from it.

CHAPTER 18

Holly woke early the next morning feeling strangely refreshed even though she had only been asleep for six hours. After posting her blog the previous night she had climbed into bed, without even cleaning her teeth, and fallen asleep almost immediately, a smile on her face and her head full of images of Philippe.

She dressed quickly in a vest top and shorts, cleaned her teeth and splashed her face with water before heading to the beach for a pre-breakfast walk, hoping for a chance encounter with Philippe. At dinner she hadn't mentioned seeing him riding his horse on the beach and he didn't mention it either, so presumably he hadn't recognised her behind her sunglasses and baseball cap.

He wasn't on the beach, even though she walked past Flic en Flac reasoning that the longer she stayed on the beach the more chance she would have of seeing him. She felt an irrational pang of disappointment when she got back to her room, having seen no one but the various hotel gardeners and a few local fisherman.

On the bright side, at least her early start meant she was on the beach before ten o'clock and her spirits lifted further when she saw the Italian couple and their gorgeous little girl already splashing around in the sea. She arranged her towel on the sun lounger, hung her sarong over the strut of the beach umbrella and crossed the few short paces on the already hot sand to the sea.

'Ciao', she ventured in her novice Italian.

The mother smiled.

'You speak Italian?'

'Not much I'm afraid,' Holly replied. 'Just a few phrases I've picked up on my travels and from restaurant menus.'

'Well I like that you try,' the woman said, moving towards Holly. 'I am Mathilda and this is Giulietta,' she said, stroking the side of her daughter's face. The little girl smiled coyly and then turned her face into her mother's shoulder.

'Ciao Giulietta,' Holly said, causing the little girl to turn back towards her. 'I'm Holly.'

At that moment a mobile phone started to ring.

'That is my husband Umberto,' Mathilda said, casting her eyes in his direction as he rushed up the beach to retrieve his phone from a brightly coloured beach bag. 'We are supposed to be on holiday but he is always working,' she continued with a hint of annoyance in her voice.

'How long are you here for?' Holly asked.

'We only came for a week,' she answered, 'and sadly

we go home tomorrow. It has been our first holiday since Giulietta was born and she has really enjoyed playing on the beach.'

On hearing her name the little girl started to wriggle, so her mother dangled her from under the arms allowing her feet to kick in the sea.

'Is it your first time here?'

'Yes,' Mathilda said. 'How about you?'

'I came here on my honeymoon,' Holly said, another effortless lie escaping her lips, to keep her cover story consistent.

'Your husband is not with you this time?' queried Mathilda.

'No,' Holly said. 'He died.'

The Italian woman looked shocked and saddened.

'I'm so sorry,' she said. 'I didn't mean to pry.'

'You weren't to know,' Holly reassured her, noticing as she spoke that Mathilda was glancing almost protectively in the direction of her own husband.

The two women continued to chat amicably while Giulietta paddled in the warm sea. Holly had been wondering about Mathilda's command of the English language and it turned out that she was bi-lingual due to an English mother and an Italian father. Apparently they had met when her mother had visited Rimini on holiday with a group of friends. Her father had been a waiter in a restaurant and it was love at first sight. They were still together thirty years and five children later.

A holiday romance with a happy ending, Holly thought, a small smile playing at the corners of her mouth and a million butterflies fluttering in her stomach.

Mathilda was asking her something but she had no idea what it was because she had been daydreaming about Philippe.

'I'm sorry Mathilda I didn't quite catch that,' admitted Holly.

'It must be my accent,' said Mathilda apologetically. 'I was just asking if you would like to join us for lunch?'

'I'd love to,' replied Holly, putting her working hat back on. It would give her a perfect opportunity to see how helpful the staff were at catering for families with small children.

In the end it was just Holly, Mathilda and Giulietta who had lunch in Waves restaurant. Whatever work problem the phone call had brought up, Umberto was clearly finding it difficult to solve. He had gone to their room which, it turned out, was in the same block as Holly's but on the ground floor, and he was sitting on their terrace frantically bashing the keys of his lap top with an exasperated expression on his face. When Mathilda went across to tell him that she was going to lunch he raised his eyes from the computer screen momentarily and waved to his daughter. With her free hand Giulietta waved back, her other hand was holding on to Holly's very tightly just as she had been told to do by her mother.

It's a good job the Internet is working today, Holly thought, or that would be one very unhappy hotel guest.

Holly spent most of the afternoon with Mathilda and Giulietta. After lunch they went to the children's play area together. It was nothing like any of the council playgrounds Holly had taken Harry to when he was little. It was themed around children's fairytales, with a life-sized gingerbread house complete with toadstool tables and log stools for the children to sit and draw. In one corner there was a low tower which was a helter skelter. There was a painting of Rapunzel's face next to a window near the top and the slide was painted yellow as though it was her hair wrapping around the tower. Giulietta loved climbing to the top with her mummy and sliding down on a mat to be caught by Holly at the bottom.

They walked back to the beach each holding one of Giulietta's hands and occasionally swinging her high in the air. Holly couldn't help thinking how sad it was that she had never been able to do that with her own child as there had only ever been her to look after him. At one point Giulietta stopped walking, let go of their hands and picked something up off the floor and carefully put it in the pocket of her yellow cotton dungarees.

'She loves to collect things,' Mathilda said, 'like the coral on the beach. I must remember to check her pocket later and remove whatever it was otherwise it will end up going through the washing machine.'

Holly smiled knowingly, remembering the time a two-year-old Harry had put a biscuit in the pocket of his shorts to eat later and then forgotten about it. The chocolate chips had melted in a forty-degree wash creating a gooey mess that she had to scrape out before re-washing them.

After walking back from the playground Giulietta was ready for a cool drink. 'It is time for your nap now. Say Ciao to Holly,' her mother said. Instead of saying anything the little girl toddled over to Holly, reached into her pocket, retrieved what she had picked up earlier and handed it to Holly.

'You're very honoured,' Mathilda said. 'She doesn't normally like to share what she has found until she has had chance to play with it.'

Holly looked down at the tiny white curled feather the little girl had given her. '*Grazie*, Giulietta.'

Holly watched mother and daughter walk across the grass towards her father who was still sitting on their terrace, working at his computer, and thought of her own father as she always did whenever she saw a white feather in an unusual place.

It had started the day of his funeral when a devastated Holly, clutching eight-month-old Harry, stayed at her father's graveside long after the other mourners had left. She had been about to leave when a solitary white feather spiralled slowly down and landed at her feet. Holly had felt that it was her dad trying to communicate with her. She had picked up the feather and later slipped it in to a compartment in her purse to always carry with her. There had been many white feathers appearing in random places over the years, usually when Holly needed comfort, reassurance or guidance. White feathers and also rainbows, the two things that she felt were a connection from beyond the grave. Holly wondered what her dad was trying to tell her this time?

Mathilda returned to the beach after putting Giulietta to bed leaving Umberto to listen out for his daughter. Holly was pleased as it gave them the opportunity to have a proper chat. They ordered a couple of colourful, non-alcoholic cocktails from the refreshment buggy that drove up and down the sandy path next to the beach, and settled on their sunbeds.

'Your husband seems to spend a lot of his holiday working,' Holly remarked.

Mathilda sipped her drink. 'He was promoted four months ago so he feels the need to always be on the end of a phone line until he has really established himself in his new role.'

'What does he do in Rimini?'

'Well in Rimini he was the import manager for a Swiss computer software company but his promotion meant that we had to move to Geneva where their head office is.'

'That must have been a bit of a wrench, leaving your family when Giulietta is so young?'

Mathilda turned to look at Holly. 'I hate it. Umberto is working so hard that Giulietta and I hardly ever see him, and of course there is no family there to help watch my baby for a few hours if I want to go shopping. I feel so isolated.'

Holly knew the feeling. She had spent the whole of Harry's early years virtually alone until he had started at primary school and she had begun to mix with other young mothers. Even then it had been awkward if they were having people to dinner as it was mostly couples.

'Have you told Umberto how you feel?'

'No. I don't want to seem ungrateful when he is working so hard for our future. It was so difficult to persuade him to come away for this holiday but despite him still working at least we have been able to spend some time together as a family. Have you ever been to Switzerland?' she asked.

'No I haven't. Most of my trips are to beach resorts,' said Holly, phrasing it in a way that was truthful and didn't mention holidays.

'Maybe you would like to come and visit us in Geneva sometime?' the Italian woman asked hopefully. 'Giulietta has really taken to you and I would certainly welcome a familiar face.'

'I would love that,' said Holly.

After they had exchanged details, Mathilda excused herself saying she needed to check on her little girl.

Holly scribbled a few lines in her notebook for the blog she would be writing later. The resort had definitely passed the 'happy parents' test.

CHAPTER 19

Holly ordered room service that evening. She was impressed to find that you could order anything off the Waves restaurant menu. The items marked with a yellow tick were part of the all-inclusive package she was on and there was plenty to choose from, particularly for vegetarians, she thought wryly.

After replacing the telephone handset she only had time for a quick shower before there was a knock at her door.

Impressive, thought Holly, back home it takes longer than that for a pizza delivery, courtesy of a dodgy old moped.

She had decided to eat on her balcony, the perfect place for a bit of people-watching as she was only fifty yards from Roberto's Italian restaurant, and she could also enjoy the soft breeze from the Indian ocean and the fragrant perfume of the frangipani carried on the balmy evening air.

As she tasted her first forkful of food she was surprised to see Umberto and Mathilda at the entrance to Roberto's waiting to be seated, without Giulietta. They were shown to a table next to the entrance which would give them a perfect view of their room, the last one of the block closest to the restaurant. Holly leaned over her balcony and could just see the baby's buggy fully reclined with netting over it to protect Giulietta from the night time bugs. Her parents would be able to hear her if she cried but Holly still felt uncomfortable that they had left her outside their room alone. That picture of Madeleine McCann and her huge haunting eyes flashed into her mind. It would be a very safe bet that her parents never got through a single day of their lives when they didn't feel regret.

Holly had never left Harry unattended for a moment, even to pop into a shop to buy a loaf of bread or a postage stamp. She would either struggle in with the buggy, often disappointed that no one volunteered to help, or she would unclip Harry from his harness and carry him into the shop, leaving the buggy outside on the pavement. Although she was short of money a buggy was replaceable if it got stolen, not so her precious child.

Maybe it was different for her because she had no one else in her life. No husband, no father and a mother who had disowned her because of one mistake.

She remembered her mother's words as if they had been spoken yesterday: 'Have a termination Holly or you will regret it for the rest of your life.'

She had been shocked by her mother's vehemence. Theirs had never been an easy relationship, with constant accusations that she was a 'daddy's girl', but that was a savage thing to say to a frightened nineteen-year-old whose boyfriend had seemingly disappeared off the face of the earth. Holly admitted that there was a good deal of truth in her accusation. She had adored her dad, but it was her mother's fault really. It was difficult to love someone who was so volatile particularly when she had been drinking. That was when she would become abusive towards Holly.

'You ruined my life,' she screamed at the terrified, cowering child on more than one occasion, along with, 'I should have got rid of you.' Holly swore that one time her mother had said in a drunken rage, 'I should have got rid of you too.' When she questioned her mother about it she was adamant that Holly had misheard, although she had sobered up pretty quickly that time.

Laughter below her balcony dragged Holly back to the present. A group of a dozen or so young people in very high spirits were heading for Roberto's. Holly wanted to tell them to shush, as they might wake the baby, but she was too late as Giulietta let out a wail. Within a few seconds Umberto was next to his daughter's pram, lifting her out to comfort her. Then he released the brake on the pushchair and wheeled it the few yards to their table in the restaurant. That was the end of his and his wife's romantic dinner for two, but in a way Holly was pleased as now she could sit back, relax and enjoy her own dinner.

A different noise attracted her attention. This time it was the sound of the almost silent golf buggy steering along the path with another room service dinner delivery. It stopped outside Robert and Rosemary's room. The waiter knocked on their door and moments later Robert appeared and took the laden tray from the waiter, rather than letting him take it into their room.

'Great minds think alike,' Holly said to herself, with a smile.

CHAPTER 20

It was Robert who had suggested dining in their room that evening. His wife looked exhausted after they had spent the day in Port Louis, the capital of Mauritius. Every trip they made to this island paradise they always went to Port Louis at least once and had lunch or dinner in the small restaurant where they had first met almost twenty years ago.

Meeting Rosemary had been the most amazing piece of good fortune. He had only returned to Mauritius to check on the progress of the building work at the Plantation House hotel the day before they met. After the initial construction period, he didn't usually return to the site of a build until the project was finished and required his final seal of approval, but there had been a problem on site which the foreman feared could prevent them from making the contracted completion date. It could have cost the company he worked for several hundreds of thousands of pounds in fines so he was immediately dispatched to sort it out.

Fortunately it transpired that someone had missed off a zero when writing down the calculations of a load-bearing wall, so there was no problem to sort out after all. As a thank you for dropping everything on his latest project in Hong Kong to fly to Mauritius, his company had told him to take a few days' holiday, all expenses paid. Not usually known for their generosity, this was too good an opportunity to miss.

He had walked into the Chez André restaurant intending only to have a glass of fruity new season Beaujolais with the owner, a friend he had made during the six months he had lived there. He was sitting at the bar looking at his own image in the mirror behind the spirit optics when a beautiful tall blonde woman appeared behind him in the reflection. She glanced around as though she was looking for someone and, on finding the place almost empty, seemed about to leave, when Robert did something completely out of character.

He swung round on his bar stool and said, 'No one here but me I'm afraid. Would you care to join me in a glass of red while you're waiting for your friends, or maybe it's just a friend, to arrive?' For a moment Robert thought he'd blown it as the slender blonde hesitated, so he quickly added, 'On the house of course, the owner's a friend of mine.'

Even to Robert's ears it had sounded crass so he was amazed when a slow smile spread across her face and she said, 'Just one then and if my friends are still a no show I'm heading back to the ship.'

That had been at 7 p.m. and it was midnight when Robert finally said goodbye to Rosemary at the gangplank of the SS *Venus*, having shared two bottles of wine, an exceptionally tasty coq au vin and an abridged version of each other's life story.

Robert knew he had met the woman he wanted to be with for the rest of his life and he had the feeling that she felt the same way.

During the course of the evening it emerged that their paths had crossed some fifteen years earlier at an engagement party in Clapham, south London. Robert had asked Rosemary what she did for a living and when she had said she was a dancer he had commented that he only knew one other dancer, his best friend's sister, Melody.

Rosemary had paused mid sip.

'What's her last name?' she asked.

'Well she's been married for fourteen years so she's Melody Brown now, but she was Melody Martin,' he replied.

'You're joking,' Rosemary exclaimed. 'We did our first dancing job together in Paris and kept in touch for years. What an amazing coincidence that you know her too.'

It turned out that they had both been at Melody's engagement party but hadn't been introduced to each other.

'Were you at the wedding?' Robert asked, surprised that he had missed noticing this stunning woman not once but twice.

'No, I was away working,' she replied. 'I had just signed my first six-month contract for the cruise line I'm still working for so I couldn't get the time off. The wedding couldn't be delayed because Mel was already pregnant with Sam. She was really upset because she wanted me to be her Maid of Honour.'

'I was Pete's Best Man,' Robert revealed. 'So we would definitely have met that day.'

They had looked deep into each other's eyes. Maybe they were meant to meet at the wedding and now fate was giving them a second chance?

Six months later they were married, with Pete as Best Man, Melody as Matron of Honour and their four children as pages and bridesmaids.

Robert looked at his beautiful, brave wife delicately picking her way through a plate of steamed vegetables and wished, as he had so many times since their meeting in Mauritius, that she had been able to go to the wedding. All those wasted years and now so little time left.

Not for the first time Robert had to swallow hard to hold back tears as he wondered what on earth he was going to do when the love of his life had gone.

CHAPTER 21

There was a message waiting for Holly at the hotel reception when she went to collect the picnic lunch she had ordered for her day out. She opened the envelope with dread, thinking that Philippe had decided to cancel, and feeling ridiculously disappointed.

The message wasn't from Philippe, it was from Rosemary.

Dear Holly (and Philippe)

Have a wonderful day out together. We would love you to join us for dinner in Roberto's this evening at 8 p.m... or for Philippe's benefit 7.45 p.m.

Love
Rosemary x

Holly didn't understand the last comment. Why would they want Philippe to get to the restaurant before her? Were they going to discuss the events of the day with him? she wondered. How very odd.

The receptionist indicated a row of cool boxes, each with a guest's name taped to it, and said the driver would lift it into the car for her when he arrived. Holly glanced at her watch. As usual she was a few minutes early so she relaxed onto a rattan sofa opposite the reception desk, waiting for the two men to arrive. She knew which one she was most looking forward to see.

The sofa was comfy and well worn and her imagination ran riot as she imagined all the various posteriors that had rested there over the years. The Plantation House was a very luxurious resort and it was rumoured that celebrities and even minor royals had stayed there since the rebuild. It had featured in the pages of glossy magazines as the backdrop for swimwear shoots and in the occasional music video, and Holly had read that it was one of the locations used in a recent Bond movie.

Who knows, she thought, maybe Daniel Craig had sat in this very spot.

'What's so funny?'

She looked up to see Philippe looking down at her with a quizzical expression on his face.

'Funny?' she repeated, jumping to her feet blushing.

'You had a big grin on your face, I thought maybe you didn't appreciate my dress sense?'

'No, no,' she said. 'I didn't even see you come in,' she continued in a fluster. 'I was daydreaming. You're early,' she stammered.

'I know,' acknowledged Philippe. 'You should feel very honoured, I am usually at least five minutes late.'

The penny dropped.

'Ah, that would explain Rosemary's note,' she said. 'They've invited us to have dinner with them tonight at Roberto's, but they gave two different times and I thought... well I'm not sure what I thought actually. Anyway you'll probably be tired of my company by then so don't feel you have to come,' she blundered on.

She felt like a schoolgirl on a first date, except that she didn't have that particular experience to draw on as she had never dated when she was in school.

It was Philippe's turn to grin. 'You're not nervous to spend the day alone with me are you?' he teased.

'Of course not,' she lied. 'Anyway we won't be alone,' she said, indicating the driver who had picked her up from the airport, who she had spotted over Philippe's shoulder.

'More is the pity,' Philippe said under his breath as he watched her move towards the driver, Sachin, hand outstretched.

Holly was explaining to him that Philippe would be joining her for the sightseeing trip, and asking if she needed to pay any extra.

'No, madam,' Sachin said. 'The price is for the car and the driver, not per person. But do you have enough picnic for two people?'

Holly unclipped the lid of the cool box and looked inside. There was fruit and salads, sandwiches and cakes, and cans of soft drink.

'There's plenty,' Holly said out loud, adding in her

head, particularly as I have totally lost my appetite since setting eyes on Philippe again.

Usually when Holly was working, going on the sightseeing tour was a necessary chore so that she could write about the experience on her blog. Not so today. She couldn't remember the last time she had enjoyed herself when it didn't revolve around her son. From the moment she had climbed into the back seat of the limo that morning, with Philippe at her side, she had felt like Holly the woman, rather than Holly the mother. Her initial nervousness at being in his company had disappeared by the time they had reached the other side of Flic en Flac. She was enjoying his proximity.

To start with Sachin had been the one answering all of Holly's many and varied questions: What was that mountain called? Who were the first inhabitants? What is the name of that tree? Is it safe to buy the fruit and coconut milk from the roadside shacks? Philippe just sat back listening and observing. His first input was when Holly asked Sachin about the colours of the Mauritian national flag.

Sachin had answered, 'The red is for the flame-flower tree. The blue is the ocean. The yellow represents the sun and the green is the wealth of vegetation on the island.'

Holly would have been quite satisfied with this explanation but Philippe interjected, 'That's the first time I have heard the red stripe described that way. I thought it represented the bloodshed during the years of slavery and more recently the fight for independence?'

Sachin regarded Philippe in his rear-view mirror. 'That is true, sir,' he confirmed, 'but peaceful Mauritians prefer to forget the past and nurture the future.'

'A good attitude,' Philippe said. 'However people usually like to know the truth.'

Holly said nothing.

'Have you also heard the interpretation regarding the four cultures who live harmoniously on the island,' Sachin asked.

Philippe nodded, but Holly, anxious to steer the conversation away from truth-telling, said, 'I haven't.'

'The red represents Hindus, the blue Creoles, yellow is the Chinese and green is Muslims,' Sachin said. 'Each has its own community but they exist happily side by side.'

The first stop on their island tour was to see the famed coloured earth at Chamarel. It could only be reached by driving along bumpy roads that were more suited to a four-wheel drive than a limo. It had rained overnight and the still-wet ground had steam rising from it as the hot sun beat down, so it was very difficult to determine the various shades of colour with the naked eye. Satisfaction rating, considering the journey and the entrance fee, was only really a five, but in Philippe's company it rose to a six.

They stopped to take some pictures of the Black River Falls. Holly had presumed the river had taken its name from the volcanic nature of the island but was corrected by Sachin who told her it was named after the African slaves who escaped and would hide out in the heavily forested area in the south of the island. Following Philippe's admonishment he had clearly decided that truth was the best policy with this tourist couple.

They drove past the huge reservoir that provided drinking water, although tourists were always advised to drink the bottled variety, to the dormant volcano called Trou au Cerfs.

Knowing Philippe's French heritage Holly turned to him and asked, 'What does Trou au Cerfs mean?'

'It's the hole of the deer,' he answered. 'There is a story that English noblemen would chase the deer for their meat, and the deer would jump into the volcano never to be seen again.'

'But it's been dormant since the island formed, hasn't it?' Holly asked.

'Someone has been doing their research,' Philippe conceded.

Funny choice of word, thought Holly, maybe he is on to me? She needn't have worried though as his next sentence confirmed.

'Or maybe you remember it from when you came here on your honeymoon?' Philippe added, his voice softening. 'Rosemary told me about your husband. It's all right Holly,' he whispered. 'You're allowed to have a life.'

She could feel the solitary tear form and then roll down the side of her nose. What precisely am I crying for? she thought. That someone has given me permission to live after all these years of self-inflicted solitude, or that I'm forced to lie to that same someone and I don't want to?

For a brief moment she toyed with the idea of telling Philippe the truth but she had only just met him and she had no idea how he would react. No doubt he would tell Robert and Rosemary and they might reveal who she was to the hotel management. She could lose her job.

Instead she simply said, 'Thank you.'

The day just got better and better. They drove through the capital Port Louis up to the north of the island where Sachin found a quiet beach backed by filaos trees so that they could enjoy their lunch out of the glare of the sun. Holly had thought she wasn't hungry, but after a bit of coaxing from Philippe she started eating and realised she was ravenous.

'I like a woman who has a healthy relationship with food,' he teased.

Is he calling me fat? she wondered for a moment, but one look at his admiring glance told her otherwise.

After lunch they walked along the beach hand in hand, like a couple in love, while Sachin packed up the lunch box and retired to his car for a nap. Holly wanted to pinch herself to make sure this was really happening and not just some cruel dream.

'This is my favourite thing to do,' she confided. 'Walking along a beach at the water's edge with the sun smiling on me.'

'Mine too,' agreed Philippe. 'But I would add in the company of someone special.'

He stepped across in front of her and took her face in both his hands. He leaned forward slightly and for a moment Holly thought he was going to kiss her.

'Don't lock yourself away from the world, Holly,' he said. 'He's gone and he's not coming back.'

Holly leant in to Philippe's chest and stayed there for several moments.

This is all happening too quickly, her sensible head told her. He knows I'm vulnerable, maybe he is just after one thing. But her heart was telling her something else. He is the first man you have felt this way about in twenty years, perhaps it's time to move on.

CHAPTER 22

Robert was worried. He wasn't sure that he should be leaving his wife for a whole day in the company of someone they had only met five days ago. And was it really fair on Holly? What if Rosemary became ill?

The alarm was due to sound in three minutes so he needed to make a decision. He could turn it off and tell Philippe he had overslept. Philippe had been very precise about the time when he had suggested the fishing trip over dinner last night. They needed to meet at 7 a.m. to catch the tide if they were to go out for the day with his fisherman friend.

'I'm awake, Bobby,' Rosemary said. 'And I know what you're thinking.' She turned to face him in the bed. 'It's only a few hours. I'll be fine and I'd like to spend some time alone with Holly. I think it would be good for both of us.'

Robert wondered which 'both of us' Rosemary was talking about. Did she mean herself and Holly, or the two of them?

'I hate the thought of being away from you for a

single minute, Rosie,' he said.

'Well I'm not coming fishing,' she teased. 'You know I get seasick on anything smaller than twenty thousand tons and anyway I wasn't invited.'

She had noticed how Robert's eyes had lit up when Philippe had suggested going fishing. He deserved a break, some time to simply enjoy himself, and she needed a break too. He had been with her twenty-four seven since she had come off the medication and although his intentions were good she was occasionally irritated by him constantly asking if she was feeling okay. Guilt overcame her at the sadness she was causing him and yet there was nothing she could have done to prevent this cancer, or was there?

When she had first been diagnosed she had asked the consultant what he thought might have caused it? He had no answers for her. Unlike lung cancer, where there was a connection with smoking, or breast cancer, where some researchers had made a connection with drinking too much alcohol, the only suggested cause for this type of leukaemia was exposure to high levels of radiation.

The shrill sound of the alarm made them both jump.

'Come on Bobby,' she urged, getting out of bed. 'You know you want to and if all goes well out on the ocean we'll be able to enjoy a fresh fish supper.'

Within twenty minutes they were showered and dressed and waiting outside the reception area with Holly for Philippe to pick them up in his car. Unsurprisingly he was late even though he was the one who had emphasised the need for punctuality in order to catch the tide.

The plan was for Rosemary and Holly to spend the day at Philippe's house while the boys were out fishing and then to cook the day's catch for supper. There had been an awkward moment when Philippe had said they would 'eat what they catch', and Rosemary had reminded him that Holly was a vegetarian. Holly had quickly said, 'I have eaten fish before just not for a while and freshly caught will taste very different from supermarket frozen, I'm sure.'

'Are you a pescatarian then?' Rosemary had asked.

'I suppose I am,' said Holly evasively. 'But just an occasional one.'

Philippe was only five minutes late and he was smiling happily as he pulled up in his old BMW.

'Sorry I am late, my friends,' he said. 'I made a quick detour into town to buy fresh croissants for Holly and Rosemary to have for breakfast, and a crate of beer for us lads,' he continued, winking at Robert.

'Don't you go getting him drunk,' Rosemary said. 'We don't want him falling overboard.'

'Don't you trust me?' Philippe asked, directing his question at Rosemary, but looking at Holly.

'I know you would never hurt anyone who is precious to me,' Rosemary answered meaningfully.

CHAPTER 23

L ight, flaky crumbs were all that remained of the breakfast croissants. They had been buttery and delicious, enjoyed with Mauritian guava jam, and strong French coffee.

The simple things, thought Holly, and then laughed at herself as she looked around at her beautiful surroundings. The view from the balcony of Philippe's house must surely be one of the best on the island and the house itself, although small, was perfectly formed.

Small compared to what? Holly asked herself. It's at least twice the size of my little two up two down back in England. I'm clearly becoming too accustomed to the five-star resorts I'm frequenting for work, she thought.

'Did Robert design this house too?' Holly asked, admiring the view from the colonial-style balcony. 'Is that how you met Philippe?'

'We did meet Philippe because of the house,' Rosemary replied, 'but no Robert didn't design it, and Philippe doesn't own it.'

She explained to Holly that they were considering buying the house and how by suggesting to Philippe that he should rent it for a year they had been able to postpone the decision.

'But why would you want to delay things if you love the house?' Holly asked. 'Surely you must be concerned that someone else may come along and steal it from under your nose?'

'It's... complicated, Holly,' the older woman said. 'I just need to be sure that it will be the right move for Robert.'

Holly didn't want to pry. There was obviously a very good reason why Robert and Rosemary hadn't yet clinched the deal on this wonderful find. It's none of my business, she thought. I'm sure Rosemary will tell me more if she wants me to know. She decided to change the subject.

'You mentioned at dinner you used to be a dancer,' Holly said. 'What type of dancing did you do, and how did you and Robert meet?'

'I met Robert twenty years ago,' Rosemary said with a wistful smile, 'and I can honestly say it was the best thing that ever happened to me. I was working for a cruise line and my ship came in, here in Mauritius, in more ways than one.'

Rosemary told Holly of the wonderful life she had enjoyed as a dancer for one of the most prestigious cruise companies in the world. Over the course of the fifteen years she had worked for the Italian-owned Goddess line, she had been a dancer, progressing to head girl and for her final five years with them she had taken on the role of choreographer as well as still performing.

Her eyes sparkled as she told Holly of all the glamorous ports of call they had visited, from the Caribbean to the Far East and most places in between. She had mixed with rich and famous clientele who could afford the five-star cruises and also celebrities who would be on board to give talks about their autobiographies, or filming for a TV holiday channel.

'I was very, very lucky, Holly, doing a job I loved and being paid for it. There's a saying isn't there? If you love your job you'll never work a day in your life.' The older woman's face was animated telling Holly about her dancing career, but then her expression changed. 'There was just one drawback,' she said. 'Because I was travelling around so much I never had the opportunity to meet someone and settle down to have a family.' She had a look of regret now as she continued. 'Goddess line had a very strict policy of not fraternising with the guests and relationships with crew members were frowned upon too. Being on a cruise ship for months on end is like being on a floating island,' she explained. 'Everyone knows each other's business, and besides most of the crew had wives back home and I've never wanted to be the "other woman".'

Holly nodded in agreement.

'So I was living this dream lifestyle but there was something missing. Love.' She looked Holly directly in the eye. 'And a life without love is really no life at all.'

Holly didn't respond to the comment which was

clearly directed at her. If only Rosemary knew how close to home that remark was. No one knew better than Holly what it was like to live for years without a meaningful physical relationship. Forget the sexual act, just to have someone touch her hair or caress her back in a protective 'you are my woman' kind of a way. Someone to tell her how beautiful she looked in a party outfit or how great her bum looked in tight jeans.

She had lavished her love on her growing child and relied upon Harry's unconditional love in return to fill the space in her heart. She had made excuses for not having boyfriends when Harry was growing up, adamant that there wouldn't be a string of 'uncles' coming and going through his childhood, driving a wedge between their special relationship. She knew it wasn't ideal for him to not have a male role model but she was determined he should have a happy, stable childhood, not like her own, where her mother had seen her as a competitor for her father's affection. But had it all been an excuse? Was she just too afraid to fall in love in case she got hurt again?

'And then I met Robert,' Rosemary said.

Having been lost in her thoughts, Holly started at the sound of Rosemary's voice.

She told Holly about the chance encounter in the restaurant in Port Louis and how they had spent the evening laughing and chatting together. They had spoken on the phone every day for the following month until the ship arrived back at its home port of Genoa. Robert had flown in from Hong Kong and was waiting on the dock side with a huge bunch of pink roses, her favourite flower.

'I walked down the gang plank to meet him knowing that I wouldn't be renewing my contract with Goddess lines,' Rosemary said, her voice full of emotion. 'I knew I'd finally met my soulmate.'

'How did you know he was the one?' Holly asked, her voice almost a whisper.

'You just do, don't you,' Rosemary replied, shrugging her shoulders slightly. 'It must have been the same for you with your husband?'

It was a probing question that demanded more than a monosyllabic response.

Holly took a deep breath. She knew that what she was about to do was risky, and might cost her her job if Rosemary decided to reveal her true identity to the hotel, but she just couldn't bear to continue with the lie to this woman who was starting to feel more like a mother to her than her own mother had ever been.

'I want to tell you something,' Holly said. 'In fact, I feel like I need to tell you, but you must promise me something first.'

'What's wrong, Holly?' she asked, reaching out for the younger woman's hand. 'What do you need to tell me?'

'Please promise me you won't repeat this to anyone, not even Robert.'

'All right, Holly,' she agreed reluctantly. 'I usually tell Robert everything, but I won't breathe a word to anyone – not even him – if you don't want me too.'

Holly felt a pang of guilt. Of course, a couple as deeply in love as Rosemary and Robert were would keep no secrets from each other. But this was her secret to tell, and the fewer people who knew about it the better. Looking into Rosemary's eyes, she felt that this was someone she could trust.

Holly's shoulders relaxed slightly and her head dropped forward as she closed her eyes momentarily, then she lifted her chin to look Rosemary in the eyes. 'I've been lying to you,' she said quietly.

'I don't understand. Why would you do that?' asked Rosemary.

'To protect my identity,' Holly replied.

'So your name isn't Holly?' Rosemary questioned, looking confused.

'No... I mean yes... my name is Holly,' she stammered, 'but the story I told you about my husband being dead is a lie.'

She could see the shocked expression on Rosemary's face and fully expected an angry response but none came. Instead she asked, 'So why would you lie about a thing like that?'

Holly could hear the incessant rumble of the waves crashing against the reef, unable to stop. She felt just as powerless to stop now that she had made her decision to tell Rosemary the truth.

'I work for Soleil Resorts as an undercover travel blogger,' she said. 'It's my job to go into their resorts and write honestly about my holiday experiences, good and bad. Not even the managers know that I am anything other than a paying guest. I usually travel alone so I need a convincing cover story, one that people won't question.'

Holly couldn't read Rosemary's expression so she ploughed on.

'When I tell people my husband is dead most of them are considerate enough not to ask for details so I can get away with telling a minimum of lies. I hate lying, it's the worst part of the job for me.'

Rosemary had still been holding Holly's hand but she let it drop.

'Well you're very good at it.' There was disappointment in her voice. 'I'm usually a very good judge of people, Holly, but you certainly fooled me with your anguished look and the depth of hurt in your eyes. I could feel your pain. I felt totally devastated for you. Perhaps you should have been an actress rather than a writer?'

Silence fell heavily between them. Holly felt dreadful as the level of concern Rosemary had felt for her became apparent.

'My mouth can lie but my eyes can't,' said Holly. Rosemary was watching her intently but she remained silent so Holly stumbled on. 'When the love of my life left me, I felt my life was over,' Holly said, stifling a sob.

'Your husband left you?' Rosemary asked, finding her voice again.

'He wasn't my husband. I've never been married. He was my boyfriend at university.'

'Oh, Holly,' said Rosemary, putting her arm around the younger woman's shoulder to comfort her. 'Everybody has their heart broken when they are young. It's part of growing up.'

'It was different for me,' Holly said. 'I was pregnant with our baby.'

'So did you have a termination?' Rosemary asked,

unable to look Holly in the eye.

'No, of course not. How could I kill my baby?'

'Your family stood by you then?'

Holly let out a small hollow laugh. 'Quite the opposite,' she said. 'I discovered I was pregnant while my boyfriend was away in America for the summer studying American football in preparation for his masters degree. I was waiting for him to come home so that we could tell both lots of parents but... he never came back,' she said, her voice faltering. 'I had to face my parents alone two days before I was due to start my second year at university. I had never seen my mother so angry. She called me a selfish ungrateful whore and she raised her hand to hit me, but my dad caught her arm before it made contact. Then my mother turned on Dad and accused him of spoiling me and this was how I'd repaid him.' Holly was crying now, huge gulping sobs in between her words. 'Then her voice turned to ice and she told me that if I didn't have an abortion she would never speak to me again.'

Rosemary had both her arms around the distraught Holly now, rocking her like a baby and stroking her hair away from her face to try and soothe her.

'But your mum calmed down and changed her mind surely?' Rosemary asked, 'once she realised you wanted to keep your baby.'

Holly shook her head sadly. 'No,' she said, 'and to make matters worse she forbade my dad from having any contact with me.'

'So she has never spoken to you since?' Rosemary asked incredulously.

'Just once,' Holly said. 'At my dad's funeral.'

Holly could still remember the venom in her mother's voice when she had spat out the words.

'I wish it was you and that bastard child of yours in that box instead of him.'

CHAPTER 24

Robert could taste the salt on his lips and feel the heat of the sun on his skin. Although he hated to admit it, Rosemary had been right to encourage him to spend the day fishing with Philippe. A few hours apart didn't mean he loved her any less and anyway it would be good for her to have a bit of female company so that they could talk about girlie things.

The *Dolphin*, skippered by Philippe's friend, Billy, had brought them out beyond the reef and they were now bobbing about on the deeper blue water with their rods trailing from the stern of the boat. There wasn't really much to this fishing lark thought Robert, taking a swig of Phoenix beer direct from the bottle and enjoying the flavour of the local brew on his tongue. Once you've baited the line you just sit back and wait for a bite.

He glanced across at Philippe who was relaxing back in a weathered old director's chair with his eyes closed and feet up on the rail. Without opening his eyes Philippe raised his beer bottle in Robert's direction and said, 'Glad you came?'

'Absolutely,' Robert replied, 'just what the doctor ordered,' he added, acutely aware of his thoughtless choice of words the moment they had left his lips. He didn't want to invite any questions about Rosemary's health, particularly as Philippe couldn't have failed to notice how tired and thin she was looking.

'I know she is hiding something,' Philippe said, causing Robert to choke on his beer.

Had Philippe been reading his mind? he wondered.

'Not used to roughing it my friend?' Philippe teased. 'It's a bit different from sipping on a fine red.'

Robert wasn't sure what to say, so he made a big deal of coughing to buy himself some time. He and Rosemary had agreed that they wouldn't tell any of their friends about her terminal condition unless asked a direct question. Neither of them liked to lie.

'Or maybe it is just the finality of it all,' Philippe continued, 'particularly coming back to Mauritius.'

Robert was floundering now. He was trying to remember if he had left Rosemary alone with Philippe and if so he wondered if she had inadvertently said something to arouse his suspicions. Unless, of course, the burden had become too great to bear on her own and she had needed to tell someone. But surely she would have told him that she had told Philippe?

'You're very quiet, Robert,' Philippe said, swinging his legs down from the rail and turning to look at his friend. 'Maybe she has asked you not to talk about it?'

'We agreed to keep it to ourselves,' Robert confirmed. 'There's no point in getting too many people involved.'

'Does Rosemary know too?' Philippe asked.

Robert could feel the colour drain from his skin as he realised that they had been talking at crossed purposes and he had almost given the game away. Philippe had obviously been talking about Holly.

'Er no,' he stammered, 'although I rather suspect they may share one or two secrets today. She really has connected with Holly. I think she views her as the daughter she never had.'

Philippe looked hurt. 'I thought I was the son she never had,' he said. 'Does she adopt all late thirty-somethings as her own?'

Robert laughed, glad to lighten the mood. 'Wrong on both counts,' he said. 'It's just the two of you that she has taken a shine to, and you're not thirty-something as I can clearly remember celebrating your fortieth birthday last time we were here!'

Philippe held his hands up. 'Guilty as charged,' he laughed, 'but don't tell Holly, she might think I'm too old for her.'

Robert was grateful for the chance to take the conversation in a different direction.

'You seem to have taken quite a shine to Holly,' he said. It wasn't a question. Philippe had been very obviously attracted to her and although hesitant at first Holly seemed to be enjoying his company too.

'I don't see how anyone wouldn't be attracted to Holly,' Philippe said, his eyes glowing. 'Yes, she is undoubtedly beautiful and she has just the sort of figure I like, with a bit of meat on her bones,' a comment that made Robert flinch. Philippe continued, unaware of what he had said. 'There is something about Holly the person that I find captivating. One moment she seems quite self-assured and confident and the next she seems like a little girl lost. She intrigues me,' he admitted. 'I am desperate to know more about her and find out if it is just the loss of her husband that has made her close herself off from people. I want to help her.'

'That's exactly what Rosemary said after the first evening we had dinner with her,' Robert said. 'There is something more that Holly isn't sharing with us yet.'

'But I thought she had confided in you, Robert,' Philippe said, looking puzzled.

Robert felt like a rabbit dazzled by bright headlights. He was so bad at lying.

'Yes, yes she has,' he said, avoiding Philippe's quizzical stare, 'but I think there is still more,' he continued, lamely. 'Maybe Rosemary will be able to get to the bottom of things,' he said, looking towards the shore in the direction of Tamarina Bay, very pleased that she wasn't there to hear his bungled explanations.

Philippe followed his gaze. 'Have you two reached a decision about the house yet?'

Robert hesitated. 'We will make our minds up once and for all on this visit.'

'You should buy it my friend,' Philippe encouraged. 'You and Rosemary seem so at home there.'

And therein lies the problem Robert thought, turning his head to look out to sea. Will it be home without Rosie?

CHAPTER 25

The two women had sat in silence for a long time after Holly's revelations, neither wanting to be the first to break the extraordinary feeling of closeness between them. Holly had never in her life felt love from another woman. She hadn't known either of her grandmothers and her mother was an only child so there were no aunties to compensate for the lack of maternal affection. There had only ever been three people who Holly had loved that had loved her back, and they were all male.

Rosemary on the other hand had had a wonderful relationship with her mother until she had died, as the result of a stroke, at the tragically early age of sixty-two.

Her mother had been so delighted when Rosemary had met Robert and they were married just six months later.

Some mothers might have questioned the haste of the marriage but Rosemary's mum, Faith, had said, 'It's taken you half a lifetime to find each other, why waste any more time?'

Their wedding had been a small affair in the tiny church of St Agatha's, in the Surrey village where she had grown up, with only close family and special friends on the guest list. They had all been hoping that the village church would see more use for the christening of babies but it hadn't worked out that way. Instead the next gathering had been to bury Faith, followed nine months later by her husband Morris who, the doctor said, had died of a broken heart.

Rosemary was still stroking Holly's hair. It was something that Robert always did to calm her when she was upset. Holly's sobbing had subsided and there was just the occasional sniff from her now as she tried to compose herself.

Rosemary was feeling a mixture of emotions. Sadness and anger that someone Holly obviously loved so much could abandon her and his unborn child, and a twinge of envy that Holly had fallen pregnant so easily, something Rosemary had been unable to do despite the best efforts of the infertility experts. Why does life have to be so unfair? she thought.

And then there was Holly's mother. Rosemary was appalled. She couldn't imagine how a mother could behave like that towards her own child. Poor girl, she thought, holding Holly close, any feeling of mistrust she had felt after the admission of the lies Holly had told was replaced by a surge of compassion.

There were so many questions she wanted to ask but they would have to wait. For now she just wanted

Holly to feel loved.

'I have never told another soul what Mum said to me at my dad's funeral,' Holly eventually said, 'not even my son.'

'So you have a little boy,' said Rosemary.

'Well he's not so little now,' Holly said, a hint of pride creeping into her voice. 'He's just celebrated his nineteenth birthday.'

'Really?' said Rosemary, the surprise evident in her voice. 'You don't look old enough to have a son that age. I thought you were only around thirty.'

Holly managed a watery smile. 'I take after my dad,' she said. 'People could never believe his age either.'

Rosemary watched Holly's smile fade as she mentioned her father. 'Do you want to talk about it?' she asked gently.

'I don't know where to start really,' said Holly. 'He was my rock to cling on to in the turbulent sea that was my mother's moods. He was such a good honest hard-working man, I often wondered why he stayed with her.'

'Maybe he stayed for you,' said Rosemary.

'Maybe he did,' said Holly, 'or maybe he was one of those people who made a life choice and felt it was his duty to see it through. Don't get me wrong,' she continued, 'I think he truly loved my mum but he didn't like the person she became when she had been drinking.'

'Your mum had a drink problem?' Rosemary asked.

Holly nodded. 'Nobody ever spoke about it but I

think she was an alcoholic. I can remember even from a very young age the smell of whisky on her breath,' Holly said, wrinkling her nose in disgust, 'although I didn't know what it was at the time.'

'Didn't your dad try to get help for her?'

'An addict can only be helped if they want to be helped,' Holly said defensively. 'She wouldn't admit that she had a drinking problem and if my dad ever suggested she should try and cut down she would become abusive towards both of us. I guess he just wanted to try and keep the fragile peace.'

'Do you know why she drank?' Rosemary asked tentatively.

'Not really,' Holly said, her lower lip trembling slightly. 'The only time I ever asked her she glared at me accusingly and said... because of you.'

Rosemary could see Holly was starting to get upset again and that was the last thing she wanted.

'Tell me about your son,' she said brightly. 'What's his name?'

'Harry,' said Holly, the cloud immediately lifting, 'although it says Harold on his birth certificate. It was Dad and my little joke and an homage to his favourite British prime minister.' She turned to face Rosemary to continue with her explanation. 'My surname is Wilson you see, so Harry is really Harold Wilson.'

Rosemary was looking confused again but not because she didn't remember the former Prime Minister's name.

'I thought you said your mum had forbidden your dad to have contact with you,' she said.

'She had, but when Mum threw me out of the

house, my dad came running after me and handed me all the money he had in his wallet. He told me he would find a way to help me and that I must keep in touch by ringing him at work, so that Mum wouldn't find out.'

'It must have been awful for your dad, loving you both and yet being forced to make a choice between you,' Rosemary said.

'Yes, I can see that now, but at the time it was just a second rejection from someone I loved. I felt totally abandoned.'

'So what did you do?'

Holly looked up at Rosemary. 'It's a long story,' she said. 'Are you sure you want to hear it?'

Rosemary nodded, knowing that until Holly had unburdened herself of the weight of guilt she was carrying she would never be able to move on with her life.

Holly recounted standing at the end of their garden path clutching the money, with the two bags she had already packed for her return to university at her feet. She watched her dad retreat behind the tatty front door of the house where she had spent most of the last nineteen years and knew it was probably the last time she would ever lay eyes on it, and possibly him. She had no idea what to do or where to go.

As she waited for the bus to take her from Clifton into Nottingham city centre she tried to think straight. Maybe she could go back to university. She had her train ticket and a room in a house share organised and she was only four months pregnant so she wasn't showing yet, and she was sure the university would be able to help her.

Then she thought of Gareth. He hadn't been in contact with her at all since he left for America. He obviously wanted nothing to do with her and she wasn't going to try and force him into marriage. She had her pride. That was when she realised that going back to university wasn't an option. She couldn't bear the thought of seeing him around campus with a new girlfriend.

Holly had used the train ticket but instead of going all the way to Bath she had got off at Reading. She and Gareth had always joked about the pronunciation, calling it reading, as in books, rather than Reading, which sounded like the colour. She always had her nose in a book. When she wasn't studying, and there was a lot of reading in her English degree coursework, she was engrossed in romantic novels. Somehow Reading had just felt right.

The council had found her a one-bedroom flat and put her in touch with Social Services. Holly knew she would need some financial support but she was determined to work for as long as she could and she managed to get a job at the local library. She contacted Bath university and explained her situation. They had wanted to know if the father of her baby was one of their students but Holly had refused to say. She also had to let her housemates know that she wouldn't be needing the room. She wrote them a very short letter with no explanation about why she was not going back to uni and no return address.

Rosemary had been watching Holly as she spoke. It was almost as though she was giving an account of something that had happened to another person. That's how some of us deal with things, Rosemary thought, remembering how unreal the first few months of her cancer treatment had felt.

'So did your dad come and visit you in Reading?'

'Not until after Harry was born,' Holly replied.

'Was no one with you when gave birth?'

'No one except the midwives,' Holly said, 'but it was okay. In a way I preferred not having to share my precious baby with anyone else. It was the most magical moment of my life when I held Harry in my arms for the first time. The love I felt for him was totally overwhelming.'

Rosemary could hear both emotion and devotion in her voice and felt a pang of jealousy that she had never been fortunate enough to experience that feeling.

'I'm so sorry, Rosemary,' Holly said. 'How selfish of me talking about how wonderful it is to be a mother when clearly it is something you wanted so much.'

'It's history now,' Rosemary said, managing a faint smile, 'and anyway we're talking about you not me. When did your father first visit you and Harry?'

Holly explained that she had phoned her dad to tell him he was a grandfather and he had taken the next day off work so that he could make the round trip from Nottingham to Reading without arousing his wife's suspicion. He was totally besotted with his grandson the moment he saw him, although surprised at his blond hair and blue eyes, so unlike his mother and grandfather.

'That was when we decided on the name Harry,' Holly said. 'I was going to call him William, my dad's name, but because they were so dissimilar in looks it didn't seem right. What I didn't tell my dad was that Harry rhymed with Gary, my pet name for Gareth. I guess at that point I still had a tiny glimmer of hope that one day he might walk back into our lives.' She shrugged. 'That was the start of regular monthly visits from my dad. He used to bring little gifts for Harry and always give me a few pounds to help with the bills. He even bought himself a mobile phone that Mum didn't know about so that we could keep in contact when he wasn't at work in case there was an emergency. The tragedy is that's what killed him,' said Holly, starting to get emotional again.

Rosemary didn't speak, she just waited until Holly was able to carry on.

'The police said afterwards that he had lost control of his car on the M1 motorway less than thirty minutes from home. Apparently he was talking to my mother on his mobile phone. He was dead by the time the emergency vehicles arrived on the scene,' said Holly, tears streaming down her face again.

Rosemary was trying to calm Holly as she said, 'Had your mother found out about his secret visits to you?'

Holly shook her head. 'No, she had no idea that Dad was visiting us. She found the mobile phone bill, saw that all the calls were to the same number and assumed my dad was having an affair, at least that's what she told the police when they called to tell her there had been a fatal accident,' Holly sobbed. 'She had called his mobile phone number to accuse him of cheating on her and he must have lost concentration wondering how he was going to protect me.' Holly was becoming hysterical now. 'So you see it was my fault. I'm responsible for my dad's death. My mum is right to hate me.'

'No, no, no,' said Rosemary, once again cradling Holly in her arms and rocking her back and forth. 'If anyone should carry the guilt for your dad's death it's your mother for putting him in such an impossible position in the first place. It's not your fault, Holly,' she reassured her. 'It's not your fault.'

Finally Rosemary was beginning to understand why Holly had spent so many years on her own, afraid of becoming too close to anyone in case they left her. And the tragedy is, thought Rosemary, she has opened up her heart to me and put her trust in me and I am going to leave her too.

CHAPTER 26

The water felt warm and soothing as it washed over her feet and her stillness emboldened the shoals of tiny fish to swim closer to examine them. Holly raised her gaze and squinted slightly, holding her hand up to shield her eyes as she looked out towards the reef and beyond at the small shapes that were the fishing boats. In her haste that morning she had forgotten her sunglasses and her sun hat but fortunately she still had her Yankees cap stuffed into the bottom of her beach bag and that was helping to lessen the glare of the afternoon sun sparkling on the sea. She wondered which of the boats was Billy's and also whether Robert and Philippe had enjoyed a successful morning fishing.

When they had waved the two men off earlier that day Holly had promised a slightly apprehensive Robert that she would take good care of his wife. I'm not sure burdening Rosemary with my life story and swearing her to secrecy was quite what Robert had in mind, thought Holly guiltily.

Rosemary had been so drained after the morning's revelations that she had barely touched the fruit and cheese that Philippe had left out for their lunch. After pushing the food around her plate for a while she had claimed a headache and gone for a lie-down. Holly rinsed the lunch plates and then knocked softly on the door of the spare room before pushing it open slightly. Rosemary was lying on top of the white waffle bed cover. Her eyes were closed and she didn't stir, so Holly decided to let her rest and pulled the door closed again.

She had no idea how long Rosemary would sleep so, rather than wasting the opportunity to explore, she climbed down the wooden steps from the verandah of the house and clambered over the dark volcanic rocks onto to the stretch of beach at Tamarina Bay. From there she could see the spot where she had walked to a couple of days earlier, before her path had been blocked by the undergrowth. Beyond the view up the coast was uninterrupted and spectacular, with soft white sands and clear blue water, just like it showed in the holiday brochures. There's certainly something magical about Mauritius, she thought, or maybe it's the people I've met that makes it feel that way.

She turned away from the sea to look up at the house just as Rosemary walked out onto the verandah. Holly waved, trying to catch her attention but Rosemary was looking out to sea in the direction of the fishing boats. Holly was about to head back to the house but Rosemary had already begun her descent of the wooden steps so she crossed the short expanse of sand and sat on a rock to wait for her friend. It seemed impossible that she had revealed so much about her life to a person she had met only a few days ago. Rosemary now knew more about her than any other living person, even her son, Holly realised. There had been no judgement of any of her actions just a calm and compassionate understanding. When Rosemary had assured her that her father's death wasn't her fault she had felt a huge weight lift from her shoulders.

'I didn't recognise you in your baseball cap,' called Rosemary as she carefully picked her way across the black rocks, 'but I thought it must be you down here as I couldn't think where else you would have gone.'

'I hope you didn't mind me leaving you,' Holly said as Rosemary approached. 'You seemed so soundly asleep I thought I would come down to the beach for a wander.'

'Not at all,' Rosemary said. 'You weren't to know it would only be a cat nap. You probably needed a breath of fresh air after the morning we've had.'

'I don't know what came over me,' Holly admitted, extending her hand to help Rosemary down from the rocks onto the warm soft sand. 'I normally keep myself to myself.'

'Have you heard the expression, a problem shared is a problem halved?' asked Rosemary.

'I have,' said Holly, 'but until today there was no one in my life that I felt I could trust enough to share my problems with. I'm sorry,' she added, looking up at the older woman whose very presence made her feel calm.

'Don't be sorry,' Rosemary said. 'I'm honoured to be the person you felt you could open up to. If I had a daughter at the age you were when you gave birth to Harry she would be your age now. I would want her to come to me with her problems not keep them hidden away. I'm not judging your mum, Holly, she obviously has issues of her own and to lose her husband so soon after choosing to disown you she must have been in a very dark place when she said those awful things to you at your dad's funeral.' Rosemary paused and linked her arm through Holly's as they started to walk back towards the shoreline. 'But I can't understand or condone what she did either. Nobody goes through life without making mistakes and unless you learn from them and share what you have learned with others you care about, the same mistakes will be repeated again and again.'

They had reached the water's edge and both women slipped their feet out of their sandals and continued into the shallow warm sea until it covered their feet.

'This is one of my favourite things to do,' said Holly, wiggling her toes in the sand, causing underwater clouds.

'And mine,' said Rosemary. 'This and watching the sun set into the water.'

'Me too.'

A tear escaped from the corner of Holly's eye which she quickly brushed away. She had learned a long time ago not to ask the question, 'Why me?' when bad things happened and had replaced it with the more positive, 'Why not me?' Something wonderful was happening to Holly on this paradise island and for once she was able to ask the question, 'Why not me?' about something good.

The two women walked along the beach chatting about everything from their favourite colour to their taste in music. They discovered that neither of them was a fan of jazz but they both loved power ballads and some classical music could reduce them to tears. Neither was particularly interested in sport although both had loved cheering Team GB on in the previous year's Olympic Games held in London. Holly admitted that she had never seen a West End musical because she had never had the money or a companion to go with. Rosemary said they would have to put that right when she and Robert returned to the UK after their extended stay in Mauritius. Holly had then asked how long they were planning to stay but Rosemary's answer had been non-committal.

'You are lucky,' Holly said. 'I would love to be able to stay somewhere like this forever. I love the fresh smell and the warmth of the sun on my skin. I guess I'm a bit of a beach bum at heart,' she confessed, 'which is why I couldn't believe my luck when I got this job working for Soleil Resorts.'

'How did you get the job?' Rosemary enquired, intrigued to know how a charity worker from Reading had become a blog writer for one of the top hotel groups in the world.

'It was all a massive stroke of luck actually,' Holly admitted. She explained how Harry had been saving his paper round money for years and also the tips from his bar job during his first year in university, to take himself and his mum on their first proper holiday. She was so thrilled by the experience that at the end of every day she had written a lengthy entry in her diary. On the plane on the way home she had read it out to Harry as a reminiscence of the wonderful holiday they had just had together. When they got home Harry, without telling his mum, had found a blog-hosting website and had posted all her diary entries over the period of a week. The response to her 'warts and all' account had been incredible, with over 50,000 views, and dozens of comments left suggesting that she should do it again from a different destination. Harry had suggested approaching Soleil Resorts and they loved the idea, seeing it as a fairly inexpensive way of gaining publicity and also a way to keep an eye on the quality of service without a resort knowing they were being checked up on.

'It sounds like your Harry is a very bright boy, recognising a gap in the market. What does he do for a living?' she asked.

'He's in his second year at university,' Holly said, and then added before Rosemary asked the inevitable question, 'he's studying to be an architect.'

Rosemary stopped in her tracks. 'So that was what you almost let slip at dinner the other night when I told you that Robert was an architect.'

'Yes,' said Holly, 'I nearly blew my cover story on the first evening with you and Robert because I am such a proud mother. You can't say anything to Robert though,' she added, panicking slightly.

'I won't say a word,' Rosemary reassured her. 'So does your blog have a title?'

'It's called Life's a Beach. It's a sort of play on words.

You know the saying "life's a bitch and then you die"?,'
Holly explained.

'Yes I know the saying,' Rosemary said. 'You know
all this walking has made me peckish,' she said,
quickening her pace as she headed towards the house.
'Was their any fruit and cheese left from lunch?'

That's an odd reaction to my blog title, thought
Holly as she followed her across the sand. She could
have just said she didn't like it.

All that was left of the watermelon was a pile of black
seeds on Holly's plate. She didn't normally bother
with watermelon as it was usually quite tasteless, but
this had been a delight for her taste buds. Along with
the locally grown pineapple it had made a very tasty
afternoon snack and was much healthier than the cup
of milky coffee with a couple of chocolate digestives
Holly would have had at this time of day back home.
The two women were sitting on the sofa on the
verandah in the shade, even though the ferocity of
the midday sun had long since passed.

Rosemary had been quiet since they had returned
to the house despite Holly's best efforts at conversation.
Holly was trying to think if she had inadvertently said
anything to upset the older woman. She didn't think
so but Rosemary had been acting strangely ever since
she had mentioned the title of her blog.

'Do you think I should call it something else?'
Holly ventured.

Rosemary looked bewildered.

'The blog,' Holly clarified. 'Do you not think it's a

good title?'

'I like the title,' Rosemary said. 'Why do you ask?'

'Well you seem to have gone all quiet on me since I mentioned it,' Holly said, looking puzzled. 'It's not because I told you Harry's studying architecture, is it? You don't think I've made friends with you so that I can make use of Robert's contacts do you?' she asked, feeling mortified.

'Hardly, Holly, particularly as I am under strict instructions not to mention any of your story to my husband!' Rosemary replied, managing a weak smile.

'So what's wrong then?' Holly persisted. 'It must be something I've said.'

Rosemary sighed. 'In a way it is, although there's no way you could have known how close to home your "life's a bitch and then you die" comment was.'

'There is no easy way to tell you this Holly and now it's my turn to swear you to secrecy. No one knows what I'm about to tell you, not my closest friends back home, not Philippe, no one, and I need it to stay that way. Can you keep a secret?'

Holly had a dreadful sense of foreboding and her mouth went suddenly dry, preventing her from speaking so she simply nodded her head.

'I'm sick, Holly,' Rosemary said gently. 'Very sick.'

Holly could hear her own voice coming from a long way away as she started to say, 'W-what's wrong...' but before she could finish her sentence Rosemary had raised her hands to stop her speaking.

'In fact, it would be more accurate to say I'm dying.'

'Nooooooo!' Holly let out an anguished cry, like a wounded animal. Her head was spinning and her heart was thundering. For a moment she thought she might faint. She felt Rosemary put her arm around her to comfort her but selfishly she pushed her away. 'No,' she said again. 'You can't leave me, it's not fair.'

Even to her own ears she could hear the childishness of the statement but she couldn't stop now. 'Maybe it's a mistake,' she rambled, 'have you had a second opinion? You can't leave me, I've only just found you... I need you,' she blurted out, tears flowing freely down her cheeks.

Rosemary reached out again and this time Holly didn't push her away she clung to her like a frightened child who was having a nightmare.

As Holly's breathing began to even out she asked in a very small voice, 'Are you absolutely sure nothing can be done?'

Rosemary was very calm as she explained to Holly about her leukaemia, resigned to the inevitable consequence that her lack of response to the various treatment drugs had brought about.

'How can you be so calm about it?' Holly asked. 'Aren't you angry or frightened?'

Rosemary was quiet for a moment looking out to the distant horizon before she answered. 'Maybe I was at first, but I soon realised that there is no point being angry, Holly, it doesn't solve anything, as I'm sure your mum has found out. I suppose I am still a little frightened but mostly I'm overwhelmingly sad that, after taking so long to find my soul mate, I'm going to leave him alone.'

Holly had seen how close they were and wondered how on earth Robert would cope with losing this incredibly courageous woman.

After a few moments Rosemary took Holly's face in her hands and looked straight into her olive green eyes. 'If I've learned anything from this life it's that if you have a chance of happiness you need to take it. It may not always turn out the way you hope it will but if you don't seize your opportunities all you will be left with is regret for what might have been.'

Holly chose to ignore the obvious reference to her blossoming romance with Philippe. 'How long do you have?' she asked, not really wanting to hear the answer.

'No one knows for sure how quickly my condition will deteriorate but we are talking months rather than years.'

Holly felt totally crushed.

'No wonder you couldn't answer when I asked how long you would be staying in Mauritius? Is that why you've come, to spend the rest of your life here?'

'No, I have something else in mind and I may need you to help me. Would you do that, Holly? Would you help a dying woman with her last wish?'

Holly was still reeling from the shock of hearing that Rosemary was dying. 'Of course. I'll do anything I can.'

'Do you promise?'

'I promise.'

'Thank you,' she said. 'You have no idea how much that means to me. I wanted to visit Mauritius one last time before I get too sick to fly, but I don't want to die here because I want Robert to be able to come to this house, where we had planned to retire together, and remember all the happy times we shared, watching beautiful sunsets like this.'

Holly raised her eyes to follow Rosemary's gaze. The sun was a fiery orange ball and was just starting to dip below the horizon, the sky around it a colourful backdrop of pinks and yellows. They sat quietly, Rosemary's hand resting on Holly's, until the final flash of orange had gone, both wondering how many more sunsets Rosemary would enjoy.

'They'll be back soon,' Rosemary said. 'We'd better start getting things ready for supper.'

CHAPTER 27

Robert and Philippe were in good spirits when they arrived home shortly after sunset with steaks from the huge yellow fin tuna that Billy had helped them land and gut. Holly was relieved that the fish was ready to grill on the barbecue. She hadn't gutted a fish since making roll-mop herrings as an eleven-year-old in her school cookery class when she had almost fainted after cutting down the fish's belly before twisting its head off. She had gone home and announced to her mum that she wanted to be a vegetarian to which her mum had replied, you'll eat what you're given.

With the tuna steaks sizzling on the hot coals of the barbecue Philippe and Robert gave a blow by blow account of how they had not only landed the yellow fin tuna but also a prized ruby snapper. Billy had grudgingly said it was beginner's luck but was nonetheless grateful when the boys had given it to him, along with the rest of their catch, as a thank you for their day out on the ocean.

'I'm surprised you didn't fall overboard, Robert,' Rosemary teased, as it was clear that he was more than a little tipsy. 'I thought I asked you to look after him, Philippe.'

'I did,' countered Philippe, winking in Robert's direction. 'He was never without a bottle of beer in his hand!'

The tuna steaks were delicious accompanied by the salad that Holly and Rosemary had prepared. Philippe offered wine but Robert declined, admitting that he had probably had enough alcohol for one day, and Rosemary also gave it a miss as she had volunteered to drive back to the Plantation House in Philippe's old BMW.

'You'll join me in a glass of white, won't you, Holly,' Philippe urged. 'I don't like to drink alone.'

Holly hesitated before replying, 'Just one glass then.'

As soon as they had finished their meal Rosemary said, 'I think I should get you back to the hotel, Robert, before you fall asleep.'

'You might be right, old girl,' Robert said.

'It's early, Holly,' Rosemary said, ignoring the old girl comment. 'If you don't want to leave just yet you could always phone the hotel for a taxi when you're ready.'

Holly could feel three pairs of eyes on her, and felt a blush begin to colour her face. Part of her wanted to make her excuses and leave with the Forresters. That would be the sensible, safe option. But running around in her head was Rosemary's advice about not living to regret missed opportunities and besides she really didn't want the evening to end yet.

CHAPTER 28

It was only a ten-minute drive to the hotel from Tamarina Bay but Robert could feel his eyelids drooping. He was feeling a bit irresponsible for letting Philippe ply him with drink all day. What if Rosemary was taken ill in the night and he was in no state to help her? he thought guiltily.

'She's a grown woman, Robert, and quite capable of making her own decisions,' said Rosemary, who had mistaken Robert's silence as disapproval of her meddling in matters of the heart. 'I was merely pointing out that the hotel could send a taxi if she wanted to stay a bit longer.'

'Never crossed my mind, old girl,' said Robert, slurring his words.

Rosemary stole an affectionate glance at her inebriated husband. It was so unlike him to drink too much but he wasn't used to beer and clearly couldn't handle it as well as he could wine.

'Once was enough, Robert,' she admonished.

'What's that?'

'Old girl,' she said. 'I let it go at Philippe's but let's nip it in the bud now. It makes you sound like the Major from *Fawlty Towers*.'

'He really likes Holly, you know,' said Robert, referring back to Rosemary's original remark. 'He told me so on the boat. Did she talk about him at all?'

'His name might have been mentioned,' Rosemary teased and then added mysteriously, 'but I have been sworn to secrecy on our conversations today so don't bother asking.' It was a clever way to avoid further discussion of her day with Holly.

'Spoilsport,' said Robert. 'We always tell each other everything.'

'Usually, Robert,' she corrected. 'We usually tell each other everything, but in this case it's off limits.'

Robert looked at the defiant angle of his wife's chin and knew that whatever the girls had been talking about all day it wasn't going to be shared with him. If he hadn't felt quite so tipsy he might have persevered in trying to break down his wife's resolve but it wasn't worth causing an argument over a load of girlie chat.

Rosemary pulled the car into a free space in the hotel car park and said, with a hint of irony, 'Come on, old boy, let's get you back to our room.'

The irony was completely lost on Robert.

CHAPTER 29

Philippe was usually confident around women but he felt ridiculously nervous at being left alone with Holly in his own home. It had been different going on the island tour with her in the company of Sachin. Even when the driver had left them alone to have a stroll on the beach there had been plenty of other people around, but here it was just the two of them. He had been surprised when Holly had agreed to Rosemary's suggestion to stay a little longer. He had purposely not said anything to encourage her to stay, frightened that she would feel he was trying to pressure her, so it was all the more pleasurable that she had opted for a later night than his other two friends. He was also surprised that she had accepted his offer of a second glass of wine.

He carried the two replenished wine glasses out towards the verandah where Holly was leaning on the rail looking out to sea. The big silver moon was lighting the night sky and from the angle he was looking as he approached her it looked like a halo around her head.

Holly could hear his footsteps as he crossed the room but only just over the hammering of her heart. She was already wondering if she had made the right decision to stay. What would they talk about? What if Philippe assumes that by agreeing to stay a while longer I'm agreeing to have sex with him? she thought. And is that why I've stayed, she wondered? Feeling confused and vulnerable she deliberately kept her back to him and looked out to the ocean.

'Your wine madam,' Philippe said as he handed her the glass, bowing slightly.

'*Merci*,' she said, responding to his French accent.

'Do you speak French, Holly?'

'Probably about a dozen words and that's if you include yes, no and what time is it,' she laughed. 'I always admire people from other countries who speak English so fluently. I suppose it came quite naturally to you,' she said, turning to face him. 'One of the benefits of having parents from different nationalities. Did you learn both from the time you could talk?'

'I speak a lot less French than you might imagine, even though I grew up in France. My father was adamant that I should learn about English history and geography so I had a tutor from the age of six. I only really mixed with the village children when I went out to play and that wasn't that often as my mother didn't like me to get dirty.'

'Oh, I just assumed you would be bi-lingual.'

'I always swear in French if that helps?'

'You swear?' she said, a look of mock horror on

her face. 'I'm shocked!'

'Doesn't everyone? Although I usually only swear when I'm writing,' he said, anxious to dispel any opinion she may be forming about him being foul-mouthed. 'And only when the words won't flow.'

Holly seized the opportunity to change the subject.

'How is your book coming along?' she asked.

'It's a work in progress,' he said, not adding that progress had been very slow.

Philippe was anticipating her next question and was wondering how to refuse allowing Holly to read his manuscript without offending her. If he hadn't lied about it being a travelogue he wouldn't have minded her reading a chapter or two.

The question never came. Before Holly could speak there was a whooshing followed by an explosion of sound and multi-coloured sparkles.

'Fireworks,' she cried. 'I love fireworks.'

'That's a relief,' said Philippe. 'I wasn't sure if you did when I organised the display.'

Holly turned to look at him and caught the twinkle in his eye.

'I hope you're not lying to me, Philippe?' she said accusingly, digging him playfully in the ribs.

'What a suggestion,' he countered, draping his arm around her shoulder as the fireworks exploded in the night sky and in Holly's heart.

The display lasted for fifteen minutes and concluded with a spectacular arch created by the exploding fireworks in the colours of the rainbow.

'That was beautiful. I love rainbows, they have a special meaning for me,' Holly said, turning to

Philippe as the final light extinguished.

'Not as beautiful as you,' Philippe said, leaning down and kissing her softly on her full inviting lips.

For a moment Holly allowed herself to be kissed and then she pulled away.

'Perhaps I should be going,' she said, turning away from Philippe so that she didn't see the look of disappointment flash across his face.

The acrid smoke from the firework display was starting to drift towards them in a coloured cloud. Philippe realised he had been too forward but he hadn't been able to resist her upturned face.

'We should both go inside before we're engulfed in the smoke,' he said, steering her gently into the living room and closing the door to the verandah. 'I don't want you to go yet, Holly, but I will call you a cab if you've had enough of me for one night.'

Philippe could see that Holly was wavering. He wanted her more than any woman he had ever met but only if she wanted him too.

'I promise I won't lay a finger on you if you don't want me to,' said Philippe.

'How do I know I can trust you?' she asked.

'I promised Rosemary I would do nothing to hurt you,' he answered. 'I would never lie to Rosemary, she is like a mother to me.'

'You and Rosemary have been discussing me?'

'I wouldn't say discussing you,' he replied quickly, 'but I did tell her I thought you were beautiful and that I fancied you like mad and she was very protective towards you.'

Holly relaxed a little. 'She feels like a mother to

me too, more so than my own mum in a lot of ways,' admitted Holly, sinking down onto the comfy sofa.

Philippe nodded sadly as he sat down beside her. 'I know what you mean,' he said. 'Do you want to talk about it?'

Holly told a watered-down version of her early life and how she had always felt that she was a burden to her mother despite her best efforts at being a model child. The harder she tried and the better behaved she was, the more her mother seemed to dislike her. It was easy to talk to Philippe. He just listened quietly. At one point she lifted her head from his shoulder, where she had been resting, to make sure he was still awake. His eyes were wide open but he was looking out towards the full moon.

'Why did you stop?' he asked looking into her deep green eyes.

'I thought I had bored you so much that you had fallen asleep,' she replied.

'I'm listening,' he said. 'I'm a good listener.'

Holly continued her story but stopped at the point where she left home to go to university.

'What did you study?' he asked.

'English,' she replied and then quickly continued before he could ask her anything about her time at university. 'So come on it's your turn to tell me about you.'

She snuggled into his chest with her legs curled up on the sofa and his arm resting around her protectively. The last thing she remembered thinking, before falling asleep, was that the story about his mother sounded vaguely familiar.

CHAPTER 30

Sleep had eluded Philippe. Once he realised that Holly was no longer listening to his story he carefully removed his body from under her head and replaced it with a cushion. He fetched the white waffle blanket from the spare room and covered her with it but he didn't pull the curtains closed as he didn't want to disturb her. He had retired to his bedroom but couldn't sleep knowing that the object of his desire was just metres away. He wanted to be close to her when she woke up in strange surroundings and guessed she might wake early when the first light of the new day filtered in through the unguarded windows, so he had lain staring at his ceiling wondering why he had such depth of feeling for someone he barely knew.

Philippe was in unfamiliar territory. To him women were objects of beauty to be enjoyed without allowing them to get too close. He had no problem attracting the opposite sex, particularly when he was working as a journalist, but he didn't have lasting relationships. Seducing a woman with his practised small-talk and laconic sense of humour was easy but it was only ever to achieve one end result: a night of sex.

Many woman, from work colleagues to nubile young glamour models, had succumbed to his charm but none had ever heard their adoring words in the heat of passion reciprocated. Philippe never misled any of them, always telling them that he wasn't looking for anything permanent, however most of his conquests believed they would be the one to change his mind. None of them had.

He hadn't uttered those three little words, that every woman longs to hear, since he was thirteen years old. His parents were separating and Philippe had asked his mother why they couldn't live together.

Her reply had been truthful but not explanatory.

'Your father doesn't love me any more,' she had said.

'But I love you, Maman,' he had pleaded.

'You don't know what love is, Philippe,' she had said dismissively. 'Maybe one day you will.'

Philippe wondered whether finally that day had arrived.

As dawn approached he quietly crept back into the living room and knelt down beside the sleeping Holly. The lust he had felt when he had first seen her in the hotel restaurant was still there but it was tempered by a desire to nurture and care for this emotionally fragile woman. The long dark lashes that framed her beautiful eyes were flickering and he knew that in a few moments she would wake. He whispered her name.

Holly had been dreaming about the holiday she and Harry went on eight months earlier that had changed her life so dramatically but she couldn't understand why he was calling her by her name.

'Mum,' she mumbled incoherently, as she started to wake from sleep. 'Call me mum.'

Philippe rested his fingers lightly on Holly's lips assuming that she had been dreaming about her mother as that was the last thing she had been talking about before falling asleep. He wondered if Holly and her mum were still in contact after the unhappy childhood she had endured. Maybe in the depths of sleep she was asking her mum to call her, but it hadn't sounded like a plea, more of an instruction.

Philippe was acutely aware that he hadn't spoken to his own mother since he had sent her a copy of his book which she had read without recognising the woman he had written about. She was upset and angry in equal measure when he had patiently explained in a telephone conversation that the title character was his perception of her through adolescent eyes.

'You should have spoken to me before you started writing and I could have told you the truth about your father and me,' she had said in an aggrieved tone of voice.

'But the book was a novel, so the character was based on you and how I saw you from my point of view, not actually who you really are, although I'm not sure I have ever known the real you.'

'The real me would have made a much better story,' she said defiantly before she abruptly ended the call.

That was over a year ago and she hadn't answered

any of his calls since.

Holly was looking up at him now her green eyes wide with questioning but not alarm. He realised he still had his fingers resting on her lips and moved them away as if they had been scalded.

'Did you need me to keep quiet?' she asked sleepily. 'Am I not supposed to be here? Is your girlfriend at the door?'

'None of the above,' Philippe replied. 'I just wanted to be close to you when you awoke. I didn't know if you would remember straightaway where you fell asleep.'

'I'm so sorry Philippe,' she said apologetically, the colour starting to rise in her cheeks I can't believe I fell asleep when you were in mid flow. Do you want to carry on where you left off?' she rambled.

'Maybe later,' he said, his sexy French voice loaded with innuendo. 'But now I need you to get up. There is something I have to do that I think you will enjoy.'

Holly was intrigued. She freshened up in the bathroom by splashing water on her face and then using some of Philippe's sun protection lotion as a moisturiser. Some men had a whole host of beauty products, thought Holly, but Philippe was very old school with just his shaving foam, after shave balm and deodorant in the bathroom cabinet. She squeezed a line of toothpaste onto her finger and rubbed it over her teeth to banish her morning breath. Her tousled curls looked like she had been dragged through a hedge backwards, she thought, using her dad's favourite phrase, so she raked her fingers through her hair and then retrieved a stretchy band from the pocket of her shorts and tied it back in a pony tail. The only other things in her pocket were a stick of lip salve, which she gratefully applied to her lips, and her hotel room key.

'Come on, Holly,' Philippe urged through the closed bathroom door. 'I don't like being late for this.'

This must be very special, she thought, unlocking the bathroom door, because he doesn't mind being late for almost everything else.

He grabbed her hand as soon as she was through the door and pulled her towards the verandah and down the wooden steps onto the beach. The sun was starting its ascent but there were still traces of red and orange in the early morning sky. They ran along the soft sand for about fifty metres and then Philippe turned away from the sea towards a small field sandwiched between two houses. In the furthest corner was a ramshackle stable and nodding his head in greeting was the magnificent black horse that Holly had seen Philippe riding on the beach a few days before.

As they approached Philippe reached his hand into the bin of feed and held it out to the appreciative animal.

'Is he yours?' Holly asked.

Philippe shook his head. 'He belongs to my fisherman friend, Billy,' he said, 'although I like to think it is the other way round. Billy won him in a poker game and had no idea how to look after him so I volunteered to help him out by exercising him three mornings a week. I could ride almost before I could walk which is funny as the Greek meaning of my name is "lover of horses". Do you ride Holly?'

'There wasn't much available cash for riding lessons when I was growing up.'

'Well you don't need money to ride this horse,' said Philippe, placing the bit in the horse's mouth, buckling the bridle and looping the reins over its head.

Holly felt uncertain about getting on this magnificent animal.

'What's his name?' she asked.

'His name is Helios, the Greek sun god. Maybe that's why he loves to go for a gallop as the sun is starting a new day.'

Holly looked at the impressive beast towering above her and then at Philippe's animated face.

'Aren't you missing a saddle?' she enquired, fearful of the answer.

'Helios and I don't like saddles,' he replied. 'We like to feel the heat and motion of each other's bodies,' he said, looking Holly straight in the eye. 'Are you going to let me teach you?'

Holly could barely breathe. She understood the power of horses, particularly one as large as this, but she felt sure Philippe wouldn't let her come to any harm. That was not why she was hesitating. It was the thought of sitting astride a horse with Philippe's arms around her and his torso pressed into her back.

'I know he's big,' said Philippe, his eyes twinkling in a mocking manner, 'but he's very well behaved. You know you want to.'

Holly knew she was being teased but she didn't

care. It was time to throw caution to the wind and live a bit. Besides she had always wanted to ride a horse bareback. It was on her 'things to do before I die' list, that Harry made such fun of.

She lifted her chin defiantly. 'How do I get up there?'

In one deft movement Philippe spun her round to face Helios, lifted her by the waist while instructing her to throw her right leg over the horse's back and then pushed her bottom upwards until she was sat astride its wide back. Moments later he too had mounted the horse and reached around Holly for the reins which he rested gently in her hands, his own hands covering hers.

It was dizzyingly high but Holly focused her eyes on Helios's dramatic black mane.

'Are you sure you want this?' Philippe asked.

'Yes I'm sure,' she said, leaning back against his firm chest, feeling the rippling of muscles in his arms and legs as he urged Helios forward at a gentle walking pace.

CHAPTER 31

There was a thundering in Robert's head almost like a horse's hooves pounding incessantly on his temples. He opened one eye very gingerly and peered through the dim light towards the motionless form of his wife lying next to him in the bed. She must have sensed the slight movement as she turned her head towards him.

'How are you feeling?'

'Pretty rough if I'm honest,' he replied. 'I've got a thumping headache.'

'I'll get you some paracetemol,' she offered, rising from the bed and making her way towards the bathroom before her husband could argue.

She returned moments later with the pills and a glass of water. Robert eased himself into a semi-sitting position to enable him to swallow the tablets and the water without choking and then rested back onto his pillow.

'What time is it?' he asked.

Rosemary glanced across at the travel clock on her bedside table. 'It's not quite six,' she replied, gently stroking his head. 'You should try and get back to sleep for a couple of hours.'

'Don't be nice to me,' Robert said. 'I've brought this on myself. I don't know what I was thinking trying to keep up with a man twenty years my junior.'

'Don't beat yourself up about it, Robert,' Rosemary said soothingly. 'You needed to unwind and enjoy yourself after the eighteen months we've had. You just didn't realise the potency of the local brew and combined with the strong sunshine it's no wonder you've got a sore head.'

Robert smiled weakly, glad of his wife's understanding and closed his eyes. He had a slight sensation of movement but nothing like the 'whirling pits' he had experienced on numerous occasions when he was a student at university and had had a heavy night out with his mates. Within moments he had drifted back to sleep.

Rosemary waited for a few minutes to make sure he was sleeping then noiselessly slipped into the sundress she had worn the previous day, which she retrieved from the chair where she had left it after helping her husband to bed seven hours earlier. She picked up the room key and quietly let herself out of their room just as the first rays of sunlight were beginning to appear in the morning sky.

Robert was blissfully unaware of the many mornings she awoke early and laid silently staring at the ceiling so as not to wake him. At least this morning she could spend her time in a more pleasurable way, she thought as she strolled barefoot across the grass, wet from the early morning sprinkler system, towards the sea. It was calm this morning with the rumble of the reef very distant.

Looking out at the ocean with the orangey-pink sky beyond as the new day dawned, Rosemary acknowledged that she had been incredibly fortunate to live the life she had. In some way she felt as though the trade-off for her happy life, particularly since she had met Robert, was that it couldn't last forever and that was why she had been afflicted with leukaemia. I wonder how many more sunrises I will witness, she thought, before I'm too ill to appreciate them. The idea that Rosemary had been toying with surfaced in her consciousness again. She knew it was the right thing to do but she would never be able to convince Robert.

A movement further along the beach caught her eye. It was a horse and rider heading in her direction. She didn't feel like getting into a conversation with anyone so she moved as swiftly as the soft sand would allow to the top of the beach and stood behind a palm tree. From her vantage point she watched the horse approach at a gallop.

As it got closer she realised there were two riders astride the magnificent beast and she immediately knew who they were. The woman was leaning back into the man's chest an expression of pure joy on her face as he masterfully guided the horse and protected her from falling at the same time.

A smile spread across Rosemary's face. Holly must have stayed with Philippe the previous night. She hoped it was the start of a new phase in Holly's life, one where she received the love she deserved.

CHAPTER 32

It was one of the most exhilarating things Holly had ever done. She was still smiling broadly as she allowed the hot water from the overhead drench shower to wash down over her. There was no denying that she had been terrified when Philippe had spurred Helios into a gallop but he held the reins in one hand, freeing his other arm to wrap firmly around her waist. It had only been for a few minutes but it had been a complete adrenalin rush. The warm air had rushed to meet her face and she could feel the power of the horse's shoulder muscles as he extended his legs into his enormous stride. All Philippe had said was grip with your knees and she had done as she was told.

Philippe had slowed Helios to a walking pace and then turned him back along the beach stopping near the water's edge in front of the hotel block where Holly's room was. He dismounted first and then formed a stirrup with his hands so that Holly could dismount properly and not spook Helios by swinging her leg over his head. As her feet hit the hard sand her legs felt wobbly enough but as Philippe cupped her face in his hands and leant down to kiss her softly on the mouth a total collapse was on the cards. She pulled away from the embrace, acutely aware of how it might look to any hotel guests who believed she was recently widowed, although, as Philippe pointed out, they were so early that no one was around yet, not even the hotel gardeners.

They made arrangements to meet in the same spot at 10 a.m. Holly said she had a couple of things she needed to do, one of which was eating breakfast. By the time she had emerged on her hotel room balcony to wave him goodbye he was already halfway down the beach towards Tamarina Bay, Helios's hooves kicking up a mix of sand and sea-spray.

Freshly showered, Holly switched on her computer to write her latest blog. She had the foresight not to write too much in her previous post so that there would be something left to write about this morning that didn't involve the time she had spent with Rosemary, Robert and Philippe yesterday, apart from mentioning all-day fishing excursions. Although Holly hadn't gone herself she had picked up enough information from the boys to enable her to give it a personal touch and she had done a bit of research on the best companies to recommend as not everyone has a fisherman friend called Billy. Somehow her blog didn't seem so vitally important to her today, but she still wanted to do a good job. She hit the publish button and then checked for emails.

There were two from Harry, which panicked Holly initially until she opened them up. He was simply concerned that he hadn't been able to get hold of her on Facetime or her mobile. She checked her phone, and sure enough there was a message from him on there too:

U ok mum? No word in 3 days - not like u.
U haven't run off with some1 have u? xx

Holly smiled. She and Harry were so close that they often knew when something special was happening in each other's lives, even if they were separated by thousands of miles and a couple of continents.

She checked her watch. It was 8.30 a.m. Mauritius time so 4.30 a.m. in the UK. Some uni students regularly stayed up until that hour but Harry was conscientious about his studies and he had a part-time job so he needed his sleep. Facetime was out of the question so she dropped him a quick text:

All gd here Harry - u wd luv it. Busy
writing & enjoying new friends. Tell all
when back. Mum xxxx.

Holly's stomach rumbled ominously. Time for breakfast, she thought, and to check that Robert hasn't got too much of a hangover.

CHAPTER 33

Rosemary had watched 'the kiss' from the privacy of her hiding place and although it hadn't been long and lingering the body language from both looked encouraging. She had waited for a few minutes after they had parted before heading back to the shoreline for the gentle pre-breakfast stroll she had promised herself.

Now she was sitting sipping black coffee at her favourite table on the verandah of the restaurant, facing the entrance so she could see if Robert roused from his sleep in time to join her. There had been no sign of him and she was just getting ready to leave when she spotted Holly in the queue of the now busy restaurant. She waved and called out, 'Holly, I'm over here,' as though she had been waiting for her friend to join her.

Holly made her way past the crowded tables and gratefully sank into the chair opposite Rosemary.

'That was lucky,' she said. 'I'm a bit later than usual this morning and I was beginning to think I would have to skip breakfast if a table didn't free up. Is Robert at the buffet?'

'Robert is slightly indisposed this morning,' Rosemary replied with a wink. 'I don't mind breakfasting alone but it's much nicer now that you are here. Go and get some food and I'll order some more coffee and then you can tell me about last night... if you want to,' she added hastily.

Minutes later Holly returned followed by a waiter carrying her bowl of fresh fruit and her plate of toast, poached eggs and tomatoes.

Rosemary allowed Holly to savour a few mouthfuls of pineapple and papaya while she sipped her replenished coffee.

'So how was your evening?'

Without hesitation Holly responded, 'I really like Philippe, in fact we're meeting on the beach at ten to spend the day together. And yes I did stay over at his house but we didn't get up to anything because I fell asleep, although I'm not sure we would have got up to anything anyway,' she rambled realising how her previous statement had sounded. 'Then this morning we woke up early and Philippe brought me home on horseback,' she continued, unable to hide her excitement. 'All that was missing from the fairy tale was a suit of shining armour.'

'I think armour would be a little warm in Mauritius,' Rosemary laughed, deciding not to divulge that she had seen them on the beach earlier.

Holly nodded her head in agreement as she took the final mouthful of fruit before swapping her plates over so that she could tuck into her cooked breakfast.

'Is that all you've had?' she asked, indicating the half-eaten croissant with a yolky fork.

'I wasn't very hungry this morning,' she replied truthfully, 'but I'll probably share some of these with Robert later,' she said less truthfully, pulling back her napkin to reveal an assortment of Danish pastries and croissants. 'So what are you and Philippe planning today?' she asked, skilfully changing the subject away from food.

'Just a lovely lazy day on the beach like proper holiday makers,' she replied. 'And then we'll meet up for dinner as planned, if that's still okay with you and Robert?'

'It's more than okay, we're looking forward to the last supper,' Rosemary said, delighted to see Holly looking so relaxed and happy.

'It won't be our last supper,' Holly corrected. 'I'm planning to visit you lots when you get home from here and remember you've promised to take me to see a West End show, which I would hope will include supper afterwards.'

'Absolutely,' Rosemary confirmed. 'We'll go to Joe Allen's,' she continued, while wondering if that occasion would be a table for three or four.

CHAPTER 34

Holly felt warm inside watching the admiring glances of women, from behind the safety of their oversized sunglasses or wide-brimmed sun hats, as Philippe walked past them looking very handsome with his golden hair still damp from the shower, wearing his knee-length, floral-patterned swim shorts, slightly transparent linen shirt and Havaiana flip flops. It felt a little surreal... she was usually one of the ones watching from afar, but today the object of their admiration was on his way to meet her.

She had arrived on the beach ten minutes early to reserve two sun loungers under a straw parasol and although she had her book in her hand she hadn't read a word.

'Good book?' Philippe said.

She glanced down to realise that she was holding the book upside down, immediately instigating the flushed cheeks that always betrayed her embarrassment. Before she could fabricate an excuse he leaned down and kissed her, rendering her speechless.

'We should enjoy the sunshine this morning,' Philippe said as he stripped off his shirt and hung it over the strut of the parasol. 'It feels like rain to me.'

Holly looked up at the clear blue sky in disbelief. 'Really?'

'Trust me – the rain can move in from the mountains in under an hour when the wind is in this direction.'

'I hope you're wrong,' Holly said. 'It's my last day and there won't be another opportunity to top up my tan for a few weeks.'

'If not months, unless you've got inside information on an early heat wave in the UK.'

Fortunately Philippe's eyes were closed so he didn't see Holly colouring up for the second time in a matter of minutes. Think before you speak, she silently admonished herself, realising that once again his proximity had almost caused her to give the game away.

Holly turned her book the right way up and tried to concentrate on reading, which wasn't easy with a semi-naked Philippe just a couple of feet from her. After reading the same page four times and still not getting the gist of it she gave it up as a bad job, closed the book and stood up. Philippe did not stir. What great company I am, she thought, he's fallen asleep!

She wandered down to the water's edge and idly moved pieces of coral with her toes. She thought of the little Italian girl, Giulietta, collecting pieces for her mama. Holly looked up the beach to where they usually sat but their sunbeds were vacant. Of course, yesterday was the last day of their holiday and she had missed saying goodbye. She was disappointed as the little girl's antics had been very entertaining and she had really connected with Mathilda. Maybe I will go and visit them in Geneva, she thought.

Her eyes travelled back to Philippe, who still appeared to be sleeping but was about to be disturbed by a beach seller. Although she had been on the beach most days during her stay Holly had not succumbed to the gentle sales pressure from the men and women who made their living from selling to the tourists. The Plantation House security staff were very good at only allowing a few of the hawkers to approach their guests before urging them to move on. Most of the sellers were young or middle-aged but the man approaching Philippe was old and bent almost double under the weight of the heavy bag of goods he was carrying. Holly started to move across the sugary soft sand to try and intercept but she wasn't quick enough. Philippe was now sitting up shaking his head at the wizened old man.

'I have T-shirts and polo shirts in all sizes and colours,' Holly could hear him say when she was within earshot. The old man looked at Holly as she approached. 'Or maybe a colourful sarong for your wife.'

Holly immediately blushed, again, while a smile played at the corner of Philippe's mouth, but he was still shaking his head about buying anything.

The old man reached into his bag and pulled out a handful of brilliantly coloured sarongs. Some were patterned with hibiscus flowers, others with the dodo, the emblem of Mauritius.

Holly found her voice. 'I have lots of sarongs, thank you,' she said kindly.

'I have something very special that I think you would like,' the old man said. He reached into an end pocket of the battered old sports bag and produced a figurine of a dodo made out of jade. Holly had seen lots of these on her day trip, sculptured from a variety of different semi-precious stones, when they had stopped at a local market but this one was different. Instead of being solid it was carved to be open at the sides and inside was a miniature dodo. It was really beautiful and Holly knew immediately that she was going to buy it as she ran her hands over the smooth olive green stone.

'I haven't seen the dodo carved like this before with the baby inside the mother. It must be very difficult to do.'

The man shrugged his shoulders. 'Things are only difficult to do if you do not have a natural talent. I have been carving stones since I was a child and it is what I love to do. I don't like walking the beach and selling cheap T-shirts and sarongs but I need to put food on the table for my family.'

'How much is it?' asked Holly, still tracing the exquisite carving with her fingertips.

'Eight hundred rupees,' the old man said without hesitation.

Philippe raised his eyebrows but he said nothing as Holly reached into her beach bag for her purse and handed the notes over.

'The dodo inside a dodo is a symbol of love and

good luck. Be sure you only give it to someone very special,' said the beach peddler, pushing the sarongs back into his bag. He zipped it up and wearily hoisted it on to his shoulder before continuing down the beach.

Holly cradled the carving in her hands.

'You know you could have bargained him down on price,' said Philippe.

'Maybe, but I felt sorry for him.'

'There is always a sob story,' scoffed Philippe. 'I'll bet he didn't even carve the dodo. Let me see it,' he said, holding his hand out. 'It was probably made by a machine in China.'

Holly said nothing but rather than hand the dodo to Philippe for inspection she slipped it into her bag along with her purse.

Philippe's tone softened. 'You can't feel sorry for them all.'

'I know, but I felt sorry for him because he's an old man and I believe he was telling the truth.'

Philippe took Holly's hand and pulled her down onto the sunbed with him. He reached up and twisted her ponytail through his fingers before gently pulling her face close enough for him to kiss the tip of her nose.

'You have a soft heart,' he whispered.

She looked into his eyes. Maybe too soft, she thought, and maybe too easily broken. She pulled away from him and stood up.

'Let's go for a walk along the beach,' she suggested. 'If you are so sure it is going to rain this will be my last chance.'

She was already moving in the direction of Tamarina Bay to the south and indicated the still clear blue sky as she called back over her shoulder.

'I mean just look at those huge black rain clouds!'

'You'll eat those words,' he said, getting to his feet and quickly making up the distance she had travelled, 'you'll see.'

They had walked as far as the undergrowth that separated the long stretch of beach from Tamarina Bay before the first dark cloud became visible over the Black Mountains but Holly and Philippe were too engrossed in each other's company to notice. They sat on a rock looking out to sea, sharing moments from their respective pasts, each carefully editing the bits they didn't want the other to know. It was only when they heard a distant rumble of thunder that they became aware of the approaching storm.

'I'm not one to say I told you so,' said Philippe smugly, 'but I told you so. You need to learn to trust me. I reckon we have twenty minutes at the most before the rain hits. Come on,' he said, grabbing her hand.

He had been right about the rain and he was right about the twenty minutes. Unfortunately they had walked for thirty minutes, so even though they hurried, risking cutting their feet on the razor sharp coral, the deluge began before they got back to their sun beds. Philippe's linen shirt, that he had slipped on to walk in, and Holly's colourful sarong were drenched and sticking to their bodies by the time they made it back to the shelter offered by the straw parasol. Shivering, Holly wrapped the beach towel around her shoulders.

'Should we wait here a few minutes for it to ease off?'

Philippe looked in the direction the storm had blown in from and then up at the drips already starting to leak through the parasol.

'I think we should make a dash for the hotel. This isn't easing up anytime soon. Your room or the restaurant?'

Collecting her bag, book and flip flops, pulling her towel over head for shelter and gesticulating with her spare hand she said, 'my room is closer. Come on.'

They raced across the lawn and up the steps at the side of the building before reaching the shelter of the verandah that ran along the back of the first floor rooms providing access for the guests. Holly unlocked the door and they tumbled in like a couple of drowned rats. Until that moment Holly hadn't given a thought as to what would happen next but looking at Philippe, drenched from head to toe, she realised it would involve removing wet clothing.

'I'll get you my bath robe,' she said, hurrying into the bathroom.

Philippe had followed her into the bathroom so that he didn't create a puddle on the bedroom floor.

'We're going to need a shower,' he said. 'Look at the state of us.'

Holly looked down at his legs and feet, splattered with sand and mud from running across the wet grass, and then at her own. Without raising her gaze, she asked in a trembling voice, 'Do you want to go first?'

'We could shower together if you like?'

The question hung in the air for what seemed like an eternity to Holly before she raised her eyes to look into his.

'It would save water I guess,' she said, fully aware of the absurdity of her response as the rain pounded down on the corrugated roof above their heads, matching the pounding of her heart. She let her beach towel fall to the floor and untied the knot behind her head which had held her sarong in place. The thin wet fabric refused to fall to the bathroom floor, instead clinging to her body and revealing her erect nipples beneath her flimsy bikini.

'Here let me,' said Philippe peeling the wet fabric away from her body like the skin from an orange. 'You're cold,' he said. 'Let's get the warm water running.'

He gently pushed her into the shower enclosure and reached for the lever with one hand, undoing the clasp of her bikini with his other in a very practised manner. This did not escape Holly, but right at that moment she didn't care. As the warm water started to fall from the overhead drench shower she turned to face him, nipples still standing to attention.

'It has nothing to do with feeling cold,' she whispered, barely able to speak.

The water flowed freely over them, as did their kisses, small and exploratory to start with, then deep and passionate. Holly hadn't felt someone else's tongue inside her mouth for the longest time and she had forgotten the desire that this unlocked in other parts of her anatomy.

Philippe was gentle and measured with his caresses, wanting to savour every moment of the intimacy. This didn't feel like his many other encounters with adoring females. He wanted it to be more than just sex. He could sense her urgency but selfishly wanted the foreplay to last.

They were both naked now, and very clean from the repeated massaging of shower gel into a foamy lather.

Holly could hear her voice pleading, 'No more playing, Philippe, I want you now.'

CHAPTER 35

The rain stayed for the rest of the afternoon. After making love in the shower they had an encore on the bed before falling asleep cuddled up like spoons, with the rhythmic patter of rain acting as a lullaby. Perhaps that was what woke Holly, the silence once the rain had stopped, or maybe it was the orange glow from the brooding sunset.

She turned to face Philippe with the intention of waking him but he was already awake and staring at her admiringly. She covered her nakedness with the sheet, feeling embarrassed now that the heat of passion had subsided.

'Why didn't you wake me? We'll be late for dinner with Rosemary and Robert,' she said.

'I'm always late anyway, so I won't need an excuse. You on the other hand....' his voice trailed away teasingly.

Panic-stricken Holly looked at the clock on her bedside table. It was 7.15 p.m. She could still be on time to meet with their friends if she showered straightaway.

She rolled off the bed taking the sheet with her, averting her gaze from Philippe's nakedness just a moment too late to notice that he was hard again.

'You need to go, Philippe. You have to go home for a shower and a change of clothes. You'll only be a few minutes late if you leave now.'

'Or I could shower here with you,' he said. 'I like your shower.'

'And wear what to dinner,' Holly demanded. 'One of my dresses?'

They both laughed.

'Even I couldn't pull that off,' Philippe said. 'Although I don't mind trying if it gives me an extra twenty minutes with you.'

'Out now,' she said, pointing to the door. 'Or do I need to phone security and tell them an intruder has broken in?'

As she watched Philippe pull on his soaking shorts and shirt and head for the door she realised that an intruder had broken in to her heart and she fervently hoped that he felt the same towards her.

CHAPTER 36

Robert was still feeling decidedly fragile even though he had spent most of the day in bed recuperating from the excesses of the previous day. Rosemary had snuggled into the bed beside him for a cuddle shortly after she got back from lunching alone. He had asked why she hadn't invited Holly to have lunch with her but Rosemary had dismissed his question, saying that she probably had better things to do on the last day of her holiday.

He had finally dragged himself out of bed around 5 p.m. and sat on the covered terrace watching the rain and breathing in huge gulps of the freshness that heavy rainfall always brought. Rosemary had made them both a cup of tea and they had sat like an elderly couple from the days of the Raj in India, the only thing missing was the servants. It was so sad to think that Rosemary, his beloved Rosie, was never going to grow old.

He turned to look at his wife now, as they sat waiting for their dinner companions in Waves restaurant. She was still a beautiful woman despite the ravages of her illness. Her eyes lit up and Robert turned to follow her gaze. On the dot of 8 p.m. Holly was being shown to their table by the waiter. She had minimal make-up on and her still damp curls were twisted up into the beautiful jewel-encrusted hair clip that she loved. She looked radiant. He rose to greet her.

'My goodness, Holly, you look even more stunning than usual,' he enthused, kissing her on each cheek.

'Are you feeling better now, Robert?'

'Much better thanks, but I think I'll stick to mineral water tonight.'

As he spoke the wine waiter, Pritesh, arrived carrying a champagne bucket with a bottle of Bollinger cooling on the ice within it. Robert started to tell the waiter that he had brought it to the wrong table but Rosemary interrupted him.

'I ordered champagne, Robert, to celebrate a wonderful week with old friends and new.'

'What a lovely idea, I wish I had thought of it,' Holly said. 'You will have one glass won't you Robert when Philippe gets here?'

Pritesh cleared his throat.

'Excuse me,' he said. 'The champagne is from Mr Philippe. He told me to cancel any other arrangements that may have been made for tonight. I hope this was the right thing to do?'

Robert was puzzled. Philippe was not known for ostentatious gestures. Maybe he was celebrating something? Just then the man himself arrived at the restaurant entrance looking only slightly less groomed than usual. He accepted Rosemary's warm hug and patted Robert on the shoulder.

'I hope you've recovered from yesterday?'

'No thanks to you,' said Rosemary reproachfully but Philippe was too engrossed in kissing Holly's hand while maintaining eye contact to respond.

'Good job it was raining really,' said Robert. 'We probably wouldn't have got up to too much anyway. It's a shame the rain came on your last day here though Holly but hopefully you managed to amuse yourself?'

Holly shot Philippe a warning look but it was Rosemary that spoke.

'Well it was only this afternoon really and I expect you've been packing.'

Holly was grateful for the interjection but she also noticed the twinkle in Rosemary's eye. She knows, thought Holly, picking up her menu to hide behind before a customary blush could give her away.

Pritesh had been busying himself with the champagne cork and at that moment it popped, spewing a tiny amount of froth onto the table before he could reach for the first glass. Philippe mopped it with his napkin while Pritesh poured the sparkling liquid into the four flutes and then raised his glass.

'To special friends and a special place. If only it could last forever.'

Philippe had meant his toast to communicate how much he cared about the people around the table so he was confused by the reaction.

Robert was acutely aware of how little time he had left with his wife and Holly was wondering if Philippe was ending any chance of a relationship before it even got started. Once again it was Rosemary who spoke.

'Nothing is forever, Philippe, so let's just enjoy tonight.'

They chinked glasses each feeling slightly less comfortable than they had moments before.

Fortunately good food, animated conversation and a second bottle of Bollinger helped get past the awkwardness and by the time they moved into the bar area to enjoy the evening's entertainment they were all feeling mellow. Holly had wanted to sit by the beach but there was still a spit of rain in the air so they sat by the open side of the bar area, sheltered but still within earshot of the waves gently lapping the shore.

There was no show featuring local dancers that evening, instead the band were playing songs from movies and encouraging the guests to dance. Rosemary was in her element performing the quickstep and tango with all the grace and passion you would expect from a former professional dancer, so much so that people applauded as 'Por Una Cabeza' from *Scent of a Woman* came to an end. The moment the first few notes of the next song began Philippe pulled Holly to her feet and said, 'Come on let's join them.'

'But I can't dance,' Holly protested.

'Everyone can do the waltz,' Philippe persisted. 'Just follow my lead.'

Holly had drunk just enough champagne to relax in his arms without feeling self-conscious, allowing him to guide her around the dance floor while the band played 'Moon River'. For the second time that day their bodies were in perfect harmony. Having been a reluctant dance partner initially Holly was sad when the song finished and the band leader announced they were taking a fifteen-minute break.

The four of them made their way back to their table.

'You should dance more often, Holly, you move beautifully,' Philippe said.

'I just needed reminding of the steps,' she replied, 'and you were an excellent teacher.'

'Beautiful song "Moon River", but I can't place the movie,' Robert said.

The other three chorused, '*Breakfast At Tiffany's*,' and Philippe added, 'My favourite film.'

'Ours is *Gone With the Wind*, isn't it, Holly,' Rosemary said. 'We discovered we both have the same favourite film over dinner the first night.'

Holly wasn't listening. *Breakfast At Tiffany's* had been her dad's favourite film too, in fact she had been named after Audrey Hepburn's character, Holly Golightly. Her dad had told her that after her birth her mother had suffered terribly with the 'baby blues' and refused to give their little daughter a name. After a week of being referred to as 'baby Wilson', during which time he had made several suggestions, she had simply said, 'Call her what you like. I couldn't care less.' Years later when Holly had told them that she was pregnant with Harry her mother had said, 'That's what you get naming your daughter after a prostitute in that stupid film you like.' Her dad hadn't even tried to argue.

Holly realised the other three were looking at her.

Had someone just asked her a question? She had no idea.

'We were just wondering if you were named after Holly Golightly,' Rosemary prompted.

'No,' she mumbled. 'I think it was probably something to do with Christmas. Would you excuse me a moment? I just need the ladies' room.'

CHAPTER 37

Rosemary was holding Robert's hand as the two couples walked along the sandy path towards their respective rooms. Philippe's arm was draped casually across Holly's shoulders and she occasionally glanced up at him to respond to his conversation.

'They make a lovely couple, don't you think?' Rosemary said in a hushed voice.

Robert looked at his wife's radiant face but he was troubled.

'You don't think it's all moving a bit too fast, do you? I mean she has only just lost her husband, it could be a rebound thing. I don't want either of them to get hurt,' he concluded.

'They fit,' said Rosemary, feeling guilty that she knew Holly's real situation when her husband didn't. 'And, as I said at dinner, nothing lasts forever. We should all make the most of each moment.'

Robert couldn't argue with that sentiment but he still felt uneasy as they reached the bottom of the steps leading to Holly's room and the two of them said goodnight to Rosemary and Robert, clearly intending to spend the night together.

'Will we see you at breakfast, Holly?' Rosemary asked.

'Of course' she replied, 'although it will be quite early as the car to take me to the airport is due here at nine thirty.'

'We'll see you around eight then.'

'Perfect,' said Holly rounding the turn in the steps and wondering, not for the first time, exactly when she was going to do her packing.

Rosemary and Robert continued on to their room in silence, each remembering the excitement of being young and in love in Mauritius.

Holly opened the door to her room feeling ridiculously nervous. This was the first time they both knew what would happen next. She reached for the switch on the bedside lamp but Philippe put his hand over hers to stop her. It felt like she had been struck by a lightning bolt.

'Let's open the curtains instead,' he whispered, his mouth so close to her ear that she could feel the warmth of his breath. 'It's a beautiful moon, it would be such a shame not to enjoy it.'

They moved over to the window together, Holly feeling strangely shy but full of anticipation for a repeat performance of the pleasure that she had denied herself for so long. He drew back the curtains then stood behind her allowing her to lean back into him as they looked out at the inky ocean with the path of the moon leading directly to them. Holly could feel Philippe's desire pressing into the small of her back as he began to kiss her neck, gently flicking his tongue into her ear and then sucking softly on her lobe, sending shivers through her whole body. He traced the outline of her shoulder blades with his tongue before easing the narrow straps of her dress down with his teeth, revealing her naked shoulders and exposing her breasts. She stood semi-naked in the moonlight not sure if anyone could see her but not caring if they could. This was a different Holly, one that had been locked away for nineteen years. She closed her eyes to fully appreciate each flick of the tongue or gentle bite, every nerve ending on full alert sending messages to the depths of her belly.

Philippe placed his fingers lightly on her shoulder to turn her to face him then let his hands drop again. He nibbled along her collar bones, then traced her breastbone with the tip of his tongue moving down towards her belly button, still without touching her with his hands. Her dress had caught on her hips so he reached behind her to unzip it, allowing it to fall to the floor in a graceful pool. He moved away from her slightly to drink in her curves and the triangle of champagne-coloured lace that was her only protection from nudity.

Holly's eyes were still closed, willing him to touch her in her most intimate place.

'Open your eyes, Holly.'

She did as instructed and caught her breath as he stood before her naked.

'Do you want this?' he asked. 'Do you want me?'

'Yes,' was all the affirmation she could muster and all the confirmation Philippe needed. He swept her off her feet and laid her on the bed and as she arched her back his lips closed around her hardened nipple. Moments later he slid into her, unable to resist any longer.

Afterwards, Holly lay on her side, her head resting on Philippe's chest while he played with the jewel-encrusted hair clip that had worked its way loose during their exertions.

'It's pretty,' he said. 'Was it a gift?'

'Yes, Harry treated me to it for Christmas last year.'

'Was Harry your husband?'

Holly's throat tightened as she realised what she had said. She wanted to tell Philippe that she had been lying about having a dead husband, and that she had a teenage son called Harry, but this wasn't the right moment. She nodded.

'Do you want to talk about it?' he asked. 'You already know I'm a very good listener.'

She shook her head.

'Are you sure?' he persevered. 'Were you thinking about him earlier in the evening when you rushed off to the loo?'

Holly took a deep breath. 'No,' she answered truthfully. 'I was thinking about my dad. I lied when I said I wasn't named after Holly Golightly. I was. It was my dad's favourite film too.'

Philippe was looking at her questioningly . 'So why didn't you just say that?'

'Because... because I don't like being named after a high-class hooker,' she replied.

'She wasn't really a hooker, Holly, she just accepted gifts from wealthy gentlemen. You should be pleased that he wanted to name you after the lead character in his favourite film. Have you spoken to him about the way you feel? You could always get your name changed you know.'

'It's too late,' Holly said wearily.

'Of course it's not, people would soon get used to calling you by a new name.'

Holly allowed herself a wry smile. People already knew her by a different name, Liberty Sands.

'I don't mean that it's too late to change my name, I mean it's too late to talk to my Dad about it. He died. It wouldn't feel right changing the name he gave me.'

'I'm so sorry, Holly,' Philippe said, genuine concern in his voice. 'You haven't had much luck with the men in your life have you?'

She looked up at him. 'I'm hoping my luck might change.'

CHAPTER 38

For the second night in a row Philippe had barely slept, not wanting to miss a moment of his time with Holly, and now the first light of the day was streaming in through the windows. His fingers toyed gently with the dark unruly curls framing her face, tangled from their lovemaking. He smiled at his choice of word. Philippe would normally have referred to it as sex but this experience had been different. He had felt emotion, possibly even love, he thought as he gazed down at her. She looked peaceful in sleep, vulnerable, and at that moment his only thought was to protect her. Obviously losing her husband had been devastating and he wondered if maybe in his desire to get to know her physically he had rushed things emotionally. She had been a responsive, willing sexual partner but she hadn't uttered those three little words that so many of his previous conquests had. He had wanted her to say it, even though he was unsure how he would have responded, but she had remained silent and then the moment was lost when he had mentioned her husband.

Philippe had noticed the look of panic in her eyes. Maybe she thought she had betrayed her husband's memory by mentioning his name while lying naked in the arms of another man. He could understand that and it made the powerful feelings he was experiencing towards her even stronger. What he was finding harder to comprehend was her behaviour at the dinner table. Why had Holly lied about being named after a character in a film? Although she had explained her reasons he felt she was holding something back. And her description of Holly Golightly as a high-class hooker. Was that accurate? Philippe had never thought of Audrey Hepburn's sensitive portrayal as that, and he had watched *Breakfast at Tiffany's* a dozen or more times. She was just a young woman alone and vulnerable, not unlike my Holly, he thought, still playing with her tousled curls.

He glanced past her to the clock on the bedside table and knew that he needed to wake her if she was to keep her breakfast rendezvous with Robert and Rosemary. He had already decided that he would say his goodbyes and head back to Tamarina Bay to avoid any awkwardness with the hotel staff. Dinner was one thing, breakfast something else entirely.

'Holly,' he said gently, 'you need to wake up.'

Holly opened her eyes and focused on the man she had spent the majority of the last two days with. It seemed longer, she thought, it feels like I've known him for years. His slight physical resemblance to Gareth may have been what had initially attracted her to Philippe, but Holly was sure that the deepening feelings she had for him were nothing to do with Harry's dad. She flinched as she remembered the near miss she had had over the hair clip. It would be so easy to simply tell Philippe the truth but there wasn't time now, she realised, as she caught sight of the clock. It was already seven thirty.

Philippe was stroking her arm, occasionally brushing her right breast as he did so.

'I don't suppose we have time for an encore?' he said, his eyes twinkling.

'Sadly not,' she replied, removing his arm from around her shoulders, but kissing the tips of his fingers as she did so. 'We have a breakfast appointment in thirty minutes.'

'You have a breakfast appointment,' he corrected.

Holly's heart missed a beat. 'Are you not coming?'

'I think it's better to say out goodbyes in private,' he said, then added, 'and anyway it's not really adieu it's au revoir,' and in case she didn't understand he translated, 'until we meet again.'

Holly released the breath she hadn't realised she had been holding. 'You do mean it Philippe? We will see each other when you come back to England?'

'I would fly back with you today if I could. You have given me a reason to get my book finished as quickly as possible so we can spend time getting to know each other properly.'

They kissed deeply but before it could lead to anything Holly pulled away.

'You take a shower first. I need to start throwing my clothes into my suitcase.'

Reluctantly Philippe did as instructed leaving the water running for Holly while he gathered his clothes from the floor by the window. It's a good job people expected linen to look crumpled, he thought, looking down at the woeful state of his trousers. He sat on the bed buttoning his shirt watching Holly through the shutters that divided the bathroom from the bedroom. She had her head back allowing the warm water to rinse away the last remnants of shampoo from her hair and all trace of him from her body. The temptation to strip off and join her in the shower was almost irresistible but Philippe stopped himself. There would be plenty more opportunities. Finally he had found a woman he could love who would love him back.

Holly towel dried her hair and combed it through, then slipped into her comfy trousers and loose-fitting tunic in preparation for the twelve-hour flight home.

They didn't speak, just held each other close, all the communication they needed. Holly opened the door to her room and they walked along the sandy path towards the main hotel building hand in hand. When they reached the fork in the path, one direction leading to the restaurant and the other to the front of the hotel, they stopped.

Philippe leaned forward and kissed her on the

forehead. In an attempt to keep the mood light he said, 'You realise if the restaurant was called Tiffany's you'd be on your way to Breakfast at Tiffany's.'

Even as he said it an idea started to form in his mind so he was only half listening when Holly said, 'Wrong Holly. I don't own a cat and if I did I'd think of a better name for it than Cat!'

CHAPTER 39

The black limo pulled up outside the Plantation
House hotel at 9.25 a.m. and despite having
Robert and Rosemary with her Holly felt alone
without Philippe at her side. She understood his
reasoning about the hotel staff and how awkward he
would have felt going to breakfast with her but a small
part of her was hoping that he would arrive in his
ageing BMW to drive her to the airport because he
wanted to be with her until the last possible moment.
There was no sign of him and, come to think of it, he
had suddenly become very distracted and positively
rushed away from her towards the hotel car park as
she stood watching him before she took the other
path to the restaurant to meet her friends.

Neither of them had mentioned Philippe at
breakfast, which was a little odd as they must have
realised the two of them had spent the night together,
until Rosemary, while checking that they had each
other's contact details, phone, mobile phone and
email address, asked if she had exchanged her details

with Philippe.

'Just email at the moment,' Holly had replied. 'Phone calls and text messages to Mauritius are expensive.'

That wasn't the only reason. She didn't want Philippe ringing her mobile and getting a foreign ringtone when she was away on her next assignment. There would be plenty of time to exchange phone numbers when he finished writing his book and came home to England. There would also be plenty of time to tell him the truth about her life, at least she hoped there would be, and she hoped he would understand the reason she had needed to lie to him.

The driver, Sachin, was holding the car door open for her.

Holly hugged Robert first. 'Look after your beautiful wife, she's a very special lady.'

'You're right she is,' said Robert.

Then she held Rosemary for a long moment. 'Keep in touch and ring me the moment you get home so that we can meet up.'

'I will,' Rosemary promised, a promise tinged with sadness as both women knew that the reason for Rosemary's return to the UK would be Rosemary's failing health.

Sachin closed the car door, climbed into the driver's seat and the limousine pulled smoothly away with Holly biting her trembling lip and unable to look back for fear of crying.

So much had happened to her in one short week and she knew the impact would stay with her for the rest of her life.

CHAPTER 40

All the way back to his rented house at Tamarina Bay Philippe had been struggling with the urge to turn his car around and walk in through the front of the hotel, witnessed by the staff who knew him well, so that he could spend a little more time with Holly, maybe even breaking his own rules about last-minute goodbyes by driving her to the airport. The only thing that stopped him was the spark of an idea for his book that would turn it from a dull 'travelogue' to a romance with a twist. He was running out of time to deliver the rewrite of his first draft as had been made crystal clear by the frosty email from his publisher that had been waiting for him yesterday when he had arrived home after his afternoon of lovemaking:

Phil,

You have two months to deliver before you are in breach of contract, let me know if this is going to be a problem for you. My neck is on the line too – you know how hard I worked to get you the three-book deal before we knew if Maman would be the success it was.

KR

Jo

KR, he thought with annoyance. His editor, Jo, had criticised his writing ability and she couldn't even write 'kind regards'. He could feel a bubble of anger starting to swell but he quickly quashed it knowing, despite his irritation, that she had a point. *Maman* had flowed easily but this latest book had lacked the same depth of emotion, his fabricated characters feeling shallow and unrealistic. Even his English teacher at his boarding school in Kent would have made him go back to the drawing board to flesh out his characters until they felt like real people that you believed in and cared about. That's the secret, he thought, my characters have to be based on real people and now I know who 'Tiffany' is.

He turned the key in the lock of his front door and headed straight for his desk and laptop impatient to get started on the rewrite. There would be plenty of time to spend with Holly once his book was finished and he was back in England. As he had reassured Holly, it was *au revoir* not *adieu*.

CHAPTER 41

Holly stood on the station platform at Gatwick airport waiting for the next train to Clapham Junction from where she could catch a train home to Reading. Soleil Resorts footed the bill for everything while she was on location but travel arrangements in the UK were her own responsibility. She allowed herself a wry smile. It was a very different journey in prospect from her arrival at Dubai International airport in the back of a black stretch limousine for her flight home, some seven hours earlier.

It had been a crazy eight weeks. She had arrived home from Mauritius to find a manuscript requiring her copy-editing attention. It was a second book from a former daytime television presenter and sadly it was no better written than his first. He had particularly requested Holly as she had 'licked his first book into shape'.

That was one way of putting it, Holly thought, but a more accurate description might have been that I totally re-wrote it. Holly had not only corrected the punctuation and grammar, but also made dialogue suggestions as the writer in question seemed to have his characters speaking in language more relevant to the early twentieth century rather than a hundred years later. Even the plot had been too straightforward with no twists and turns and little to keep the reader interested, so Holly had tweaked that too. The resulting book had been well received but even with her changes Holly doubted that it would have made the Bestseller List if it hadn't been bought by all his adoring female fans.

Instead of the 'light touch' instruction she usually received from the publishing company, meaning let the author's voice be heard, the accompanying note had said:

Hi Hols

Another hatchet job required to make this fit to publish I'm afraid. Do exactly as you did with his last masterpiece please and can I have it by the end of next week?

Cheers

DD

PS I keep telling you that you should write a book of your own instead of making other people believe they can write xx

How many times had Holly thought of doing just that over the years she had been working as a freelance for DD, a nickname they used that had nothing to do with her friend's real name. It had been her bra cup size when they had met in their first year at university and instantly become friends but was now a bit of a misnomer as DD was constantly on the latest fad diet.

When Holly had failed to return to university for her second year DD had tried phoning and even writing to Holly's home address anxious to find out what had happened that had caused her talented friend to abandon her degree and her friends. Holly's embarrassment at the situation she found herself in had prevented her from responding to either. Several years later, after completing her English degree with the Open University and having been rejected from most of the publishing companies she had approached for freelance work, she had read that her former friend, Joanna Thomas, had been promoted to editor at Ripped Publishing, a company she had already been rejected from. She had re-sent her CV and a covering letter and a couple of days later DD had called her. Holly wasn't sure whether her vague explanation of family issues had satisfied DD's curiosity but she had been prepared to give her friend a chance. Holly didn't let her friend down. She always did a thorough job and met the deadline, even if it meant staying up late into the night, and she never turned down work, regardless of how badly written it was because, as a freelancer, you have to take what you are given. Through her work for Ripped she had built a good reputation and other companies began to use her too.

It had taken her the best part of two weeks to finish *A Perfect Swine* and she had changed almost everything apart from the dreadful title which unfortunately was beyond her remit.

With the manuscript out of the way Holly had gone to visit Harry in Bath. She had been itching to tell her son about Philippe but she wanted to tell him face to face.

'Have you heard from him since you got back?' was his first question.

Typical Harry, always trying to protect her. He had done it all his life even getting into fights with the boys at his school if they ever made nasty remarks about his mum not being married to his dad.

'We've been in touch by email several times,' Holly replied, although in truth she was a little disappointed at both the length and the infrequency of the emails.

Philippe had apologised, explaining that he had been tied to his computer as he was 'on a roll' with his book which he had virtually entirely rewritten. Holly had smiled as she imagined them both feverishly tapping the computer keys on book rewrites.

In the last email she had received from him a few days previously he said that he was almost ready to send the rewritten version to his editor and if approved he could start to pack up the house in Mauritius and be home within a fortnight. He had added that he couldn't wait to see her again and just reading that had made Holly go weak at the knees.

Harry had also asked if she had been in touch with the older couple she had mentioned meeting.

Rosemary had emailed a few times, mainly to say that they hadn't seen much of Philippe since she had left as he was holed up writing his latest book.

'I hope it's as good as his first one,' Rosemary had written on one email.

Holly had replied, 'Which destination did he write about in his first book?'

She hadn't heard from Rosemary for a couple of days after that and when she did there was no mention of either Philippe or his first book.

It had been such a joy to spend time with Harry and she left Bath feeling proud of the young man she had single-handedly guided through his early life. As they hugged he had asked where she was off to next for Soleil Resorts, and when she answered Cuba followed by Dubai he had laughed and said, 'I've created a jet-setter.'

Jet-setter, Holly thought, climbing aboard the Gatwick Express, jet-lagged more like. She settled in her seat and closed her eyes for a power nap.

CHAPTER 42

A fly was buzzing round the room, occasionally landing for a few seconds before taking flight again. It was annoying Philippe but he was so tired he couldn't be bothered to drag himself out of bed to swat it or open the door to the verandah to set it free. He hadn't slept for more than a few hours a night for the past eight weeks but last night he had finally finished the book and emailed it to his publisher. He had crawled into bed at 2 a.m. without even brushing his teeth, which he now regretted as they felt positively furry, and fallen asleep within minutes.

The fly landed on his hand and he took an ineffectual swipe at it. It's no good, he thought, I'm not going to get back to sleep. He rolled over to check his bedside clock and was astonished to see that it was 4 p.m. Reluctantly he swung his legs out of bed and headed to the bathroom. While he was brushing his teeth he decided he would go over to the Plantation House hotel that evening to have dinner with Robert and Rosemary. He had barely seen them in two months and he was feeling guilty for neglecting them, particularly as they had introduced him to Holly. He was still looking at his unshaven reflection in the mirror, after rinsing the foamy toothpaste away, and noticed with amusement that even the thought of her caused him to smile. Although he loved Mauritius he was anxious to pack his things and head back to the UK to see her again. Who would have thought that he would find love at his age?

He desperately wanted a shower and a shave but first he needed to check his email to make sure that his editor had received his manuscript. He moved towards his desk feeling a flutter of nerves in his belly and clicked the inbox on his laptop. Sure enough there was an email from Jo, and even without opening it he could see the first few words:

OMG Phil, this is bloody...

Bloody what, thought Philippe? He couldn't bear it if his editor hated what he had spent every waking hour working on for the last two months. He hovered the arrow over the email then closed his eyes as he clicked the left button. He took a deep breath and opened one eye... the next word was BRILLIANT.

Philippe didn't read the rest of the email, he let out a shriek and then started jumping around the room shouting, 'YES... YES... YES,' at the top of his voice! His only disappointment was that there was no one there to share his happy news with. Right, he thought, I'm going to shower and head to the Plantation House early. I'll buy the champagne and Robert, Rosemary and I can have our own Happy Hour before dinner.

Less than an hour later a freshly showered and shaved Philippe was striding up the front steps of the hotel two at a time. The first person he saw in the vaulted reception area was the assistant manager Vikram.

'Afternoon, Vikram. Do you happen to know where my friends the Forresters are? I've got some fantastic news I want to share with them.'

'I'm sorry, Mr Philippe, they checked out two days ago.'

Philippe stopped mid-stride, unable to believe what he was hearing.

'Are you sure, Vikram? I'm certain they wouldn't have left without saying goodbye.'

'I'm sure, sir, but they did leave a note for you.'

Vikram went behind the front desk and retrieved an envelope with the solitary word Philippe scribbled on the front in Robert's handwriting. Philippe opened it:

Philippe,

I'm afraid we have to go back to England. It's a shame that your latest book prevented us from spending more time together. We both hope it is as successful as your first book was.

Robert and Rosemary

Philippe looked down at the sheet of paper in his hand in disbelief. It was always more difficult to interpret the written word rather than the spoken word but this felt almost like a rebuke. And why had Robert written it rather than Rosemary? Was she that annoyed with him that she couldn't even bring herself to write him a note?

He muttered under his breath, 'I thought she understood that a writer needs time to write!'

He crumpled the paper in his fist, tossed it into a wastepaper bin, and left as quickly as he had arrived, all feeling of elation replaced with outrage.

CHAPTER 43

Holly woke with a start as the train jolted to a halt at Clapham Junction. It was a good job, she thought, or I would have ended up at Victoria and then had to get a train back to Clapham Junction for the connection to Reading. A quick glance up at the departures screen told her the platform number of the next train to Reading and also that she had precisely four minutes to negotiate the two lots of steps with her suitcase bumping along behind her.

Fortunately it was the middle of the day so the train carriage was not busy and she was able to stand her case in front of the seat next to her to keep an eye on it. Not that there's much in my suitcase worth pinching, she thought, apart from my laptop, but a thief wouldn't know that until they had forced the case open.

It wasn't until the train was pulling out of the station at Virginia Water more than thirty minutes later that Holly realised she hadn't switched on her mobile phone. She reached into her handbag, turned it on and keyed in her four-digit security code. A minute later her phoned beeped to alert her that she had new messages. She looked at the screen. There were eight missed calls and three new messages. Crikey, I'm popular, she thought, hitting the button that would identify the missed callers details.

As well as the number of her voicemail service and Harry's number, there was a mobile number she didn't recognise that had called her six times. She dialled 901 intrigued. The most recent voice message was from Harry: 'Hi, Mum. Give me a call to let me know you got back safely.'

She was smiling broadly thinking of her caring son as she began to listen to the second message, but her smile soon faded:

'Holly, it's Robert Forrester. I hope you are well. I've tried your number several times as I didn't really want to leave you a message but I guess I'll have to.' That would explain the missed calls from the number I didn't recognise, thought Holly. She had only taken Rosemary's mobile number not that of her husband. 'I don't want to worry you but we're back in the UK and Rosemary is asking if you can come and visit as a matter of urgency. Please give me a call when you get this message.'

Holly's heart plummeted and her hands were shaking as she dropped the phone back into her bag. If the Forresters were back in the UK it could mean only one thing: Rosemary's health must have deteriorated. She would ring from her land-line the moment she got home. This was a conversation she couldn't have with a signal dropping in and out on a mobile phone.

The rest of the journey to Reading seemed to take an age and when the train finally pulled in to the station Holly rushed for the taxi rank as quickly as her luggage would allow. Typical, she thought, seeing at least a dozen people already queuing and no taxis in sight. One rounded the corner and in desperation Holly did something completely out of character.

She went to the front of the queue and said to the smartly dressed man carrying a briefcase, 'I wouldn't normally ask but would you mind terribly if I took this cab? I've just heard that my friend is dying and I need to see her.'

The man took one look at her pale face and panic-stricken eyes then stood aside holding the taxi door open for her. There were a few glares and mutterings from people further back in line who hadn't heard the exchange but Holly didn't care. She was thinking through what she had just said. How bad was Rosemary? Was she actually dying? Tears spilled down Holly's cheeks.

Fifteen minutes later Holly let herself into her little terraced house, reached into the desk drawer for her address book and found the Forresters' home number. Robert answered on the fourth ring.

'Forrester speaking.'

'Robert, it's Holly. What's happened. Is Rosemary OK?'

'Holly, thank God it's you. Rosie has been asking for you.'

In the background Holly could just make out Rosemary's voice. 'Can she come, Bobby?'

Without waiting for him to ask the question Holly said, 'I'll be there as quickly as I can but you have to tell me what's happened.'

Robert told her that Rosemary had started to feel unwell about a month after Holly had flown home. She was having excruciating headaches that no amount of paracetamol could touch and she was starting to have dizzy spells. Then one morning Robert had been unable to wake her.

'I thought I'd lost her, Holly,' Robert said in a muffled voice, fighting back tears. 'I phoned for the hotel doctor but by the time he arrived I had managed to rouse Rosie. He wanted her admitted to the hospital in Port Louis for tests but Rosie was adamant that she wanted to come home so they sent an ambulance to take us to the airport instead. It was all such a rush I barely had time to pack. Thankfully she slept for most of the flight and then an ambulance met us at Gatwick to take her straight to University College Hospital. It was during the ambulance ride that she told me you knew everything and begged me to ring you. That was two days ago and I've been trying to reach you since.'

Holly groaned. 'I've just got back from Dubai and I didn't have my phone on the last day I was there because I was fed up with constant interruptions when I was trying to work.'

There was a pause on the other end of the phone and then a confused Robert said, 'You've been working in Dubai?'

Holly was too tired to try and explain. 'I'll tell you all about it when I see you. So how is Rosemary now?'

'Well, they hooked her up to an intravenous drip with the experimental drug they wanted her to try months ago and it seems to be working for the moment. They kept her in overnight and gave her another chemotherapy session yesterday before letting her come home. We were back at the hospital this morning for another three hours, in fact we only got home about ten minutes before you rang.'

Robert sounded exhausted and Holly was furious with herself for not being on the other end of the phone when her friends needed her.

'How did you explain it to Philippe?' she asked.

'We left in such a rush that I just scribbled him a quick note to tell him we had to come home and left it with the hotel reception. We hadn't really seen much of him after you left because he's been busy writing, which of course I totally understand with deadlines to meet.'

'Maybe you should let him know what's really going on with Rosemary?'

'I agree, Holly, but it's Rosie's decision and at the moment she doesn't want to tell anyone else but us.'

Holly heard Rosemary's voice in the background again. 'What time will she be here Bobby?'

'Tell her I'm leaving right now,' said Holly grabbing her car keys.

CHAPTER 44

The traffic on the M4 and M25 motorways had been fairly light as Holly had beaten the afternoon rush hour but it was still almost two hours before she took the exit at junction 6 onto the A22 towards Woldingham. She followed the directions Robert had hastily given her, turning left up the hill by the station and then right into a private road. There were no house numbers, instead she was looking out for a house called 'Valley View' which he had simply described as single storey at the front and painted white. She spotted it on the right-hand side and turned into the gravel driveway, pulling up outside the dark oak, double front doors. Before she had even got out of the car the front door was open and Robert was crunching across the gravel to greet her.

He flung his arms around her. 'Thank you so much for coming so quickly.'

Holly was taken aback by his appearance. Gone was the suave elegant Robert she had met in Mauritius nine weeks previously. He had lost weight, his eyes were sunken and dark-rimmed and he had the look of a desperate man.

'It's all right, Robert. I'm here now,' she said gently.

She followed him into the house and, despite the reason for the visit, couldn't help but gasp in wonder at the magnificence of the interior. She was standing on a galleried landing with stairs descending from either side down to the reception area on the lower level. There was a huge double height window the width of the room showcasing the most amazing view of the valley and the wooded Surrey hillside beyond. Of course, she reminded herself, you would expect no less from an architect of Robert's reputation. She hoped Harry would one day design something so stunning.

'Holly, is that you?' Rosemary's voice brought her sharply back to the present. 'I'm down here. Robert, you're forgetting your manners. Offer Holly something to drink.'

Robert raised his eyebrows and for a moment a twinkle returned to his anxious eyes.

'Tea or something stronger?'

'I could murder a cuppa. I haven't had a decent one in over a week.'

'How do you take it?'

'A drop of milk and one sugar please,' she replied, following him down the stairs.

Rosemary was sitting on a plump, three-seater sofa which was beautifully upholstered in a pale grey-and-white striped fabric. She was wearing a loose-fitting, navy-blue silk shirt over winter-white tailored trousers and the tan from her recent time in

Mauritius was lifted by a touch of blusher and lip-gloss. Although she didn't attempt to get up as Holly approached, the younger woman was pleased to see that Rosemary looked almost exactly the same as the last time she had seen her at the Plantation House hotel, just slightly thinner. It was a relief as she had been fretting on the drive over not really knowing what to expect with all the talk of chemotherapy drips.

'Holly, I'm so happy to see you. I've been driving Robert crazy trying to get in touch with you. I thought maybe you were away again.' As she pulled Holly into an embrace she whispered, 'I haven't told Robert about your alter ego. Your secret's safe with me.'

'Rosemary, you look amazing,' Holly said. 'I appreciate you not telling Robert but it's really not that important in the grand scheme of things.'

'Well, I promised I wouldn't tell him so I haven't. I keep my promises and I'm hoping that you do too.'

Holly racked her brain to try and remember what she had promised Rosemary but jet lag wasn't helping her powers of recollection.

'You promised you would help me do something when the time came,' prompted Rosemary. 'Well, the time has come.'

Holly felt a little shiver run down her back.

'Oh yes, I remember. That day at Philippe's house you said you might need me to help you with something. What do you need me to do?'

'I can't talk in front of Robert but I'll send him out to the shops in a little while to buy something to make dinner. You will stay for dinner won't you?' It was less a question, more an assumption. 'And while he's out we can talk properly.'

Right on cue Robert walked into the room carrying a tray filled with bone china cups and saucers and a plate of biscuits. She reached to take the cup of tea that Robert was offering, wondering what Rosemary wanted to ask of her that she couldn't talk about in front of her husband.

CHAPTER 45

There was a hammering in Philippe's head brought on, no doubt, by downing the entire contents of the bottle of champagne that he had intended to share with the Forresters in celebration of his publisher's email. He had followed that with half a dozen bottles of beer, the only alcohol in the house, as he waited for a reply to the email he had sent Holly. At first he had assumed that, due to the time difference, she might be at work with no access to her personal emails, but as one beer turned into five or six and the time ticked on past midnight, Philippe finally staggered off to bed while he could still walk.

The hammering was getting louder and Philippe realised it was not just in his head, there was someone at his front door. Who could it be? he wondered. His cleaner, Delphine, had her own key so that she could let herself in and out without disturbing him while he was writing. He gingerly hauled himself into an upright position and crossed towards the door, shuffling his feet to minimise any jarring to his head. He tried unsuccessfully to open the door before noticing that he had put the deadlock on. He flicked the button and the door swung open to reveal a very worried-looking Delphine.

'Mr Philippe, you scared me,' she said. 'When I couldn't open the door I thought something was wrong. You look terrible.'

'Sshhh, please, my head,' was all Philippe could muster.

'Ah, the demon drink. I've told you before you should be teetotal like me. You sit down and I'll make you some strong coffee.'

Philippe slumped onto the sofa. 'You're an angel.'

Half an hour later, somewhat revived by the bitter dark liquid, Philippe turned on his computer and was disappointed to see that there was still no word from Holly. There was however another email from his editor:

Phil,

How soon can you pack up there and get back to the UK?

I've got the team working on the cover and the sleeve blurb, and I've already sent it to the copy editor with instructions for the lightest touch.

I want to get the publicity on this started asap so I need you here... it's going to be monster. Talk about the pressure of a deadline – I guess that's the journalist in you.

LOVE the title, and love the title character, she feels so real... not sure whether to feel sorry for her or whether she's just a money-grabbing bitch! Poor Pierre!

I'm already thinking bidding wars for the film rights.

Let me know when you've got your flight booked.

Jo

CHAPTER 46

The late afternoon April sunshine was streaming in through the double-height windows, flooding the room with a soft amber glow. Not only was Valley View a stunning piece of architecture it also had a south-westerly aspect at the rear. Holly was standing by the window gazing out at the beautiful garden which was coming into bloom with red and white camellia bushes and fresh green leaves on the cherry trees preceding their frothy pink blossom. If I had a home like this I would never want to leave it, she thought.

She wondered whether she should wake Rosemary who had dozed off halfway through her cup of tea. She knew Rosemary wanted to talk to her privately and Robert would be back from his trip to the shops soon. He had seized the opportunity to nip out while his wife was sleeping but had company so she would not wake up alone.

'It's beautiful isn't it?' Holly turned at the sound of Rosemary's voice. The decision to wake her had been taken out of her hands. 'Sometimes I wonder how Robert and I could ever have left this place to go on holidays.'

'I was just thinking the same thing. How are you feeling?' she asked, crossing back to the sofa where Rosemary was reclining.

Rosemary sidestepped the question. 'I think the house at Tamarina Bay is the only one I could have given all this up for and now I won't need to make a choice between them. Don't get me wrong, Holly, I know how blessed I've been in my life to have all this and Bobby too, but I just wish it could have been for a little longer.'

There was no anger just a quiet acceptance that her time was almost up.

'But Robert said the experimental drugs they have given you for the past three days are working and you look amazing considering what your body is going through.'

'I know, it's ironic isn't it? I'm the one dying of leukaemia but I feel like it's killing Bobby. I can't bear to see what prolonging my life week by week, or at the very most month by month, is doing to him. It has to stop and that's why I need your help.' She paused. 'I've been investigating a clinic in Switzerland.'

Hope sparked in Holly. 'Have they discovered a new treatment that doesn't involve chemotherapy?'

'It's not a treatment clinic, Holly,' she said, reaching across to hold her hand. 'It's a place where I can end my life in dignity when I'm ready to go.'

Holly felt an icy grip on her heart. She could feel the blood draining from her face. She couldn't speak. This frail, beautiful woman, totally calm and composed, was talking about ending her own life.

She swallowed hard, 'I... I...'

'Please help me Holly. I will make all the arrangements. I only need you to help me persuade Bobby that I would benefit from some fresh Swiss mountain air and to tell him that you will organise where we are staying and come with us for an extra pair of hands. When we get to Switzerland I will tell him the truth. Please say you'll help me, Holly.'

Still no words would come to Holly. While Rosemary had been asleep, she had wondered whether maybe Rosemary wanted her to help plan her funeral so that a distressed Robert wouldn't have to. She had steeled herself waiting for the request but was still dreading hearing Rosemary talk about the finer points of her own funeral service. But this... this was something else entirely. She wasn't sure she could keep her promise to help and in the process deceive Robert.

Finally she found her voice, albeit tightly squeezed from the back of her throat. 'You can't mean this Rosemary. You can't give up hope. One of the experimental drugs might work for you. You and Robert could have years more together. You could live happily at the house in Tamarina Bay with Robert taking care of you.' There was desperation in her voice and she was fighting back tears. 'Robert loves you so much you can't just leave him like that, it's... it's... selfish.'

'I want to do this because he loves me and I love my husband more than any other living being on this planet. I want him to see me die peacefully with people I love, not hooked up to machines with frantic nurses trying squeeze another few days of painful existence out of this poor diseased body of mine, in a London cancer hospital.'

They both heard the sound of tyres on the gravel.

'He's back, Holly. Please say you'll help me,' she implored, squeezing her hand more tightly, emphasising the urgency.

'I don't know, I need time to think.'

'I don't have time, Holly. If I get too sick I wouldn't be able to travel or sign the documents in Switzerland.'

Robert's keys were in the lock now.

'When?' asked Holly.

'Next week.'

The front door opened.

'I'm back, girls,' said Robert.

Holly released Rosemary's hand and moved into the centre of the room from where she could see Robert on the galleried landing, a Waitrose bag in each hand. Despite his bright tone of voice he was a shadow of his former self, someone whose world was about to crash around his ears and there was nothing he, or anyone, could do to stop it.

Looking down at Rosemary's pleading eyes Holly understood that these two had a rare and special love that most people only dream of. She closed her eyes and nodded her head slightly.

CHAPTER 47

The headlights coming in the opposite direction flashed periodically into Holly's already tired eyes making her squint at the road ahead. A little bit of her was wishing she had accepted the Forresters' offer to stay overnight with them but she needed to get home to unpack. She had texted Harry a very brief message to let him know she was home safe and sound but she had promised to ring him later to have a catch up. I wonder if his ears have been burning, Holly mused.

Over a dinner of mushroom risotto, which Robert had prepared under careful guidance from Rosemary, Holly had confessed her reason for being in Mauritius and Dubai, and had apologised for lying. Robert said he was disappointed that she hadn't felt able to confide in him too but he seemed to accept the explanation that the fewer people who knew the truth, the less likely that someone would accidentally give the game away.

He had asked then if she was married. Holly was surprised by the question. Did he honestly think that she would have got into a relationship with Philippe if she had someone waiting at home? Next came the inevitable question about whether or not Philippe knew the truth to which she replied, 'Not yet.'

'So do you have family at all, Holly?' Robert had asked, and that was when she had finally been able to tell him about her beautiful boy studying architecture at Bath University. Robert had shown an immediate interest in him, encouraging Holly to bring him to visit next time he was home.

By this point in the evening Rosemary had tired of chasing grains of carnaroli rice around her plate and was struggling to keep her eyes open. That was when she had offered Holly a bed for the night but Holly had declined. There really didn't seem much point in staying as the two of them needed to be up early again the next morning to get to the hospital for 9 a.m.

The M4 had never seemed so long but finally Holly pulled up outside her little house. The downstairs lights were on because they were on a timer when she was away but Holly knew there was no one home to greet her except her suitcase standing in the hall.

'It can wait until tomorrow,' she said to nobody, giving it a little kick as she walked passed on her way to the kitchen. Two minutes later she was snuggled up on her sofa with a mug of camomile and honey tea in one hand and the phone in her other. It was just after ten, early for Harry, and he answered on the second ring.

'Lucky you caught me in, Mum. I'm off out with the guys in a bit.'

After the traumatic day she had had it was a

relief to speak to someone so young and vibrant and carefree.

'It's a bit late to be starting your evening isn't it?'

'I can't believe you said that, Mum. You were young once, you know.'

Holly didn't point out that by the time she was his age she already had him as a young baby, and she was up half the night for quite different reasons. And when he was a toddler her evenings were spent studying for her English degree through the Open University.

'Anyway how are you? How was Dubai?'

'Dubai was hot outside and like a fridge inside because of the air conditioning. It was a really well-run resort though and you would love the building, it has a kind of twist in it.'

'I think I've seen pictures in class of a couple of the newer buildings there. Awesome aren't they. Hope I'll be good enough to come up with stuff like that after I've graduated. You sound a bit knackered. Have you just woken up after a nap?'

I wish, thought Holly.

'No, I've just been to see the Forresters. Oh my God, you should see their house. It's absolutely gorgeous. Do you remember I told you he is an architect?'

'Yes, and you couldn't tell him about me because of your double life. Honestly, Mum, you're not exactly a secret agent. Would it really hurt that much if they knew about the undercover blog writing?'

She smiled at his bluntness. 'Well, they both know now, I told them over dinner and Robert said he'd very much like to meet you.'

'Really? I could come up next weekend maybe?'

'That might not work for me Harry. I may be going to Switzerland for a few days.'

'I didn't know Soleil had a resort in Switzerland.'

'They don't. I might be going on a little trip with the Forresters.'

'Blimey, Mum, have they got a place there too?'

'No.' Holly chose her words carefully. 'Rosemary's not well. She wants me to accompany her to a clinic.'

'It's not one of those euthanasia places is it,' Harry said jokingly. ' You know you can get banged up for helping people top themselves.'

'Don't, Harry, that's not funny.'

'I was just joking, Mum.'

'I know. I'm sorry. It's been a long day. Listen, have a great night out and I'll check with Robert when would be a good time to get together. Love you.'

'Love you too, Mum.'

Holly finished her camomile tea and toyed with the idea of curling up on the couch but she knew she would regret it in the morning. Wearily she dragged herself upstairs to the bedroom, kicked off her shoes, undressed, leaving a trail of clothes on the floor behind her and climbed between the sheets. Tired as she was, her last thought before sleep enveloped her was a line from *Gone With the Wind* ...

'I can't think about this now, I'll think about it tomorrow...' She didn't even complete the quote before she was fast asleep.

CHAPTER 48

Holly reached over to her bedside table to turn off the alarm. She had hit the button several times before realising it wasn't her alarm clock making the noise but her mobile phone ringing and it had now stopped of its own accord. It was usually turned off overnight but she had been so tired she must have forgotten. As she hauled herself upright it started ringing again. It's either a message or someone is keen to get hold of me, she thought, sliding her feet into her sheepskin slippers and trying to remember where she had left her phone.

Although she had slept for ten hours she wasn't feeling at all rested. Too much going on, she thought, glancing at the clock. It was 9.15 a.m. and her thoughts immediately went to Rosemary who would be sitting in a hospital bed waiting to have the intravenous drip hooked up. Holly was still shocked that the ever-composed Rosemary could be considering assisted suicide. There had been many news reports on television about people in a near vegetative state wanting to end their own lives but that was not Rosemary's situation. She was still bright and lucid and relatively mobile. Why wouldn't she want to hold on to life for as long as possible? Holly leaned forward resting her elbows on her knees and massaged her temples. She knew the answer to her own question. Rosemary didn't want anyone else to be implicated in her death, so she had to act while she was still able. Far from being selfish, Holly thought, it's a totally selfless act to relieve the suffering of her adoring husband.

The phone started to ring again. For a moment Holly panicked, wondering if Robert was trying to reach her, but then she reasoned that he would be at his wife's bedside in the hospital, so his phone would be turned off. Harry wouldn't have surfaced yet as he had been out last night, so it wouldn't be him either. She made her way downstairs in search of her phone which she found still zipped up in the pocket of her handbag, abandoned on the kitchen work surface when she had made her camomile tea last evening. On glancing at the screen she could see that the last two calls were indeed from her message service. She wanted to know who was calling her so early on a Tuesday morning but decided they could wait a few more minutes as she headed back upstairs to the bathroom retrieving her toothbrush and cleansing balm from the overnight bag she had dumped in her hallway yesterday afternoon.

After applying the balm as a cleanser and removing it with a cotton cloth, she re-applied it as a mask to put a little moisture back into her parched skin. All this flying was playing havoc with her skin, in fact, with her body generally. Her doctor had prescribed some special eye drops because her eyes felt constantly dry and itchy, and her normally regular menstrual cycle had been totally erratic since she had started her job with Soleil. She wondered if air-stewardesses suffered the same problems.

Right, she thought, dialling her messaging service, let's see who is trying to get hold of me:

'Hi Hols, it's DD. Did you get my email? I've sent you a new manuscript and don't panic it's not another "celebrity turned author". This is your reward for doing such a good job on *A Perfect Swine*, and by the way I had no control over that awful title either! This one is definitely a bestseller, a bit raunchy in places, but you're a grown-up if you get my drift! Really well-written so only needs checking for punctuation and grammar. Just one thing: I need it back as soon as possible. I know you're good with deadlines so... any chance by the end of the week? I can't wait to hear what you think. Can you tell I'm excited? Drop me an email to let me know you've got it.'

Holly hadn't heard her friend this enthusiastic about a book in ages. She was intrigued but also hungry. Thank goodness there was some cereal and long-life milk in the cupboard.

Half an hour later Holly had finished her breakfast, unpacked her clothes straight into the machine for a wash, her laptop was back on her desk, turned on in anticipation, and the suitcase was back in the cupboard under the stairs for another three weeks. She nipped back upstairs to change into her comfy jeggings and a light sweater, and twisted her hair into a scrunchie to keep it off her face while working.

With a second cup of peppermint tea in her hand she sat down at her desk. Okay, let's see what all the excitement is about, she said to herself.

She clicked on her inbox and there was the email from DD. There was also one from Philippe which set her pulse racing. Although the new manuscript was important, for once she let her heart rule her head as eagerly opened his message:

Holly, my darling,

Sorry I haven't been in touch for a few days but I was up against this stupid deadline. The good news is I finished the book. I'm just waiting to hear back from the editor whether or not they like it and if they do I'll be packing up here and back in England in a couple of weeks. I can't wait to see you again (all of you) – I've really missed you. You had better email your address so that I will know where to tell the taxi to take me to when I get off the plane at Gatwick.

Missing you

Philippe xxxx

Holly checked the date on the email. It had been sent two days previously. It must have arrived just after she had packed her case to come home from Dubai so she had missed seeing it. She was pleased he had finally finished his book and hoped that his editor would give it the all clear to go into print.

She clicked reply.

Hello Philippe,

It's lovely to hear from you, I thought maybe you were starting to forget about me? I'm really pleased you finished your book. Did you hear back from the editor yet? I hope it's good news. Can't wait to see you (all of you)! Let me have your flight details once you've booked it, and don't worry about having my address, you won't need a taxi, I'll come and meet you.

Missing you too

Holly xxxx

Holly had been very careful to only put the same number of kisses that Philippe had, not wanting to appear too keen even though the butterflies were back in her stomach just thinking about him. She knew there was a bit of explaining to do when he got back to England but she was sure he would understand her reasons for lying to him. She was so looking forward to spending long hours getting to know him better... she blushed at the thought.

Right, she thought, concentrate. After sending a quick email to DD, letting her know she had received the manuscript and that, although it was a tall order, she would try and have it finished by the end of the week, she opened the attached Word document, hoping that DD's exuberance was justified.

'Oh my God!' exclaimed Holly. 'I don't believe it!'

She was staring at the four words on her computer screen:

TIFFANY

by

Veronica Phillips

She brought her hands together in mock prayer, raised her eyes to the heavens and said out loud, 'Thank you DD.'

Holly could hardly believe that she was being entrusted to copy-edit this woman's long awaited follow-up to her best-selling first novel *Maman*. There was mystery surrounding the author as there had been no photograph of her on the book sleeve and she had refused to do any radio or television interviews for promotion. Some people said that the book was so good that it must be an already established novelist writing under a pseudonym. Holly didn't care. All she could think was that she, Holly Wilson, could potentially get an acknowledgement for copy-editing this new book. Dad would have been so proud of me, she thought. Maybe at last her luck really was changing both professionally and personally.

She began to read:

Chapter 1

He drained the last few drops of amber-coloured ice-cold beer from his glass. He placed it on the bar and carefully traced rivulets of condensation with the tip of his index finger, grateful for the distraction. Overhead the ceiling fan whirred quietly but efficiently. The breeze, although welcome, was not sufficient to prevent perspiration causing his white linen shirt to cling to his back. He barely noticed. He could only think about the blunt email he had received that morning from his publisher. She was right about the first draft of his book but did she need to be so cruel? Writing, always a solitary business, became positively lonely when inspiration deserted you, he thought miserably. He ran his hands through his light blond hair observing his reflection in the mirror behind the spirit optics. He looked tired, dispirited, older than his forty-one years. Regret replaced optimism. Giving up his lucrative career as a journalist to pursue his dream of becoming a novelist seemed reckless now.

A small movement caught the corner of his eye. A woman in a coral dress stood at the entrance to the bar. She seemed to hesitate for a moment before crossing the room to slip onto the bar stool next to his.

'May I?' she asked.

'Help yourself,' he replied. He guessed she was a little younger than him, dark-haired and curvaceous, but what really caught his attention were her deep green eyes.

How weird is that? Holly thought. It could be a description of me. I even own a coral dress.

'Can I get you a drink?'
    'That's kind of you,' the woman said, maintaining eye contact for a few moments, 'but save your money, I'm staying here on an all-inclusive deal.'
    He persisted. 'Well, at least, let me order for you, that way it will feel like I'm buying you a drink.'
    A slow smile spread across her face.'I'll have a piña colada please,' she said, 'and if you're getting me a drink we should at least be on first-name terms. I'm Tiffany,' she said, holding her hand out to shake his.
    'Pierre,' he replied, raising her outstretched hand to his lips and lingering slightly before letting it drop.

Holly was starting to feel vaguely uncomfortable. There was something familiar about this, a kind of déjà vu, but surely Veronica Phillips wouldn't copy anyone else's work? Then she realised. This was not something she had read before, it was something she had been part of. A Frenchman kissing her hand on their first meeting. It was not so unusual, in fact a typically French thing to do, but how odd that she should be reading about it in a book just weeks after she herself had experienced it. But it was the next line that really resonated with Holly.

'So what brings you to Mauritius, business or pleasure?'

This was beyond coincidence, Holly thought, her heart starting to thump in her chest, what on earth was going on?

'Difficult question,' she replied, avoiding an answer. The two of them watched in silence as the barman shook pineapple juice, rum and coconut milk in a cocktail shaker with crushed ice then poured the thick white liquid into a glass before pushing it across the bar to Tiffany.
    Pierre tried again. 'So are you here with your family or maybe work colleagues?'
    'Neither,' she replied taking a sip of the sweet liquid. 'I'm here alone.'
    Pierre was intrigued. The journalist in him couldn't let it drop. 'Do you often holiday alone?' he ventured, knowing his persistence may cause her to finish her drink and leave.
    Tiffany lowered her drink. She was looking at him intently with her beautiful green eyes which he now noticed held a deep sadness.
    'The last time I came to Mauritius was with my husband on our honeymoon but now he's dead. I've come here for closure.'

Holly gasped. What the hell? That was her cover story. How could that be? She felt her skin begin to prickle and then the heat of a flush that started on her neck and spread to her face. Unless? The pieces of a very complicated jigsaw started to fall into place. She remembered the quizzical look Rosemary had given Philippe when he had said he was writing a travelogue the first evening they all had dinner together. Philippe had told her he had been struggling with his book for months but suddenly he'd become inspired and finished it within weeks. Even Rosemary's email about Philippe's first book made sense now. Veronica Phillips was not just the pen name of a famous author wanting to remain incognito. Veronica Phillips was not even a woman. Holly was absolutely certain that Veronica Phillips was in fact Philippe and, judging by what she had just read, she was Tiffany.

Holly didn't know how to feel. Part of her was flattered that she had made such an impression on him that she had become the title character of his latest book, but another part of her was upset and angry that he hadn't told her the truth about who he was. You hypocrite, she thought. Philippe has written about a woman with a tragic story that he thinks is you and that tragic story is the biggest lie of all.

Holly leant her elbows on the desk either side of her laptop and rested her forehead in her hands unsure what to do. Should she email DD and tell her that she knew the author? It was unethical to work on the book of someone you know without telling them. No, she couldn't do that because DD would tell Philippe and he didn't know that she was a copy-editor, he thought she worked for a charity. She could work on the book but ask for her name to be left off any acknowledgements but DD would want to know why she didn't want a credit. She thought about emailing Philippe to try and explain why she had lied to him, but instantly changed her mind. She couldn't bear the thought of him not understanding her reasons and finishing with her.

'Damn it,' she said to the empty room. 'Why do things have to be so complicated?'

Eventually she decided that she didn't want to let anyone down. DD thought she was the best copy editor for this book and she was going to do a professional job on it, regardless of who had written it. Decision made, she continued reading.

CHAPTER 49

For the third day running Rosemary had refused a wheelchair to transport her down in the hospital lift to the waiting cab for their journey home. She leaned against her husband as they waited for the lift to arrive, fighting back nausea and tears.

Robert held her close, lightly squeezing the top of her shoulder.

'You'll be all right when we get some fresh air,' he said unconvincingly. They both knew that wasn't true and that she would be feeling sick for most of the journey back.

'There's nothing fresh about London air, Bobby. I can taste the exhaust fumes.'

'We'll be home soon, Rosie,' he said soothingly. 'If you feel up to it I'll push the sofa over to the patio doors, open them up and wrap you in a blanket with a nice cup of tea. At least the air in Woldingham is cleaner than here.'

'True,' she said, 'but not exactly Mauritius. Is Holly coming over this afternoon?'

'I'll call her when we're in the car. I'm so pleased she knows. It makes such a difference for you to have someone other than me to talk to. Although you were tired last night she really seemed to have raised your spirits.'

'She gave me hope.'

Robert said nothing, his face an impassive mask, but his heart was aching. His conversation with the Rosemary's consultant that morning had not been a pleasant one.

'She should have started this treatment earlier,' he had lectured, 'instead of running away and sticking your heads in the sand. I fear the positive effects she is currently experiencing won't last long.'

'So what will we do then?'

The consultant had shaken his head. 'We'll just try and keep her pain free.'

Once they were settled into the back of the car Robert dialled Holly's mobile number. She picked up on the third ring.

'Hi Robert, how did it go at the hospital?'

'Pretty much the same. Rosemary is glad to be out. We wondered if you might be able to come over again this afternoon?'

Holly had been expecting this and hated making excuses but, to keep on the right side of DD, she had to get Philippe's book finished by the end of the week.

'I'm really sorry, Robert, but I don't think I can make it today. Something has cropped up at work that I can't get out of.'

Although Robert and Rosemary both now knew about her travel blog-writing job she hadn't told them she also worked as a freelance copy-editor. The coincidence of Philippe being published by Ripped, the main company she worked for, was strange enough, but to be selected to edit his book was a little surreal. She knew she would have to broach the subject next time she saw them and also ask why they had gone along with Philippe's little deception. Holly had been wondering why he didn't want her to know he was the author of *Maman*. Maybe he thought she would leak his identity to the press, or maybe he didn't want her to like him just because he was a best-selling author. Either way she felt almost relieved that he too would have to own up to keeping secrets when he arrived back from Mauritius.

'Oh, that's a shame,' Robert was saying. 'It was so lovely to spend time with you yesterday.' He had worded his response carefully, not wanting to put pressure on Holly.

'I know, I feel the same.' She paused, still unsure if what she was about to suggest was the right thing to do. 'Listen, Robert, I've had an idea. Do you think Rosemary might be up for a little trip to raise her spirits?'

Robert looked at his wife's ashen face doubtfully. 'What did you have in mind?'

'Well,' Holly swallowed hard, even though she had become an adept liar over the past few months she wasn't sure she could carry this off. 'Do you remember the Italian family in Mauritius with their gorgeous little girl Giulietta?'

'Of course she was an adorable little thing.'

'They live in Switzerland at the moment because of

Umberto's new job and Mathilda gets very lonely on her own. She's invited me to go and visit. Perhaps we could all go? The mountain air might do Rosemary some good.'

Holly held her breath.

'I don't think Rosie is up to flying, Holly.'

Rosemary, who had been dozing, was suddenly fully awake.

'No, I realise that. I thought we could drive and take the ferry and then we could stop on the way if we need to.'

'I don't know, Holly. It's a long way.'

'What's a long way, Bobby?' Rosemary asked.

He put his hand over the mouthpiece of the phone. 'Holly is suggesting a trip to Switzerland. She thinks the mountain air will do you good but—'

'I'd really like that, Bobby.'

Robert had always found it difficult to deny his wife anything but he wasn't convinced that this was a good idea. He spoke into the phone. 'I'll ask at the hospital when we're there tomorrow. When were you thinking of going?'

'Maybe next week?'

'Well I'll ask. She will have finished this course of chemo by then but I don't think they will be keen for her to go travelling again. Are you sure you can't make it today? It gave Rosie such a lift to spend time with you yesterday.'

'I'm really sorry, Robert, I'm up to my neck in it but I'll come tomorrow afternoon I promise. Please give Rosemary my apologies.'

Rosemary was looking at him expectantly.

'Holly's a bit busy this afternoon but she's promised to come over tomorrow.'

Instead of the disappointment Robert was expecting, Rosemary smiled.

'That's alright, Bobby, if she's promised to come tomorrow then she will. Holly keeps her promises, and besides we'll have plenty of time to chat on the way to Switzerland.'

Typical Rosie, thought Robert, she's made her mind up about Switzerland regardless of what the doctors say. He looked down at her face which now seemed to have a bit more colour. Who am I to try and change her mind? he thought.

CHAPTER 50

Once the initial shock of realising that Philippe's character Tiffany was based on her had subsided, Holly set about doing her job. Considering she knew how quickly the book had been written there were surprisingly few typos and grammatical errors she noticed as she continued with the read through. The first couple of chapters were about Pierre and Tiffany getting to know each other. It was a little odd to be reading about the two characters who were so clearly herself and Philippe. He had even made Pierre a struggling writer although she now knew that was not exactly based on himself following the success of his first book. She had to admit she liked the empathetic way he wrote. No wonder people, including myself, she thought, had believed that the writer of *Maman* was a woman. He was descriptive and caring, helping the reader to understand Tiffany's great sadness at her loss, while suggesting that maybe Pierre could help her get past this tragedy in her life.

From Holly's point of view it was fascinating to read about Pierre's first impression of Tiffany and the instant attraction he felt for her. Was that really how

Philippe felt the first time he saw me, she thought, blushing slightly but unable suppress the smile forming on her lips. Holly's confidence had taken such a battering after Gareth had deserted her that she found it hard to accept that anyone could be so smitten with her.

In Philippe's book the couple moved from the hotel bar to the restaurant and enjoyed dinner together, but at the end of the evening Pierre was disappointed when Tiffany made the excuse that she was tired after her journey and went back to her hotel room alone.

Holly was also disappointed. Was that how Philippe had felt? Had she misread their blossoming relationship? Had he just been after sex from the start? Get a grip, Holly, she thought, the characters are based on you and Philippe but it is not your story, you have to be able to separate fact from fiction. Again Holly wondered if she should have come clean with DD and refused the manuscript.

Holly was relieved that the next chapter didn't feature Pierre and Tiffany. It was set at the home of the French Ambassador to Mauritius, Gerard Lecomte, and introduced him, his wife, Madeleine, and their two young daughters, Nicole and Mimi, to the reader. She was keen to find out how they were going to fit into the story, wondering if perhaps Tiffany was going to become the girls' nanny, but her reading had been interrupted by Robert's phone call.

After finishing the call, which had set in motion Rosemary's dubious plan, Holly couldn't concentrate. She really needed to talk to someone about her doubts that helping Rosemary dupe Robert into taking her to Switzerland was the right thing to do. The problem was that the only person should would have felt close enough to talk to was Rosemary herself. Holly rubbed her temples. Maybe I should go across to Woldingham again today, she thought, if only to try and talk Rosemary out of her plan. If I go now I could be back by 7 p.m. and have a late-night session editing. Decision made, she reached for the phone to ring Robert back but as she was dialling his number her phone beeped to tell her she had a message. It was from DD and simply said:

Have you got to chapter 8 yet?!!!!

Knowing how much most editors disliked the use of exclamation marks, herself included, Holly thought that this must be something dramatic, so, instead of connecting her call to Robert, she switched her phone to silent to avoid further interruptions. Abandoning her normal methodical working practice, she scrolled down the pages of the manuscript to chapter 8.

Tiffany stood in front of the full-length windows of the hotel room illuminated only by the moonlight streaming towards her. She was wearing a shift dress with narrow shoulder straps in the palest green silk, which clung to her in all the right places, showing the promise of the curves beneath. The door opened behind her but she didn't turn. Her heart was pounding in her chest, her pulse racing, despite taking deep breaths to calm herself. It was a mixture of anticipation and trepidation - it always was the first time.

She heard him move across the room towards the bed. Before he could reach for the light switch she whispered in a provocatively sexy voice, 'It's a beautiful moon, it would be a shame not to enjoy it.'

The words sounded familiar but Holly knew she had not spoken them. As she continued to read she knew with a growing sense of panic that Philippe was writing about their last night together in Mauritius in intimate detail... kissing, touching, hearing her own naked body described inch by inch... but he had turned the tables, making it sound as though she was the experienced lover instead of him.

Holly could feel herself colouring up with a mix of embarrassment and anger. This was something beautiful that had happened between the two of them and now it was being shared with potentially millions of readers. She felt sick at the thought that her friend DD had already read it and found it so titillating that she had drawn Holly's attention specifically to this chapter. Holly was mortified. Was that all it had been for Philippe? Was she merely research for the new book that he had been struggling to write? They say you should write about what you know but surely some things were off limits? Apparently not in Philippe's world. Holly was trembling and her throat felt tight, but the biggest shock was still to come.

'You came highly recommended and you did not disappoint,' Gerard said, emerging from the bathroom, having showered away the evidence of the sex he had recently enjoyed with Tiffany.

It felt like Holly had been physically struck. She had assumed she was reading about a developing romance and a first night of passion between Pierre and Tiffany. Even in those circumstances she found Philippe's betrayal of their intimacy devastating but this was unforgivable. For one moment Holly wondered if Philippe had discovered her cover story was fake and believed she was a high-class call-girl? Who am I kidding, she thought, to say I am a little rusty in the art of seduction would be an understatement. Then, like the last few pieces of a jigsaw puzzle, everything fell into place, she understood where his newly found inspiration for his book had come from.

On their last evening together she had confided in him about her mother's view of Holly Golightly in *Breakfast at Tiffany's*. She had poured her heart out to him as she had done to no other, not even Gareth, and he had seemed to understand, comforting her and reassuring her, even questioning her mother's opinion of Holly Golightly's profession. But seemingly all the tenderness was a facade.

Whatever he really thought of Holly was inconsequential. In his book he had made her a high-class hooker and for that she could never forgive him.

She could no longer focus on the words in front of her, not that she wanted to read any more anyway, as tears filled her eyes and poured down her hot cheeks. How could she have been so stupid to trust this man so completely when she had only known him a few days? She was angry with herself for being so gullible but mostly she was furious with Philippe for using her. She felt violated and ashamed and she had a burning desire to go and scrub herself clean as the ambassador had done in Philippe's book, but there were two things she needed to do first.

After sending an email to Philippe, she dialled DD's number not sure what she was going to say.

DD answered almost immediately: 'Did you read chapter 8? It gets even better later in the book. I tell you this could be hotter than *Fifty Shades*!'

'DD, I... I don't think...'

'Are you okay, Hols? Are you crying? What's wrong?'

'It's my friend, Rosemary, she's dying. She hasn't got long and I want to be able to spend time with her.'

'Oh my God, I'm so sorry. When did you find out?'

'She told me yesterday,' Holly said truthfully but nevertheless feeling wretched that she was using Rosemary's illness as an excuse not to edit Philippe's book. 'Her husband rang on their way back from the hospital a little while ago. She wants me to accompany them on a trip, probably her last one, and I really feel I should go.'

'Of course you must,' said DD. 'Don't you worry I'll find someone else to do the edit, your friend is much more important. Did you make a start on it?'

'No,' Holly lied.

'Sorry to be a pain at a time like this but would you

mind deleting the file?'

'Of course, no problem, consider it done.'

'I'm really sorry that you won't get to do this one but maybe I can push book three in your direction.'

'Thanks for understanding,' said Holly as she ended the call, thinking that she never wanted to read another word written by Veronica Phillips.

She deleted the file as requested and then ran herself a hot bath.

CHAPTER 51

One battered brown suitcase stood packed and ready by the door and the other lay open on the bed in the spare room. The wardrobe was almost empty of clothes apart from the necessities he would need for the next two days. There was still space for Philippe's toiletries bag and computer but he would keep them out until the last possible moment. He checked periodically but there was still no response from Holly after his last email telling her he had managed to get a flight back to the UK on Thursday. He wasn't worried, she had seemed pretty keen to see him and just because he had now time on his hands it didn't mean that she was any less busy than usual.

I'm going to miss this place, he thought, stepping out onto the verandah and drinking in the glorious view. He wondered if the Forresters had reached a decision yet on whether to buy it. There was another three weeks of his rental agreement that he had pre-paid but presumably after that it would be back on the market for sale or rent. He was still a bit annoyed at the way Robert and Rosemary had left without saying goodbye but he was genuinely fond of them so he decided that once he and Holly had spent a bit of time together getting reacquainted, they would all meet up for dinner in London, his treat.

In a way it was a shame that his editor was pressurising him to get back to London so quickly. It would have been good to use the time for a holiday, maybe even fly Holly over if she could have taken the time off work. Too late now, thought Philippe, my flight is booked.

The sun was beginning to set and Philippe wandered through to the kitchen to see what he might rustle up for his penultimate dinner in paradise. Delphine hadn't brought him any fresh fish yet this week and now she wouldn't need to. She had been really upset when had rung her earlier in the day to tell her he was going home. Philippe liked to think it was more than just the regular income she would miss.

Even the best chef in the world wouldn't be able to make a decent dinner out of the contents of this refrigerator, Philippe thought, surveying a couple of bits of cheese and some wilted salad leaves. There weren't even any eggs to make an omelette. He closed the fridge door and grabbed his car keys. He had decided that he would give the battered old BMW to his friend Billy as a thank you for all the pleasurable morning rides on Helios. He took the road towards Flic en Flac and the Dolphin Bar, already salivating at the thought of all the freshly caught fish options there would be on the menu.

If he had been ten minutes later leaving he might have seen the email from Holly which would definitely have ruined his appetite.

The Dolphin Bar was unusually crowded for a Tuesday night with most of the little round tables occupied with three or four people. As Philippe scanned the cramped room looking for a free table he saw an arm frantically waving from the back corner and heard his name being called. He squeezed his way through the warm, perspiring bodies, some reeking of the fish they had landed that day, to find his friend, Billy, sitting at a table with another man who looked vaguely familiar.

'You'll join us won't you, Philippe?'

'If you're sure you and your friend don't mind I'd be happy to. What's going on in here tonight? I've never seen it so busy midweek.'

'Jacques here has organised some exotic dancers as a thank you to all the lads who risked life and limb saving the fishing boats from sinking in the big storm a couple of weeks ago.'

Philippe looked bemused.

'You probably didn't even notice the storm you had your head so deeply buried in your computer. I'm actually quite surprised you found time to take Helios out for his morning rides.'

Philippe accepted the rebuke good naturedly. 'I know, I know, I'm always a rubbish friend when I'm busy writing.'

The other man, Jacques, spoke. 'Delphine says you have finished your book now and are packing up to leave.'

At the mention of Delphine's name the penny dropped. Jacques was Delphine's brother whom she had introduced him to when he had first arrived in

Mauritius. 'Anything you need, Jacques is your man,' she had said, but there was something about Jacques that Philippe didn't like so he had never taken her up on the offer. Philippe suspected that Jacques dealt in drugs and while he wasn't averse to an occasional joint himself, when he needed to relax, he hated the pushers and dealers that created addicts from the weak-minded.

He managed a smile. 'Yes it's all happened quite quickly really. My publishing company need me back in the UK and I managed to get a flight on Thursday.'

'I hope you're paying Delphine a month's notice?'

Philippe was regretting his decision to join Billy at the table with this odious man but it was too late to change his mind now. Again he forced a smile. 'Don't worry, Delphine won't be short-changed.'

There was an uncomfortable silence before Billy said, 'I can't believe you are going to let me have the car. Are you sure? You could sell it for a decent price, you know.'

'You've been a good friend to me Billy, just as Delphine has, and I like to show my appreciation,' Philippe said pointedly.

'It must be nice to be in a position to be so generous,' Jacques grinned.

There's no winning with this man, Philippe thought, clenching his fist tightly under the table, but he knew from experience not to get into an argument with his type so instead he said pleasantly, 'Can I get you both a drink?'

It was a relief to go up to the bar to get the beers and while he was there he ordered himself a shot of whisky, which he downed in one, wincing at the burn on the back of his throat. It's going to be hard work with Jacques as a dinner companion, he thought, I'm going to need a bit of alcoholic anaesthetic.

By the time the grilled red snapper arrived, Philippe had been to the bar a further three times, downing a shot of whisky on each visit, so he was now impervious to the constant sniping from Jacques.

Just before the dancers began their performance Delphine slid into the vacant chair at their table.

'Jacques texted to tell me you were here. Is everything okay?' she asked anxiously.

Not for the first time Philippe wondered how these two could possibly be siblings. He raised his glass.

'Better now you are here,' he slurred as the music started and the scantily clad girls gyrated to the beat.

CHAPTER 52

'Are you sure you'll be all right?' Robert asked, nervously fiddling with his car keys. He had moved the sofa across the room so that his wife could enjoy the warmth of the afternoon sun streaming in through the long open windows from the shelter of the lounge. Although it was early May there was still a chill in the air and the same elevated position that afforded them their glorious view of the Surrey Hills often caught the cooling breeze.

'I'll be fine,' Rosemary said. 'I'll probably just dose while you are out, or read something on my Kindle.'

'With everything that's going on I had totally forgotten the car was due its MOT. What a good job we stopped at the village shop for milk and saw Dave from the garage. If he hadn't jogged my memory I'd have been driving around blissfully unaware that I was breaking the law.'

'I've always said everything happens for a reason. If we hadn't got talking to Holly in Mauritius I wouldn't have this trip to Switzerland to look forward too.'

'Rosie, it's not definitely on, you know, not until we've cleared it with Professor Lang anyway.'

'He'll probably be glad to see the back of me and let's face it, once this week is over, I wouldn't be able to have any more of the new treatment for two weeks at least, until they know if it's really making any difference.'

Robert turned away. He knew he was a terrible liar and if his wife asked what the professor had been talking to him about that morning he wouldn't be able to withhold the truth.

'Go on, off you go, Bobby, it's nearly three o'clock now and Dave squeezed you in as a favour.'

She didn't want to sound too keen to get rid of him but she needed some time alone to get on with things before the tiredness, caused by the drugs, kicked in.

'I'll drop the car off and walk back,' he said. 'It'll only take ten or fifteen minutes.'

'And then you'll have to walk back and fetch it. You might as well just wait there, it will probably only be half an hour if it passes the test.'

'You're right of course, you always are. When I get back I'll make us a nice cup of tea and we can have the scones I bought at the supermarket yesterday. It was just the milk I forgot,' he said smiling.

Once the front door had closed behind him Rosemary swung her legs down from the foot stool and stood up carefully. She slowly moved across the room and opened the door to Robert's office. It was a wonderful light and airy space, again enjoying the magnificent view. His desk and easel were set up at the far end but just inside the door on the left was a smaller desk where Rosemary kept all her papers. She opened the shallow central drawer, above the leg well, and pulled out a large white envelope that had nothing written on it. It was already quite full with smaller envelopes, each printed with the name of her closest friends, two CDs, a larger envelope and a sheet of paper. Her hands were trembling as she read the words that headed the paper:

Rosemary's Funeral Service

Rosemary closed her eyes, remembering the anguish she had felt trying to organise first her mother's funeral and then her father's a few months later. Although she had known them all her life, she didn't really know what their favourite pieces of music were, what reading from the Bible or otherwise they would have chosen, their favourite flowers or even whether they wanted to be cremated or buried. She had felt horribly unprepared and had allowed the funeral directors to make some of the decisions which she later regretted. Robert had been wonderful, helping her to track down friends and relatives, putting an announcement in the local paper and choosing flowers and music but Rosemary decided that when her time came she would have everything planned so that no one else would have to stress over it, particularly not her beloved husband.

When she was first diagnosed with CML Rosemary had started her secret envelope even though her initial response to the treatment drugs was so promising. Just as well, she thought, looking at the contents strewn on her desktop, I've still got things to finish and there's so little time. She picked up the largest of the envelopes and slid out the correspondence from within. Every line was committed to memory but she wanted to check the details for a final time before shredding the evidence of the real reason she was travelling to Switzerland. It would be difficult enough when they crossed the Swiss border to persuade Robert to change destination from Geneva to Zurich, but she couldn't risk him getting suspicious by mentioning Zurich at this stage. They had both watched the news recently about an on-going court case regarding the right to die. Rosemary could understand how a change in the law could be misused in certain circumstances, particularly in people with a mental disability or in a vegetative state but it was different for her. She had all her faculties and was making a considered decision. She didn't want the State interfering in her personal life. It was a relief that Holly would be with them though to back her up as Robert's views were very different from her own.

She picked up a fresh sheet of paper and began to write.

My darling Bobby,

If you are reading this it is because my plan has worked and I have left this world to wait for you until the time comes when you join me... hopefully that won't be anytime soon, although I will miss you more than you could ever know. I hope you will understand and forgive me for choosing my own destiny. I wanted to spend my final few hours calmly saying my goodbyes to people I love. You mustn't blame Holly, she knew nothing of my intentions once we got to Switzerland. As far as she knew it was one of my final wishes to visit the country so she just helped me devise a plan to get you to agree to drive us there. I hope you will comfort each other and that you may be able to help her son Harry, just as if he was the child we were never fortunate enough to have.

In this envelope you will find letters I have written to my closest friends, explaining why things had to be this way and why I couldn't tell them my plan. I have also planned my own funeral service, with all the contact numbers you will need and with CDs of the music I would like played.

I know this will be a difficult time for you, Bobby, but please try and remember how happy we have been together and how lucky we were to be given a second chance. Some people never find their soulmate, the person who makes them feel complete, but I did and for that I am truly grateful.

This next bit is very difficult for me to write but please believe me when I say I don't want you to be sad and lonely for the rest of your life. If you meet someone who brings you comfort and makes you feel alive again, don't let her slip through your fingers because of me.

I love you, Bobby, and have always loved you since the first night we met but our lives together on this planet have ended and I want you to be happy.

Rosie xx

Rosemary could taste the saltiness of her tears as she carefully folded the paper and slipped it into an envelope on which she simply wrote 'Bobby'. She was about to seal it but that made it feel too final.

Glancing at her watch she realised that Robert would be back soon. She gathered everything up and slipped it back into the large envelope, apart from the letter from the clinic. She slid the white envelope back into her desk drawer and then shredded the letter before returning to the sofa where Robert found her sleeping peacefully fifteen minutes later.

CHAPTER 53

For the second time in as many days Philippe surfaced with a thundering in his head, his usually cool bedroom feeling oppressively warm and his skin clammy to the touch. I must have been so drunk last night that I forgot to put the air conditioning on when I got in, he thought. For a moment he struggled to remember how he had got home, hoping that his friends hadn't allowed him to drive in the condition he was in. Then realisation began to dawn on him. This was not his bedroom, this was not his bed, and he had a horrible feeling that he might not be alone. He didn't want to draw attention to himself by turning over so he tentatively reached his left hand behind him and was met with skin. His hand recoiled as if he had been stung by a bee and the sudden movement disturbed his companion.

A female voice asked, 'Are you feeling okay? Do you need the bathroom?'

Philippe did feel sick but not just because of the alcohol. He recognised the voice as one of the exotic dancers from the previous evening, a petite pretty girl called Candice who Delphine had set him up with on a couple of previous occasions when he had been in need of female company.

'Where are we?' he asked.

'Upstairs at The Dolphin,' she replied. 'Your friend Billy wouldn't let you drive home in the state you were in so he asked the bar owner, Denis, if you could have a room for the night. Jacques suggested you might want a bit of company,' she added coyly.

Philippe was not sure who he was more mad at, himself for not being in a position to say he didn't want female company, or Jacques for suggesting it in the first place. One thing was for sure it was not Candice's fault, she was a sweet girl and she was just doing her job. He dressed as quickly as his thumping head would allow and reached into his wallet for some rupees which he handed to Candice.

'Will you pay Denis for the room and keep the rest for yourself,' he said, managing to avoid looking her in the eye, before he grabbed his keys from the chest by the door, where they had been discarded the previous night, and headed down the stairs and out into the blinding brightness of the midday sun. He unlocked his car door and then slumped forward over the steering wheel feeling absolutely wretched. He knew he was probably still not sober enough to drive but he was desperate to get away from the scene of his infidelity. He sat there for at least ten minutes trying to excuse his behaviour. It was Jacques' fault for being such an obnoxious git that I had to drink so much to get me through the evening, he thought. And it was Jacques that suggested Candice should spend the night with me. And it's not as though I haven't slept with Candice before so it's not really cheating on Holly is it?

'Of course it is you bloody idiot,' he said out loud, banging the steering wheel with his fist. 'There's no one to blame but yourself.'

Sitting in the car park of the Dolphin Bar in Mauritius, Philippe made himself two promises. He would never drink to excess again and he would never be unfaithful to Holly again. He had fallen in love for the first time in his life and he didn't want to mess it up. He decided not to tell Holly about his indiscretion because what would be gained by her knowing? he reasoned. She would be hurt unnecessarily and that was the last thing he wanted to do.

He drove back to Tamarina Bay carefully and let himself into the house. He went through to the kitchen to brew some coffee and stopped in his tracks. There was a paper bag containing fresh croissants holding down a scrawled note:

I thought you might need these to soak up the alcohol. Hope you're okay. Delphine.

Again Philippe marvelled at how different Delphine and her brother Jacques were. She had a heart of gold and he was going to miss her. Even though the last thing he felt like doing was eating, he took Delphine's advice and began to nibble on one of the freshly baked croissants. Leaving a trail of crumbs Hansel and Gretel would have been proud of he crossed over to the French doors and opened them to let some air into the room. He was going to sit out on the verandah in the shade but decided to check his email first. His heart leapt when he saw there was one from Holly:

How COULD you? I can't believe you've done this. I trusted you.

NEVER try to contact me again... I'm blocking you from my email.

Philippe stared at the screen in disbelief. How the hell could Holly have found out about last night... unless? He looked down at the croissant crumbs scattered on his desk... no, it couldn't be Delphine.

CHAPTER 54

The bath had not helped. Holly had lain up to her neck in the warm scented water with tears streaming down her cheeks wondering if she had over-reacted by sending Philippe the email without giving him a chance to explain. She was angry at Philippe for taking advantage of the Holly he thought she was, the one who had been recently widowed. But that wasn't the real Holly and she was partly to blame for not trusting him enough to tell him the truth that he was the first person she had been intimate with since Gareth had left her twenty years previously. If he had known the depth of her feelings for him, if she had said those three little words, would he have behaved differently?

Then she thought about the graphic descriptions of their lovemaking, even her most private feelings whispered to him in the throes of passion, written in black and white for the world to see, and she realised that was what really stung. The words, her words, had been uttered by a high-class hooker in his book.

Holly could feel the bitter taste of bile rising into her mouth. She felt physically sick and emotionally violated. There was no acceptable excuse that Philippe could give for his total lack of respect for her feelings, whoever he thought she was.

The email had been the right thing to do. She never wanted to see or hear from him again. There had been such a sense of finality when she had pressed send and then blocked him. At least he has no other way of contacting me, she thought, always assuming he would want to. That was the bit she found hardest to accept. He had been so keen to see her again knowing that he had written about their most private moments. Maybe he needed to do some research for another book, she thought sarcastically, thankful she hadn't given him her phone number or address and that he had no idea about her work.

A thought occurred to her. Would Philippe be brazen enough to try and get her contact details from the Forresters? The moment she thought it she knew that if he did want to contact her that is exactly what he would do.

She climbed out of the bath, almost slipping on the shiny surface in her haste, wrapped her towelling bathrobe around herself without bothering to dry with a towel first and rushed downstairs to phone Robert and Rosemary giving no thought to what she was going to say. Robert must have been standing next to the phone because he answered on the first ring.

'Hello,' he said in a hushed tone.

'Robert, it's Holly. Have I caught you at a bad moment?'

'Hang on a minute, Holly.' Holly could hear Robert

close the door to the living room. 'Sorry about that,' he said in a more normal tone. 'Rosie's just having a nap on the sofa.'

'I didn't wake her, did I?'

'No I think I caught the phone in time. Everything all right, you sound a bit flustered?'

'Erm... yes. Actually I was just ringing to say I can come over today if you'd still like me to. I got through my work quicker than expected.'

'We'd love you to come of course but it's four fifteen, so if you leave now you'll be stuck in all the rush hour traffic on the M25. Why don't you come a bit later for dinner and stay over as you were planning on visiting tomorrow anyway?'

'That's a lovely idea, if you're sure I'm not putting you to any trouble,' Holly said, relieved that she wouldn't be spending the evening alone.

'No trouble at all, Rosemary will be delighted.'

'Okay, well I'll try and get there just after seven. One other thing,' Holly said, trying to keep her voice as natural as possible, 'Philippe and I have split up.'

'I'm sorry to hear that, Holly. I thought you two were really well suited.'

So did I, thought Holly, but instead said, 'Oh you know... just a holiday romance. If... if Philippe asks you for my phone number can you tell him you can't give it out without asking me first. Sorry to land this on you with everything else you have going on.'

'Of course. I would never give your number to anyone without your permission.'

'Thanks, Robert, I appreciate that. I'll see you a bit later then.'

As Holly put the phone back in it's cradle she noticed a green car pulling up outside the house. She ran to the front door and flung it open as a tall blond young man reached into the back seat for his duffle bag.

'Harry!' she cried, flinging her arms around her son and promptly bursting into tears..

Harry ushered his mum back into the house and then stood in the cramped hallway holding her until her sobs subsided.

'Not quite the reaction I was expecting, Mum,' he said, trying to lighten the mood. 'What's up?'

'Sorry, Harry. You just caught me at a bad moment and I was so surprised to see you. I was just overwhelmed. What are you doing here anyway?'

He steered her through to the kitchen and sat her down on a chair while he filled the kettle and put it on to boil.

'Tea?'

Holly nodded.

'My lecturer called in sick this morning and they couldn't get a replacement at such short notice so I've got a couple of days off. I decided I'd come home to see my mum and no I haven't brought any dirty washing. I thought maybe you could take me to meet Robert Forrester as you mentioned you might be away next week.'

'Actually that was who I was on the phone to when you pulled up outside. I've just arranged to go to theirs for dinner tonight and to stay over. If I ring

Robert back I might be able to cancel before he tells Rosemary. I would hate to disappoint her.'

'Do you have to cancel? Couldn't you just ask if I could tag along?' Harry asked, handing his mum her cup of tea. 'You did say he was keen to meet me.'

Holly looked at her son who was clearly a bit star-struck at the thought of meeting such an eminent architect.

'Well I could ask if it's all right for you to come to dinner but we'll have to drive back here tonight, I wouldn't want to put them to any trouble making up an extra bed. I'll call them in a little while, Rosemary was sleeping and I don't want to risk disturbing her. She really is very sick, Harry.'

'Is that why you were so upset, Mum?'

Holly never lied to her son, and she wasn't about to start now. 'No, Harry. I've broken things off with Philippe.'

'Why? When we spoke last night you were all loved up and couldn't wait to see him. What's happened?'

Holly chose her words carefully.

'I found out that he has done something which shows a total lack of respect for me.'

'Has he been seeing someone else?' Harry asked in a threatening tone.

'Not exactly. Look, I don't really want to talk about it at the moment but suffice to say he has made me feel like a complete idiot. I just want him out of my life without a trace, erased from my memory as if I never met him. I thought he was someone special but he's not. That's all.'

'Okay, Mum, but if you change your mind and

want to talk I'm a big boy now.'

Holly looked at the earnest young man sat next to her on the sofa, the image of his father the last time she had seen him, but different in so many ways. She was sure Gareth would have approved of the way she had raised their son. It will be a very lucky girl who ends up with my Harry, she thought, her heart swelling with pride, before realising that all mothers must think that about their boys, maybe even Philippe's *maman*.

CHAPTER 55

Philippe sat staring at his computer screen. He had read the words over and over again. At first he had thought that maybe Holly was bluffing about blocking his emails but he had tried sending one and it had been returned by the postmaster, and besides how could he possibly expect her to forgive him after sleeping with someone else.

One word kept running through his mind: why? Why would Delphine tell Holly about his unfaithfulness? It didn't make sense. Delphine had been his friend since he arrived in Mauritius and she knew that he had fallen in love with Holly because he had told her. Unless... Oh no, he thought, is Delphine secretly in love with me and will do anything to stop me leaving? He decided that must be it. That must be how Holly had found out, and so quickly too. He checked his sent box looking for an email sent to Holly by Delphine from his computer but there was nothing. She must have written Holly's email address down and emailed her from somewhere else. You're being ridiculous, he told himself, you're clutching at straws. Delphine loves her husband and she is much too nice a person to do anything like this.

Then another thought occurred to him. What if Delphine had not been alone when she had brought the croissants for him? Maybe while Delphine was leaving the scrawled note in the kitchen, her brother Jacques was reading through his emails and it was he who had taken Holly's email address to tell her what her darling Philippe had been up to in her absence? The more Philippe thought about it the more he convinced himself that this is what must have happened. He had never liked Jacques and the feeling was obviously mutual and now this low-life had found a way to punish him. He had set him up with Candice deliberately, when Philippe was in no condition to say no, and then he had emailed Holly and told her.

'The bastard!' Philippe shouted, anger rising in him. 'The low-life, sleazy, cheating bastard!'

Philippe was pacing the room now, punching his fist into his hand, wishing all the time it was Jacques' smarmy face. There must be something I can do, he thought, I can't just let Holly go without a fight.

With sudden clarity, Philippe grabbed his car keys and headed back into town to look for Jacques. He would confront him and force him to send Holly another email, telling her that the whole thing was a set-up when Philippe was too inebriated to know better. Holly will understand he convinced himself, she'll give me another chance, he thought desperately.

The tyres of the old BMW screeched to a halt in the car park of the Dolphin Bar. Philippe strode across the sun-hardened earth and pushed the swing doors of the bar open aggressively. He didn't need to ask where Jacques was, he could see him in the far corner of the room laughing and joking with some friends.

Probably laughing at my expense, fumed Philippe irrationally, marching over to them.

'What the hell did you do that for?' demanded Philippe.

Jacques looked surprised. 'I don't know what you're talking about.'

'Yes you damn well do. You set me up with that dancer just so you could email my girlfriend and tell her I've cheated on her.'

'Why would I do that, Philippe?'

'That's what I've been wondering. Did it give you some kind of thrill to know that you're wrecking my life?'

'I think you are still drunk from last night, my friend.'

'I am not your bloody friend, and I am not drunk. I just need you to email Holly again and tell her you set me up,' Philippe shouted.

The Dolphin Bar had cleared of all people except those at Jacques' table.

'I have no idea who this Holly is.'

'You're lying,' raged Philippe.

'That's the last time I do you a favour,' said Jacques, remaining calm. 'I thought you liked Candice.'

'This is not about Candice this is about you interfering in my life. You have to tell Holly what you did or I'll... I'll...'

'You'll what, Philippe?'

Philippe lunged across the small round table, launching his fist in the direction of Jacques' face but Jacques was too quick for him and stepped backwards avoiding the contact. Philippe clattered to the floor amidst the sound of smashing glass which brought Denis rushing from behind the bar.

'Break it up, break it up,' he said, his large bulk positioned in front of Jacques to prevent the fight from getting out of hand.

Jacques held his hands up. 'I didn't start this one.'

'I know. I saw what happened. Maybe you should head home and I'll sort this out with Philippe.'

As Jacques and his friends headed towards the exit, Denis turned to help Philippe up. He had known this mild-mannered Frenchman for almost a year and had never seen him raise his voice, let alone his fist before. Whatever had caused the outburst must be pretty serious.

'Come on Philippe, let's get you tidied up,' he said, but Philippe didn't move.

Denis leaned down into the jumble of table, chairs and broken glass to take hold of Philippe's arm. As he started to lift him off the floor he noticed a bright red stain spreading rapidly across Philippe's white linen shirt. It wasn't red wine.

'Oh my God, somebody call an ambulance,' he shouted.

CHAPTER 56

The traffic on the M25 was flowing freely by the time Harry steered Toby, his old green Corsa, on to it at junction 12. He had insisted on driving as he thought his mother was too agitated to concentrate and Holly had put up no resistance.

Holly had left it about an hour before calling Robert back to ask if it was okay to bring an extra guest to dinner and Robert had been very enthusiastic, saying that another distraction might keep Rosemary's spirits up. He had also insisted that they both stay over, despite Holly's protestations, as they always had rooms made up ready for unexpected guests. This wasn't exactly true, but he knew where the clean bedding was and making up two beds rather than one was no big deal.

Harry knew a short cut via Bracknell, which avoided the busiest bit of the M25 near Heathrow airport, so they were making very good time. He was chatting excitedly about meeting Robert, which was just as well as Holly didn't feel like talking.

'If your friend is as sick as you say she is, Mum, you're going to have to cheer up a bit otherwise she'll feel even worse.'

'Don't worry, I'll put on a brave face in front of Rosemary. They were responsible for introducing me to Philippe in the first place so the last thing I want them to feel is guilt now that we have broken up,' she said, a slight tremor in her voice.

'What's wrong with Rosemary?'

Holly sighed.

'She has leukaemia.'

'I thought it was usually kids who got leukaemia,' Harry said, remembering a school friend of his whose younger brother had spent months in hospital undergoing chemotherapy causing him to lose all his hair.

'So did I until I met Rosemary, but apparently there are lots of different types of leukaemia that can strike anyone at any age. The form she has is quite rare, only a few hundred cases a year in the UK, and is usually controllable with the new drugs that are being developed all the time. The really sad thing is she was responding well to treatment but then she developed a mutation that is even rarer and very difficult to treat.'

'So how are they treating her now?'

'Well at the moment they are experimenting with different drugs administered intravenously but if they don't work there is nothing else they can do.'

'Isn't it leukaemia where you can have a stem cell transplant?'

'She's not well enough. I think she was on a register for a while but they couldn't find a match and now she is too weak for them to even consider the operation.'

'I'm sorry, Mum. I can tell she has made a real impression on you. It would have been nice for you to have her as a kind of surrogate mother.'

Holly shot a sidelong glance at her son. When he was very young he had come home from school one day with a project to complete about his family. It had been awkward enough for him not having a father but then having to explain to him that his granddad was dead and that his grandma was no longer in contact with them would have floored most children. Not Harry. His project had been called, 'My Mum is All the Family I Need'. The teacher had been moved to tears by some of the things seven-year-old Harry had written about his relationship with his mum and had awarded him the highest mark in the class.

'Do you ever think about your grandma?'

'Why would I, Mum? She obviously never thinks about her grandson.'

'She never knew you, Harry. When Dad died she never wanted to lay eyes on either of us again.'

'It's her loss, Mum. We didn't need her, we have each other. We'll always have each other.'

Holly turned to look out of the window, her eyes misting with tears. She knew one day Harry would have a wife and family of his own and she wanted that for him. Maybe that was why she had rushed headlong into the relationship with Philippe. She couldn't bear the thought of being alone when Harry was ready to spread his wings.

As though he knew what she was thinking and with a wisdom way beyond his nineteen years he said, 'Don't take things too seriously too soon in relationships, Mum, they have to be built on trust and trust is earned over time. Maybe things were just moving too fast between you and the Frenchman.'

'Nice try, Harry,' she said raising a smile. 'But I'm still not ready to talk about it.'

CHAPTER 57

'Apologies,' said Robert. 'I'm certainly no Jamie Oliver.'

'Judging by the swearing coming out of the kitchen when you were preparing things earlier I would have said you had more in common with Gordon Ramsay,' laughed Rosemary, her eyes bright, clearly enjoying the evening. 'It's a good job you only had to put it in the oven when our guests arrived as that would have been some introduction!'

'The lasagne was delicious, Robert, you'll have to give me the recipe,' said Holly, but Robert wasn't paying attention he was watching his animated wife. She looked so happy and alive it was hard to believe that there would probably be so few more evenings like this one.

'Do you do much cooking, Harry, or are you a typical university student living off Pot Noodles and takeaway pizza?' asked Rosemary.

'I don't cook a lot, I must admit, but Mum taught me how to make soup out of virtually anything so I make a big pot to last three or four days and have it for either lunch or dinner depending if I'm working or not.'

'Where do you work?' Rosemary asked.

'Just in a bar,' he replied. 'The wages aren't much but if you're nice to the customers the tips are good.'

Robert nodded his head in approval. 'I'm pleased to hear that you're working your way through university rather than getting yourself further in debt with a hefty student loan. Some of the young architects I know are still paying off their tuition fees in their thirties. Tiramisu anyone?' he added. 'And no I can't claim it as my own. It's a Waitrose special.'

Rosemary declined but the others tucked in to the creamy, alcoholic confection.

'It's a good job I'm not driving back,' said Harry. 'I think that dessert would have pushed me over the legal limit.'

'Well, as you're not driving, can I top up your wine or would you like a brandy with your coffee?'

'I'll just have the coffee, thanks Robert. Mum and I are not really big drinkers.'

At this remark Holly flushed, remembering her admission of over-imbibing on her first night in Mauritius.

'Right, well, I'll put the coffee on and I'll show you some of my latest drawings if you like, Harry, as I think the girls want a bit of time on their own,' Robert said winking in Harry's direction.

'Oh right,' said Harry, cottoning on immediately. 'I'd be honoured to have a look at some of your work.' He followed Robert through to the kitchen while the older man set the filter coffee machine going and then into his office.

The moment the door was closed Rosemary turned to Holly.

'What a lovely young man, you must be so proud of him, Holly, and so handsome too.'

'If I had been told I could only have one child, Harry would have been top of my list. I look at him sometimes and can't believe my luck. He's kind and caring and unbelievably intuitive for a teenager. I keep waiting for him to do something wrong but so far he hasn't put a foot out of line.'

'It's more than luck, Holly, it's the way you have brought him up. You two have a wonderful relationship, it's so heart-warming to see.' She paused. 'Talking of relationships, Robert tells me you have finished things with Philippe?'

Holly knew how much Rosemary liked the charismatic Frenchman and she didn't want to spoil their friendship so she hesitated before saying, 'I think perhaps I got carried away with the moment in Mauritius. It was the perfect setting for romance and I fell in love with someone I barely knew. I don't regret a moment of it,' she added, acutely aware that Rosemary had encouraged her to follow her heart. 'But Philippe is too different from me for things to ever work out long term so I thought it best to end it now before we got too involved.'

Rosemary was watching Holly closely. 'Something must have happened for you to have done such a complete U-turn with your feelings overnight. Has Philippe said something or done something to upset you? It could all be a lost-in-translation misunderstanding?'

'You have known Philippe much longer than you have known me and I don't want you to take sides. I don't want anything to affect our friendship and I don't want you to think any less of Philippe. He has done something which to me is unforgivable but other people might think I'm making a big fuss about nothing. I can't risk telling you what it is and losing you as my friend.'

'You are going to lose me soon anyway, Holly, and I would hate to go to my grave without knowing if there was something I could have done to resolve things between the two of you.'

Holly was really struggling with her emotions now. The stark reminder that her friend's life was almost over almost reduced her to tears again but she pressed her lips together and closed her eyes for a moment giving her time to clarify her thoughts.

'I know that Philippe is the novelist Veronica Phillips.'

'How…?' Rosemary started to ask, but Holly raised her hand to stop the question.

'I know because, as well as writing my travel blog, I also work as a freelance copy-editor. Yesterday I received a new manuscript to work on and, as chance would have it, it was the new book from Veronica Phillips.' Holly was watching for Rosemary's reaction, but the older woman remained impassive so she continued. 'The book Philippe was struggling to write has been brought to life by some very explicit love scenes. I don't think I need to say any more.'

'I can understand that you would find that very upsetting. You must feel that he has used and betrayed you but, for what it is worth, I don't think that was his intention. I think Philippe is only a good writer when he writes about something he has experienced. *Maman* was a beautifully written account of his own young life with a fictional story developed around it. I think he is wrong to have used this particular experience but, in his head, he may well have thought he was honouring you by writing about you.'

'He wrote about me as a high-class prostitute. Forgive me if I don't see that as a compliment.'

At that moment the office door opened and Robert emerged followed by Harry who was grinning from ear to ear.

'You've got a very talented boy here, Holly. He's just given me a few ideas for my latest hotel project in Barbados.'

CHAPTER 58

Philippe lay unconscious in the recovery room of the hospital in Port Louis. Denis had travelled in the ambulance with him and en route he had called Delphine who had immediately jumped in her car and arrived fifteen minutes after them.

While Philippe was on the operating table, having the shard of glass that had almost ended his life carefully removed from its position perilously close to his heart, Denis had filled Delphine in on the argument in the bar between Philippe and Jacques.

Although he was her brother, Delphine knew that Jacques was a trouble-maker, never shy of getting involved in an alcohol-fuelled brawl, so she found it hard to believe Denis when he said that Philippe was the one shouting and throwing the first, and as it turned out, only punch.

She rang Jacques. 'Are you aware that Philippe is lying in a hospital bed close to death?' she shouted into her phone the moment he answered. 'What did you say to him to make him so angry?'

'Thanks for your sisterly support,' he replied icily. 'I have no idea what had made the Frenchman so angry when he stormed into the bar throwing wild accusations around.'

'What accusations?' she asked, calming her tone of voice as there was a little bit of Delphine that was afraid of her younger brother.

'He was ranting on about someone called Holly. He said I had deliberately set him up with Candice to split him and his girlfriend up. He was demanding that I email her again... Not sure why he said again when I have never even heard of the woman.'

Delphine was puzzled too. What had Philippe meant?

Jacques broke through her silence. 'Haven't you got something to say?'

'I'm sorry I accused you of starting things... I was upset.'

'Well if this becomes a police investigation just remember your family loyalty,' Jacques said menacingly.

Delphine had needed to lie for him to the police on many previous occasions but it would seem that this time, confirmed by Denis's account of what had taken place in the Dolphin Bar, she would be telling the truth.

'You're my brother, Jacques, and family comes first.'

The phone call had only served to confuse Delphine further as to the cause of the seemingly unprovoked attack on her brother, and to make matters worse she was now in his bad books. It was possible that Candice may know something, she thought, so she dialled her number but it went straight to voicemail.

'Candice, this is Delphine. I'm at the hospital in Port Louis with Philippe. He's had an accident and I wondered if maybe he was upset when he left you earlier? Please ring me when you get this message.'

Delphine then made her way back to Denis in the visitor's room to wait anxiously for news.

CHAPTER 59

As he had done every morning that week, Robert slid out of bed as silently as possible so that he could wake his wife with a cup of tea and a piece of hot buttered toast. She never ate more than a bite or two but Robert reasoned that two bites were better than none. His beautiful Rosie was wasting away in front of his eyes. She had made a valiant effort to eat the previous evening but it was still like watching a sparrow peck at its food.

While he waited for the kettle to boil and the toast to pop up, he set the wooden tray with a white napkin and pulled another pink rose out of the arrangement in the lounge to lay across the tray just as he had always done for his Rosie when he brought her breakfast in bed.

As he was climbing the stairs he heard the now familiar sound of retching. He quickened his pace, careful not to spill the tea, and was surprised that the sound was coming from the main bathroom rather than their en-suite. He tapped lightly on the door.

'Rosie, are you alright in there?'

There was no response, just more retching.

Robert tried the door handle but for some reason she had locked the door. He raised his voice slightly, in case she hadn't heard him.

'Rosie are you okay?'

'I'm fine Bobby,' she answered sleepily from their bedroom.

Relief washed over Robert for a moment to be replaced by concern. That was either Holly or Harry throwing up in the bathroom and he was hoping his cooking wasn't the cause. He continued towards the bedroom to tend to his wife.

Inside the bathroom Holly pressed her face against the smooth, cool porcelain of the outside of the toilet bowl. The nausea was starting to subside now and again she wondered if she should pay a visit to her doctor as the sickness bug that had started in Dubai last week didn't seem to be showing any sign of abating. She had read in the hotel information booklet that if you developed persistent sneezing after a trip to Dubai you should consult your doctor and she wondered whether the same was true of a tummy bug but they simply hadn't mentioned it.

Like they didn't mention the jelly fish washed up on the beach with the incoming tide every day, she thought. She had never seen so many and different types too. There were the pale blue ones with fat squid-like tentacles, the clear jelly ones and some with purpley-blue markings on their back. Despite feeling so rough she smiled as she remembered finding the first one, unsure whether it was a jelly fish or a discarded silicone breast implant

Well, at least I've mentioned it in my blog, she thought, so now people, particularly those with young children, can decide whether or not to go in the sea.

The nausea had passed so Holly pulled herself up onto her feet and rinsed her mouth with cold water. She had heard a tap on the bathroom door while she was being sick and Robert's voice asking if she was okay. I hope he doesn't think there was anything wrong with his cooking, she thought.

CHAPTER 60

Before her treatment started at 9.30 a.m. Rosemary had been called into the office of her consultant. As she entered the room with Robert at her side, Professor Lang indicated for her to sit down. 'How are you feeling today?' It was the same question he always asked her.

Rosemary's normal response was, 'You are the one with my blood test results, you tell me'. Today, however, she replied, 'I'm feeling surprisingly well. Maybe finally we've found a treatment that's working.'

The professor studied her over the top of his rimless spectacles perched on the end of his aquiline nose. Everything about him was long and slim, from his legs, which contributed to his towering six-foot-three-inch height, to his elegant fingers, which he was tapping thoughtfully on the table.

'Well it's good to hear that you are feeling a bit better although we won't have the results of the latest tests for a week or so. Today is your last treatment until we get those results and then we'll decide when to bring you back in for the next course of this drug if the response has been positive.'

'When would that be do you think?' asked Robert. 'Only Rosemary is quite keen to go away for a few days while she is feeling brighter.'

'I'm presuming you are not planning on jetting off to Mauritius again as I most certainly wouldn't recommend a long-haul flight, or a flight of any description for that matter.'

'No of course not,' Rosemary said, quickly replying before Robert could let slip that they were going to Switzerland. 'We were thinking of somewhere much closer to home that we can get to by car.'

'Then I don't see any problem, provided Robert will be doing the driving, and so long as you get plenty of rest.'

Rosemary wasn't sure whether that was Professor Lang's attempt at humour but she made no comment as she wanted to get out of the office without further questioning.

'Make sure you take the hospital contact numbers with you, and Rosemary,' he said as she made for the door. 'Try to eat a bit more if you can. Nutrition plays a big part in the body's ability to recover. I can tell the pharmacy to give you some liquid meals if that would help?'

The thought of the cartons of thick pink, disgusting-tasting liquid almost made Rosemary heave, and she had no intention of ever subjecting her taste buds to them again. 'Yes of course, if it will help keep my strength up.'

The professor raised his eyebrows questioningly in Robert's direction but Robert just shrugged before shaking Professor Lang's hand and following his wife out of the room.

'You weren't lying to the professor about feeling better, were you, Rosie, just so that he would agree to let you go away for a few days?'

She turned and looked her husband straight in the eye so that he would know she was telling the truth.

'This last two days I have felt better than I have in a long time,' she said, which was certainly true of her emotional state. Then she turned away unable to deal with the flicker of hope in her husband's eyes. Physically it was a different matter. She didn't need to wait for the results of lab-controlled tests to know that she was rapidly deteriorating and may soon need to be permanently hospitalised. That's simply not going to happen, she thought, raising her chin defiantly as she sat down on the edge of the hospital bed waiting to be connected to the intravenous drip for a final time.

'Now that we've got the all clear from the professor we might as well bring our Switzerland jaunt forward to this weekend if Holly's not doing anything,' Rosemary said.

'If she's feeling well enough. I heard one of them being sick in the bathroom this morning. I thought it was you so I called out and as I brought your tray through to you Harry popped his head round his bedroom door so it must have been Holly. I hope she hasn't got a bug or something because the last thing we want is you catching anything while your white cell count is too low to deal with it. You don't think it was the lasagne do you?'

'No I'm pretty sure it wasn't that or we would all

have been unwell,' she answered, adding silently to herself, and I don't think it's a bug either.

CHAPTER 61

The tyres crunching on the gravel of the driveway signalled to Holly and Harry that their hosts had returned. Before Robert and Rosemary had left for the hospital Holly had said that she would prepare some lunch for them all, and true to her word she had found enough vegetables to make one of her famous soups. Harry had walked into the village to buy some fresh bread and had come back full of praise for Woldingham and the surrounding countryside which he had only seen in the semi-dark the previous evening.

'One day, Mum, when I'm a famous architect, I'll buy us a plot of land somewhere like this and design us the most beautiful house you have ever seen,' he had enthused.

She had no doubt that with his ability and determination to succeed at his chosen career he would do exactly that and she didn't burst his bubble by suggesting that maybe he would want to share his dream home with someone other than his ageing mother.

Holly was pleased to see that both Robert and

Rosemary were smiling as they slowly descended the sweeping staircase, Rosemary holding the banister with one hand and supported under her elbow on the other side by her husband.

'Judging by your expressions it was a good hospital visit,' Holly said, taking Rosemary's other arm as she let go of the banister on reaching the bottom of the stairs and guiding her towards the table which Harry had laid ready for lunch.

'We'll talk about it after lunch,' said Rosemary, 'which smells delicious, by the way.'

'It's only vegetable soup but I thought it would be nice and light for all of us.'

'It's one of my favourite lunches at the moment, particularly with some crusty fresh bread softened in it. Did you pop into the village for that?'

'I went,' chimed in Harry. 'It's a lovely village. How long have you lived here?'

'I was brought up here,' said Rosemary, pride creeping into her voice. 'We've won best-kept Surrey Downs village many times.'

'Was this your family home?'

'No, we had a much smaller house on Station Road but when my parents died we were able to afford this place, which Robert then set about rebuilding.'

'He's done an awesome job,' Harry said. 'Exactly what I would have done.'

Three pairs of eyes turned in Harry's direction, each face registering amusement.

'What did I say?' he asked.

'It just sounded funny,' Holly said. 'The apprentice complimenting the master by saying it is what he would have done.'

'I didn't mean it like that, Robert. I hope you don't think I'm a smartarse who thinks he knows everything and isn't willing to listen to the voice of experience?'

A smile was playing at the corner of Robert's mouth. 'I can see I'm going to have to watch my back with you around, Harry. You'll be stealing all my contracts when they see your fresh young ideas.'

Then he started to laugh, a sight which warmed Rosemary to the core.

Holly was reflecting on Robert's words: 'with you around'. Did that mean he would be willing to give Harry a helping hand to get started? Despite her own devastation at what she still considered was a betrayal of trust from Philippe she joined in with the laughter.

The vegetable soup was a success with Robert and Harry having a second helping. Even Rosemary managed to finish the small bowl Holly had put in front of her.

Throughout lunch the older trio had been chatting about the exotic locations they had been fortunate to visit as a result of their respective occupations.

'You are making me feel left out,' said Harry at one point.

'You've got a lifetime ahead of you, Harry,' said Rosemary. 'What you do with it is your choice but, whatever you choose, live each day as if it's your last and then you will have no regrets. Life is not a race it's a journey with all its twists and turns,' she said, laying her hand gently on Robert's. 'Speaking of journeys, Professor Lang was pleased that I am feeling better and has given me the all clear to go on our little road trip.'

Holly didn't want to say too much in front of Harry so she asked him to clear the table and do the dishes. Robert sensed that the two women wanted to chat without Harry around so he offered to help and then whisked him off to his office again to chat about other projects he had in the pipeline.

Holly helped Rosemary to the sofa and lifted her feet up onto the footstool and then settled into the depths of an armchair opposite her.

'I am so pleased that it was good news at the hospital this morning,' Holly said. 'Does that mean we can postpone the trip to Switzerland for a while?'

'On the contrary, I was hoping that maybe we could bring it forward to this weekend if you're not doing anything else,' Rosemary said.

'But why would you want to bring it forward if the new drugs seem to be working? Shouldn't you give them a proper chance?'

'They're not working, Holly.'

'How do you know? You told the professor you were feeling better.'

'And that was true in part. I have felt better for having you here, and better for meeting your lovely boy, but physically it is a battle to pretend I'm all right so that Robert doesn't get too upset. My head is aching for most of my waking hours and my bones hurt. I don't need the results of the latest tests to tell me that I am past the point of no return.'

Holly was trembling as she realised the enormous effort Rosemary was going to each day to protect her husband, an effort that was fuelled by love.

'My biggest fear is that once they know the drugs aren't working they will incarcerate me in a hospital room and fill me full of painkillers to die a lingering death possibly all alone. Robert wouldn't be able to be with me all day, every day, and I could just slip away while he was sleeping or taking a loo break. I think it would break him if he wasn't there at the end with me. I can't let that happen, Holly. My father died of a broken heart. I don't want that to be Robert's fate. You do understand don't you?'

Holly did understand. Night after night, that turned into week after week and month after month, she had had nightmares about her dad dying alone in the wreck of his car. If I could have just held his hand at the end, she thought. If he had just had someone with him. The pain, anguish, and of course the terrible guilt, would still have been there but Holly was sure she would have come to terms with it sooner if she had just been able to say her goodbyes.

'Holly?'

'Yes... I understand. I think you are the most amazing, courageous woman I have ever met. I wish I could have known you longer.'

She moved from the chair to the sofa and the two women hugged each other, both battling to keep the tears at bay.

Holly whispered into Rosemary's shoulder, 'I love you like I should have been able to love my mother. Thank you for giving me the opportunity to know what it feels like.'

'I love you too, Holly, you're a very special girl.'

After a few minutes Rosemary pulled away from the embrace. 'So will this weekend be all right for you to travel?'

Holly nodded. 'Yes. Harry has to go back to uni first thing in the morning as he has a lecture tomorrow afternoon. Do you want me to make the ferry booking?'

'It would help if you could. I need to ring the clinic to bring the dates forward by a couple of days and I can do that when Robert goes out to the shops later but he doesn't like to be away from me for long.'

'Do you want Dover to Calais and what time should I book?'

'The earlier the better for me Holly as I don't sleep much anyway, but what about you? Will you be well enough to travel in the early morning?'

Holly hadn't been sure if Rosemary knew about her vomiting episode that morning, but clearly she did. It was still an odd question to ask though, unless... surely Rosemary wasn't hinting that she thought Holly may be pregnant? Suddenly Holly thought back to the nausea she had experienced in Dubai the previous week. She had thought it was a bug, but what if Rosemary was right? She tried to remember the last time she had a period but realised it was months ago as the constant travelling to different time zones seemed to reek havoc on her body clock.

'Oh my God, do you think I'm pregnant?'

'Is it a possibility?'

Holly nodded slowly, the colour draining from her face. Of course she would have to do a pregnancy test but Holly already felt certain that she was carrying

Philippe's baby.

'I don't suppose Philippe has tried to contact me through you and Robert, has he?' she whispered.

'No, I'm sorry, Holly. We've heard nothing from him since we left Mauritius.'

CHAPTER 62

Philippe was drifting in and out of consciousness, occasionally hearing voices he thought he recognised and odd words of whispered conversation. He was aware of people entering and leaving his room but he couldn't turn his head to see who it was, and anyway it required a tremendous effort to open his eyes. He had tried to speak but his mouth was dry and his mumbling was enclosed by the oxygen mask that covered his mouth and nose.

Someone was speaking his name. It was coming from the end of a long tunnel. He tried to say 'Holly' but drifted back into unconsciousness with the word still forming on his lips.

Delphine noticed the slight movement of his mouth and leaned forward to try and catch what he said but she was too late. She crossed to the door and called to the nurse, 'I think he was trying to say something.'

The nurse raised her head from the report she was filling in for the doctor. 'Did he open his eyes?' she asked.

'No, it was just a small movement opening his

mouth but now he seems to be sleeping again.'

'Why don't you take a break,' the nurse said kindly. 'You've been sitting at his bedside for hours. I'll stay with him a while if you like. Has he no other friends or relatives who could share the vigil with you? You look exhausted.'

Delphine looked over to the still form of Philippe laying on his hospital bed with tubes and wires connecting him to the life-saving machines. She had sat with him for the last thirty-six hours, sometimes dozing in her chair, only leaving him to get herself water or to use the toilet. She hadn't eaten, despite encouragement from the various nurses who had come and gone as their shifts dictated, and she realized that she was now feeling ravenous.

'That would be wonderful if you're not too busy,' Delphine said. 'I'll just go and get myself a sandwich, stretch my legs and get a breath of fresh air outside. I shouldn't be more than an hour.'

She felt guilty at leaving Philippe but knew that a break from the confines of the stuffy hospital room would do her good. The nurse's words were rolling around her mind as she paid for her sandwich at the counter of the hospital cafeteria and then took it outside to eat, blinking in the bright morning sunshine.

Denis hadn't been back to visit since the emergency dash in the ambulance and Delphine was disappointed that she had heard nothing from Candice. As she bit into her sandwich a thought occurred to Delphine. Maybe she should try and contact someone in England. She was sure Mr Robert would want to know what had happened to his friend, and of course his new girlfriend Holly would want to be at his side. Philippe's mobile phone was not among the scant possessions lying on his bedside cabinet so Delphine presumed it must be at the house in Tamarina Bay. She didn't really want to leave him alone for the two hours it would take to make the round trip to collect the phone but the more she thought about it the more she knew that it was her responsibility to let his friends in England know what was happening.

She pulled her own mobile phone out of her bag and was surprised for a moment to see she had a message, before remembering that the phone had been on silent inside the hospital. The message was from Candice:

Oh no that is terrible. I feel it is my fault. Can I come and visit?

Delphine checked the time the message was sent. Yesterday afternoon! She was annoyed with herself for not checking her phone earlier. She replied immediately:

Can u come asap?

Less than a minute later she received a reply:

Is he worse? I'm on my way - there in an hour.

Delphine quickly sent a message of reassurance, realising that she might have panicked Candice unnecessarily :

```
No still the same but I need someone to sit
with him while I go to his house for his
phone. I'll be as quick as I can.
```

Delphine went back into the hospital to tell the nurse, who true to her word was sat at Philippe's bedside, that someone was coming to relieve her for a while. Then she headed for the car park, climbed into her ancient Peugeot and headed south out of Port Louis.

An hour later she was unlocking the front door of Philippe's house. It was already losing Philippe's personality as he had packed away his pictures from the walls and the knick-knacks he had collected since arriving in Mauritius. She glanced at the small table near the front door but there was no sign of his phone. She checked his bedside table and the bathroom before moving into the kitchen. The remainder of the croissants she had thoughtfully left for him two days earlier were now hard and stale so she threw them in the bin as she scanned the kitchen work surfaces. How odd, she thought, if he had stormed out of the house in a temper he may well have forgotten his mobile but surely it would be lying in a prominent position. Delphine crossed to his desk, normally piled high with papers, but now empty apart from his laptop. Nothing. She was just starting to stick her hand down the side of the sofa, in case it had slipped down there, when she realised the easiest way to find the missing phone would be to ring it. She dialled his number and waited. It was ringing on her handset but there was no sound from within the house.

Damn, she thought, what a wasted journey and then her eyes rested on the laptop again. The top was not quite closed down and as she opened it, it sprang into life. Of course, she thought, if I can't call Philippe's friends maybe I can email them. Delphine was not particularly computer literate but she knew the basics, so how hard could it be to find a couple of email addresses, she reasoned. She typed the word Holly into the search bar at the top of the screen and before she had even finished the five letters an address popped up. She clicked on it and then sat down to compose an email that wouldn't alarm Holly but instead would ask her to contact Delphine as soon as possible. She pressed send and then started to look for Mr Robert. This time several addresses popped up after typing the first three letters and Delphine had no way of knowing which was the correct one. Obviously she didn't want to send emails to all of the Roberts in Philippe's address book so how was she going to find the one she needed. Maybe he had emailed Philippe recently? Although she didn't want to pry by reading private emails she figured it was a necessary evil. She clicked on the inbox and the top message was to say that her email to Holly had failed to be delivered. What did I do wrong? she wondered. This was not going too well.

The next message down started with the words, 'Where the hell are you?' It was from someone called Jo, a name Delphine had heard Philippe speak about in connection with his book. As it was work-related rather than personal, she didn't feel too bad reading it:

Where the hell are you? The car I sent to meet you waited at the airport for two hours before ringing me, waking me up, I might add, to tell me you hadn't arrived. I tried to ring you but you didn't pick up and so I checked with the airline and you weren't on the flight. What's going on, Phil?

Jo

With everything that had happened Delphine had forgotten that Philippe was supposed to have been on a flight back to the UK the previous evening. Clearly this Jo had been expecting him and was now concerned as to his whereabouts. Again Delphine composed an email, but this time she was a little more specific as Jo was asking a direct question:

I am Mr Philippe's housekeeper. I am sorry to tell you he has been involved in an incident and is currently in Intensive Care in the hospital at Port Louis.

Kind Regards

Delphine Deveraux

Delphine glanced at her watch. It was just past midday which meant in the UK it would only be 8 a.m. and she couldn't imagine that this person would be checking her emails that early, particularly as she had been disturbed with a late night phone call. Delphine wanted to get back to the hospital as soon as possible so decided she couldn't wait for a response from Jo.

More worrying was that the message she had sent to Holly had not gone. Perhaps it wasn't the right address after all, although it had been the only

Holly. She scrolled down the inbox and came to an email from Holly. Perhaps I can just reply to this thought Delphine as she opened it. She stared at the contents in disbelief. So that was why her message to Holly hadn't sent. No wonder he was so upset on Wednesday at the Dolphin Bar, but what had any of it to do with her brother Jacques?

In a state of total confusion, Delphine let herself out of the house and headed back to the hospital.

CHAPTER 63

Harry clattered down the stairs and flung his bag on the hall floor ready for his return journey to Bath before heading into the kitchen to make some breakfast for himself and his mum. He was elated since meeting Robert Forrester and being asked for his ideas on a couple of Robert's projects. It really felt as though he might have a future in his chosen career that would amount to more than designing boring council buildings. Robert had more or less promised him a job once he had finished his degree and had even suggested that he should write his dissertation about hotel architecture around the world, featuring Robert Forrester. Talk about inside information, Harry thought, I'll be able to ask Robert first hand about inspiration and technical problems without having to rely on misinformation on the Internet.

He was grinning from ear to ear when Holly walked into the kitchen in her dressing gown looking pale and tired.

'Kettle's on, Mum,' he said. 'Do you want tea, coffee or hot flavoured water?' He was referring to her penchant for fruit infusions which he thought were disgusting.

The thought of tea or coffee turned Holly's already fragile stomach. 'Camomile and Honey for me please.'

Harry pulled a face. 'Is that what I'll start drinking in middle age?'

'Less of your cheek, young man,' Holly countered, not really feeling up to his playful banter but not wanting to ruin his ebullient mood. She was aware that she had been quiet on the journey home from Woldingham and over supper last evening but she had a lot on her mind. They had been caught in heavy traffic on the way home so had arrived back in Reading too late for Holly to nip out to the chemist for a pregnancy test. There was no rush really. She already knew that she was pregnant, the test would simply confirm it, and she had decided that she wasn't going to tell Harry until he had finished his term at Bath University in a few weeks' time.

And then there was Rosemary. When she had hugged her yesterday she had been shocked to discover that she was little more than a bag of bones. Clever dressing disguised it but surely Robert couldn't be blind to the fact that his wife was simply wasting away.

'Toast or cereal?' asked Harry, spreading a thick layer of butter on his own charred bread that had just popped out of the toaster.

'Just one piece for me, with no butter thanks.'

'You're not watching your weight, are you, Mum? Cos you didn't have much for supper last night either. Don't go all skinny, you look better with curves.'

Just as well, thought Holly, as I'm going to have

one great big curve around my middle soon enough.

'Is that a compliment?'

'Just an observation,' he replied. 'You've got a better figure than half the girls in my year. They eat a load of junk, drink too much and then wonder why their waist measures the same as their bum!'

'Is that your way of telling me that you haven't got a girlfriend yet?'

'No time at the moment, Mum, and no one I fancy to be honest, so don't go getting any ideas about being a grandma anytime soon.'

Holly was sure she had coloured up so she kept her back to her son. What an awful thought that she could potentially have a grandchild that would be older than the baby she was carrying.

'There you go, one delicious piece of dry toast,' Harry said pushing a plate across the work surface towards her.

She nibbled the corner of her toast and sipped at her drink, trying to keep the feelings of nausea at bay.

CHAPTER 64

Robert was sitting in his car which was illegally parked on a single yellow line, keeping an eye out for traffic wardens in his rear-view mirror. He had driven round the block in Caterham several times looking for a parking space but none had become available, so he pulled up outside Renato's Hair and Beauty in the hope that his wife would soon be finished. He had been surprised the previous afternoon, after Harry and Holly had left, when Rosemary had asked him to pop in to the beauty salon and book an appointment for her to have a manicure and her hair coloured and blow-dried. He was pleased. It was obviously a sign that she was feeling much better if she was taking such an interest in her appearance again.

Maybe this trip to Switzerland wasn't such a bad idea after all, although why she was in such an almighty rush he couldn't imagine.

Holly was making all the travel and accommodation arrangements, all he needed to do was drive. He had even put Holly on his car insurance, at her suggestion, in case he got tired and needed a break. What a lovely young woman she is, he thought, and what a shame it didn't work out for her and Philippe. She had asked him not to pass on any of her contact details should Philippe try to get in touch with her through them, but there had been no word from the Frenchman, which, both surprised and disappointed Robert.

The door to Renato's opened and Rosemary emerged looking beautiful, followed by a small portly Italian man who was planting air kisses either side of her face and saying, 'Ciao, Bella.'

She looked happy and relaxed as she climbed into the waiting car. 'Have you been waiting long?'

'Just a couple of minutes. I didn't want you hanging around in case someone else whisked you away.'

'Bobby, you're such a charmer. Do you fancy going to the Harrow for a pub lunch, like we used to before I got ill, instead of going straight home?'

'Great idea, gives me a chance to show you off.'

CHAPTER 65

Incident? What type of bloody incident, thought Jo, as she reread the email from Delphine for the umpteenth time. She had emailed back after first reading the message three hours ago but there was still no response.

The phone call to the Dr AG Jeetoo Hospital in Port Louis had told her nothing except that Philippe was indeed a patient there and that he was in Intensive Care.

She tapped her long gel-manicured fingernails on the desk trying to decide what to do next. The publicity machine was ready and waiting for the big reveal. She had managed to pull a few favours with the features editor of the biggest circulating Sunday supplement magazine, in which there was supposed to be a four-page spread, revealing the identity of Veronica Phillips, followed by excerpts from the new book, *Tiffany*, that weekend. In fact, at that very moment, a photographer was waiting in a studio in Holborn for the 'mystery lady' to appear.

She couldn't delay any longer.

'Alice,' she called to her PA, 'get Mike Rowbotham

on the phone please, and then Susie at the magazine.' The phone connected almost immediately. 'Mike, I'm really sorry but the shoot is off. Of course we'll pay for your time and the hire of the studio. I'll make sure I put a nice juicy autobiography cover your way and you can invoice double on it. Sorry, Mike.'

The next call was much trickier, but in the end Jo was able to persuade Susie, the magazine features editor, that the book was so good, the excerpts alone would leave the readers wanting more without the added bonus of the author reveal. Not a pleasant phone call but at this late stage Susie didn't really have any other option and Jo knew that as a consequence she would have favours to repay at a later date.

'Alice,' she called again, 'call the airlines and get me on the next flight to Mauritius.'

CHAPTER 66

Delphine arrived back at the hospital a little after 2 p.m. She was hot and bothered, not only because of the soaring midday temperatures in Mauritius in May, but also because of the grid-locked traffic which meant she had spent the last two hours cooped up in her little car without the benefit of air-conditioning. The fresh clothes, which she had changed into when she called briefly at her home on her way back from Philippe's, were now sticking to her in large damp patches.

Throughout the drive back she had been trying to establish a link between Holly's email, her brother Jacques, and Philippe's accusations, but she couldn't piece things together. She hoped Candice would still be at the hospital as she wanted to ask her a couple of questions, including whether or not Philippe had his phone with him when he had left her in the upstairs room of the Dolphin on Wednesday lunchtime.

She walked briskly along the corridor towards Philippe's room, grateful for the blast of cool air from the air-conditioning units, and pushed open the door to his room. Candice was sat at Philippe's bedside stroking his hand. Although Delphine didn't necessarily approve of Candice's chosen profession she liked the girl and had introduced her to Philippe because she had thought he would treat her kindly.

'How has he been?' Delphine asked anxiously.

'He has been sleeping mostly but he did open his eyes at one point and was talking about holly? I called the nurse and she said it was a plant used to decorate at Christmas time in England and that he was obviously still delirious.'

Delphine decided nothing would be gained by mentioning that Holly was actually the name of his girlfriend, or rather his former girlfriend. She saw no reason to upset Candice who clearly had a soft spot for him.

'What happened, Delphine? Why would Philippe attack your brother? He always seemed such a gentleman to me.'

'I was hoping you may have the answer. Was he angry when he left you on Wednesday lunchtime?'

'No, but he did seem very anxious to leave. I think he was surprised to wake up at the Dolphin. He was very very drunk the night before, we didn't even... you know. Maybe he doesn't like me any more,' she said, looking sadly at Philippe.

There was a little piece of Delphine that was relieved that Philippe hadn't had sex with Candice at the Dolphin, even though he had slept with her on several previous occasions. Although Holly's email was breaking off their relationship, it could just be a lover's tiff that would all be sorted when Philippe got back to England. Delphine was pretty sure he would have resisted Jacques' suggestion of Candice spending the night with him had he not been almost comatose from drink. Was that what this was all about, she wondered. Had he attacked Jacques because he had set him up with a prostitute for the night?

Candice was looking up at her with tears starting to form in her huge brown eyes. 'He likes you just fine,' reassured Delphine, 'although you do know he is leaving to go back to England soon so you probably won't see him again.'

'I know. I wish he had liked me enough to take me with him away from the life I lead here.'

'I don't suppose you noticed if he had his mobile phone with him at the Dolphin?'

Candice furrowed her brow. 'I remember him picking up his keys and leaving me some money but I don't think I saw his phone. I paid Dennis for the room and I've brought the rest of the money back,' she said, indicating a pile of notes on Philippe's bedside table. 'It didn't seem right to take money for doing nothing.'

'Take the money,' Delphine said, acutely aware of how difficult it was for girls like Candice to make ends meet. 'Philippe gave it to you because he wanted you to have it.'

Candice looked doubtful but she picked up the money anyway as she rose to leave. 'Please let me know how he is doing.'

'I will, don't you worry, and thank you for coming to sit with him. You're a good girl.'

Candice turned away but not before Delphine saw tears rolling down her beautiful young face.

CHAPTER 67

Holly stared down at the word written in blue on the white pregnancy test stick she was holding. Not only did it say 'pregnant' it also confirmed that she was three-plus weeks, which she already knew, as the only opportunity for her to have become pregnant were the two days she had spent with Philippe in Mauritius. She couldn't believe that her body was still so fertile at her age.

Memories came flooding back from the only other time, almost twenty years ago, that she had experienced what she was feeling now. Her boyfriend, Gareth, had left for America two weeks previously and she had heard no word from him. Initially she had thought the feelings of nausea were because she was afraid he had dumped her until, after checking her diary, she realised her period was late. She could still remember the cold fear that crept through her body as, sitting on the edge of the bath, she waited a couple of minutes for the test to develop. She had sat staring at the thin blue line that confirmed she was pregnant until her mother had banged on the bathroom door telling her to hurry up because other people needed to use the toilet.

She had kept the pregnancy to herself for the whole of the summer believing, or simply hoping, that it would all be all right when Gareth came back from America, but he hadn't come back. There had been no long-distance phone call, no letter sent via airmail, in fact, no contact at all. Two days before she was due back at university, and with her bags already packed in readiness, she had finally told her parents and things had turned ugly.

Holly shuddered. At least this time there was no one she needed to ask for help, and although she was unsure how Harry would take the news she knew in her heart that he would eventually accept it and give her the emotional support she was going to need. She rested her hands protectively on her tummy and allowed herself to wonder whether the baby would be a little brother or sister for Harry.

Once again there was never a moment when she considered a termination. True, she was furious with Philippe for the total disregard he had shown for her feelings when writing about their most intimate moments but the tiny person growing inside her was not responsible for the shortcomings of its father.

There was of course the question as to whether or not she should tell Philippe about the baby. Part of her believed he had a right to know but the other part of her decided that someone who could thoughtlessly reveal to the world the very act that had led to the conception, deserved no consideration from her at all.

At least she had been through all this before, and

at a time when she was not financially self-sufficient, so she knew how lonely but rewarding being a single mum could be. Holly smiled. Although she would never have planned to have another baby under the same circumstances, she loved being a mum and had always yearned for more children. Maybe it was simply the cosmos granting her unspoken request.

CHAPTER 68

Philippe was aware of voices that seemed to be coming from a long way away. Why were there people in his bedroom when he was trying to sleep? he thought. His eyelids fluttered open and he struggled to focus on the two people who were talking in lowered tones by his bedroom door. Realisation began to dawn on him. This was not his bedroom.

'Where am I?' he asked, surprised by the croaking sound that came out of his own mouth.

The two people by the door turned.

'I'll get the nurse,' said Delphine, hurrying from the room, while the other woman approached his bed.

As she came closer Philippe could see it was Jo from his publisher's.

Confused, Philippe asked, 'What are you doing in Mauritius?' and then added, 'I am still in Mauritius, aren't I?'

Jo perched on the edge of the chair at his bedside and said soothingly, 'You're in the hospital in Port Louis. Do you remember what happened?'

'Hospital? Am I sick?' he croaked.

At that moment a nurse bustled into the room. 'I'll have to ask you to wait outside for a few moments please,' she said to Jo who immediately obliged. She then turned her attention to Philippe. 'How are you feeling?' she asked, lifting his arm from the bed to take his pulse. 'You've had us all quite worried.'

'Why am I here?'

The nurse chose her words carefully. 'You were involved in an incident in a bar in Flic en Flac and you were seriously injured.'

Philippe closed his eyes to try and think and in front of him he could see Jacques' face taunting him.

'I think I punched someone,' Philippe said.

'Don't try to talk now,' instructed the nurse, whose badge said her name was Grace. 'Once the doctor has checked you over your sister can come back in and maybe she can help you piece things together.'

Philippe was about to say that he didn't have a sister but realised just in time that Jo must have claimed to be his sibling thinking she would need to be a relative in order to visit out of hours. He smiled weakly, wondering if Delphine had claimed to be his half-sister.

'It's good to see you smile,' said Grace. 'There hasn't been much to smile about since you were rushed here on Wednesday.'

'What day is it?'

'It's Saturday,' Grace replied.

'Did anyone tell Holly?' he asked.

'I think your friend Delphine contacted as many people as she could.'

'Is Holly here?' he asked hopefully.

'No, only Delphine and your sister, although yesterday there was another young lady here, Candice.'

The door opened and a man in a white coat entered the room. 'I'm Dr Lamb,' he said, 'and you are a very lucky man.'

He explained to Philippe how the broken glass he had fallen onto had missed puncturing his heart by a fraction of a millimetre. It had however caused a massive internal bleed which had required urgent life-saving surgery upon his arrival at the hospital. All the time Dr Lamb was speaking he was checking the various monitoring devices that were hooked up to Philippe and also the chart on the end of his bed listing the medication that was being administered.

Philippe's eyes were getting heavy again with sleep. He wanted to speak to Jo and Delphine but he could feel himself drifting off.

'Sleep is the best thing for him at this point,' Doctor Lamb said to Grace. 'Please keep his visitors out until he wakes of his own accord,' he added as he left the room.

CHAPTER 69

It was barely light as Holly pulled into the driveway of the Forresters' home. Robert was already outside, loading two small suitcases into the boot of his Jaguar. Holly pulled up behind his car and climbed out with her small overnight bag.

'You travel light, Holly,' said Robert, greeting her with a kiss to each cheek. 'Something Rosie and I have never quite mastered,' he added with a rueful glance towards the luggage in their car boot.

Holly's face flushed slightly as she realised she had almost given the game away by only packing for a couple of days when they were supposed to be away for a week. 'You'd be surprised how much I have in that little bag. I guess it's one of the bonuses of constantly travelling for work. I've learnt to only take what I'm actually going to need.'

'Rosie is just finishing her tea and toast, have you eaten?'

'It was a bit too early when I left so I think I'll wait until we are on the ferry,' she said, not wanting to risk her fragile stomach until she could make an excuse of sea sickness to Robert who, she assumed, knew nothing of her condition.

'We should be setting off really,' she added, checking her watch. 'It's almost six.'

Three hours later, with Robert's Jaguar safely parked on the lower deck of the ferry, the three of them stood on the upper deck as the boat left the English coast bound for France.

Rosemary was gripping the rail so hard that her knuckles had turned white. She was fighting back the urge to cry as she watched the towering white cliffs of Dover receding into the distance while the ferry ploughed inexorably forward out into the open but crowded water of the English Channel. She hadn't expected to feel quite so emotional leaving England. She had spent almost as much of her life in foreign climes as she had in the country of her birth but there was a finality to this departure. She shivered.

'You're cold, Rosie, let's get you inside. We don't want you coming down with anything while we're away, and besides, Holly hasn't had any breakfast yet.'

The two women exchanged a look as they followed Robert to the cafeteria. Fortunately Holly had remembered to bring some of her camomile tea bags with her as the insipid liquid Robert was sipping would almost certainly have made her feel queasy. She nibbled the corner of a piece of toast while she listened to Rosemary making the comparison between the ferry and the cruise ships she had danced on for so many years.

'As you can imagine the ships were much bigger

than this, although quite small by today's standards. I sometimes wonder how those enormous vessels stay afloat. The decor was opulent, similar to a five-star hotel, and you had to dress in evening gowns for dinner every night, not just for the Captain's cocktail party.'

'Did you ever get sea sick?' Holly asked.

'Only right at the very start. We were sailing from Southampton through the Bay of Biscay and it lived up to its reputation. I wondered what I had let myself in for. The ship was crashing through mountainous waves and I sat wrapped in a blanket out on the promenade deck because I didn't want to be trapped down in my cabin if the ship sank. I think I had just seen the original version of *The Poseidon Adventure*, which wasn't very smart when you're about to spend the next six months of your life at sea.'

'Had you always wanted to work on a cruise ship?' Holly asked.

'It had never crossed my mind really until I was successful at the audition. I've always loved travelling abroad and in my opinion there is no better way of seeing lots of different countries and cultures than from the comfort of a ship.'

'Can you believe this is the first boat I have ever been on?' Holly said. 'I've never even crossed the Thames on a ferry, or been on a pleasure boat on the River Trent.'

'Really?' exclaimed Robert. 'Well what do you think of it so far?'

'So far so good, but you don't really get much sensation of movement from in here. I think I'll go back on deck if you two don't mind.'

'You go, Holly. We'll meet you back at the car when we're coming into Calais.'

Holly was feeling fragile but it was not morning sickness or sea sickness that was causing it. Her mind and heart were in turmoil. She hated deceiving Robert and wanted to avoid any questions about meeting up with her Italian friends for as long as possible. As she climbed the steep metal steps to the outside deck she wondered again if she was doing the right thing by helping Rosemary. She moved towards the front of the boat and was surprised to see the French coastline already coming into view across the smooth grey-blue expanse of water.

La Manche, she thought randomly, wasn't that what the French called the English Channel? She had learnt it in geography as a ten-year-old and it had always helped her remember the French word for sleeve. Fleetingly she thought of the evening she had spent with Philippe at his house in Tamarina Bay when he had asked her if she spoke French. She remembered the electricity between them and the excitement she felt at having finally met someone she thought was special enough to lay her past to rest. How could I have got it so wrong? she thought sadly.

Salty sea spray splashed onto her face and mixed with the salty tears that were already there. I feel so emotional right now, she thought, how do I know I'm doing the right thing in helping Rosemary to take her own life? It's not too late to change my mind. I can make an excuse that I don't feel well and say I have to go home. Robert would believe me because he knows

I was vomiting earlier in the week. Will I be able to live with a clear conscience if I go ahead with this? Will I be able to if I don't? If only there was someone else I could ask for guidance. She lifted her gaze to the almost cloudless blue sky. Two fluffy white clouds merged momentarily to form a cloud that looked like a giant white feather. Holly gasped.

This wasn't about her, it was about helping a friend in desperate need. She had promised Rosemary and she wasn't about to break that promise.

'Thank you, Dad,' she whispered. 'I love you.'

CHAPTER 70

Jo had been waiting patiently in the hospital's relatives room for Philippe to wake and be allowed visitors. The nurse had warned her that it might be a long wait as Dr Lamb had instructed that Philippe must be allowed to sleep until he woke naturally. Thank goodness it's Saturday, she thought, at least I'm not missing work.

She had spoken with Delphine about the brawl at the Dolphin Bar but the Mauritian woman hadn't been present at the time so was only able to give her a bare bones account of what had happened, although Jo got the feeling that she was holding something back. When Jo asked if the police had been in to question Philippe she detected a look of panic in the other woman's eyes before she replied that the incident hadn't been reported to the police as the victim wasn't pressing charges. That's odd, Jo had thought, I know I would press charges if someone had tried to punch me without provocation.

After their conversation she had suggested that Delphine go home for a rest as she looked shattered and there was no point them both hanging around in the visitor room. It wasn't a totally kind and thoughtful gesture. She needed to spend time with Philippe alone and explain to him her view that maybe this was not the best time to reveal his true identity. There was no way of knowing if anyone had captured the attack on their mobile phone. If they had, and subsequently made the connection that the perpetrator was a famous author, it could adversely affect sales of the book. Worse, someone might even consider blackmail to keep the whole thing quiet. Again Jo wondered what on earth had caused Philippe to lunge at this local guy.

These days it was completely out of character but when she had first met Philippe, when they were both working for the same newspaper, he frequently got drunk and could be quite aggressive if someone expressed an opinion that differed from his own.

Jo was fresh out of university and had immediately fallen for his blond good looks and his charming French accent, which she later discovered he laid on more thickly when he was trying to impress a female. It had worked. They had dated for several months, but although they had fun and great sex – just the thought of which caused a stirring deep in her belly – there was never the feeling that theirs was a relationship that was going anywhere. Philippe had been the main reason she had eventually left the newspaper and moved into publishing and, considering her meteoric rise with Ripped, he had done her a massive favour professionally, despite breaking her heart.

It had come as a big surprise when, having not heard from him in twelve years, he sent her the manuscript of his first book for an opinion before he started approaching literary agents. It was so good that Jo had instantly negotiated a three-book deal for him, negating the need for an agent, something of a rarity in modern publishing. He had never claimed that *Maman* was written about his own young life but Jo had her suspicions and realised, after reading it, that was probably why he found committing to a relationship so difficult. He hadn't found a woman he felt he could trust.

Philippe had been afraid that some of his newspaper colleagues would ridicule the subject matter of *Maman*, so together they had come up with the idea to write under the pen name of Veronica Phillips and keep the author's identity a secret. The mystery surrounding the author had added to the success of his book and Jo was confident that revealing 'she' was actually a 'he' would be a great future publicity stunt. Now this scrape Philippe had got himself into had ruined the planned revelation for the *Tiffany* book launch. Fortunately, this new book is so good it will sell itself, she thought. We'll save the reveal for his next book which, if this one is anything to go by, won't be for at least another eighteen months, by which time this entire incident will be long forgotten.

Jo yawned. She was really tired from the flight and the jet lag but this conversation with Philippe needed to be face to face so there would be no argument. Her flight back to London was booked for the following morning but, if necessary, she could take the evening flight and still be back at her desk on Monday morning. The sacrifice for being successful in my career, she thought. I have no life apart from chasing wayward authors halfway round the world. Even as she thought it Jo knew that she wouldn't have done it for anyone else and that in truth she hoped that Philippe had sought her out when he had written his first book not just because Ripped was such a great publishing house, but because he still had feelings for her too.

There was a quiet tap on the door and Grace popped her head round. 'You can go back in now, he's just woken up.'

Jo picked up her overnight bag and followed the nurse back along the corridor to Philippe's room. He was propped up on his pillows looking better than when she had seen him a few hours previously.

He was obviously feeling a little better too as he winked and greeted her with, 'Hello, sis.'

'I'll give you fifteen minutes and then come back and see how he's doing,' said Grace, closing the door behind her.

Although she was relieved to see him looking so much better Jo had already decided that she needed to be quite stern with him.

'What the hell were you doing punching someone in a bar?' she demanded.

'Trying to punch someone,' he corrected. 'I'm obviously out of practice.'

'It's not funny, Phil. We're already right up to the deadline on your book and I was seriously considering the possibility of having to delay its publication.'

'I'm sorry,' he said. 'The red mist just descended. I suppose you could call it a crime of passion.'

He went on to explain the circumstances that had led up to the altercation with Jacques in the Dolphin Bar. 'I was so stupid,' he said. 'I found the perfect woman and then I lost her again through a drunken mistake.'

I'm the stupid one, thought Jo, chasing halfway round the world in the hope that since they had come back into each other's lives, Philippe might realise that she was the one.

Barely able to conceal her dreadful disappointment she asked, 'So is Tiffany her real name?'

'No. It's Holly.'

That's an odd coincidence, Jo thought. I had my friend Holly lined up to copy edit Philippe's book. 'Has anyone told her you're in hospital?'

'Delphine tried but she has blocked me from emailing her.'

'But you must have a phone number for her?'

'No. She works for a charity so she doesn't earn much money and she didn't want to be tempted to call me long distance. We were supposed to be reunited on Thursday and then I went and cocked it up.'

Philippe was starting to get upset, and Jo knew she didn't have much more time with him before Grace came back to check his stats. At which point I will probably be told to leave, she thought.

'It's okay, Phil,' she said, trying to calm him. 'I'll try and find her and tell her what has happened, although you haven't given me much to go on. Which charity does she work for?'

'I don't know,' he said despairingly. 'We didn't really talk about work.'

'Well, I'll do what I can. Holly isn't a common name but I'll need her last name. You do have it?'

'No, but the Plantation House hotel will know.'

'Good thinking, I'll email them when I get home. Now listen,' she said. 'About the book. I think it's strong enough without the big "Veronica Phillips is a man" reveal and in the circumstances we don't want to risk any adverse publicity. I suggest we continue to keep your identity secret until your next book is done. What do you think?'

The effort of all the talking had tired Philippe and his eyes were starting to close as he nestled back into his pillows.

'Do what ever you think is best, Jo, but promise me you'll try and find Holly.'

'You need to rest now,' Jo said, as she stood and leaned over to kiss his forehead, before turning away abruptly, tears prickling the back of her eyes. Why couldn't he love me the way he loves this Holly woman? she thought, her hopes for rekindling their relationship totally crushed.

Weariness enveloped her as she trudged to the front of the hospital and fell into the back of a waiting cab to go to her hotel. At least I'll be on the morning flight, she thought, now I know there is no point me hanging around here.

Jo was not a vindictive person so she would try and find Philippe's new love, but she didn't see any need to rush.